"YOU . . . YOU BELIEVE ME?"

Gulliver was astonished.

"Yes," said Steiger, helping him into the bedroom and easing him down to the bed. "Yes, I believe you."

"How can you be so certain?" Gulliver said. "You have but my word."

"And I'm sure it's the word of a gentleman," said Steiger. "But for now, please be patient with me because it's urgent that I complete this report—"

Gulliver cried out suddenly, and Sandy spun around. He felt a sharp searing pain across his cheek. As he brought his hand up to his face, he spotted his attacker firing once more . . . *a tiny man, no more than six or seven inches tall, firing a miniature laser pistol.*

The beam struck him in his left eye and Sandy screamed in agony. More tiny people were materializing out of thin air, equipped with floater paks and firing tiny weapons.

The room was filled with a crisscrossing webwork of brilliant and deadly light . . .

9 TIMEWARS

THE LILLIPUT LEGION

SIMON HAWKE

ACE BOOKS, NEW YORK

This book is an Ace
original edition, and has never
been previously published.

THE LILLIPUT LEGION

An Ace Book / published by arrangement with
the author

PRINTING HISTORY
Ace edition / August 1989

ISBN: 0-441-50395-0

Ace Books are published by
The Berkley Publishing Group,
200 Madison Avenue, New York, New York 10016
The name "ACE" and the "A" logo
are trademarks belonging to Charter Communications, Inc.

PRINTED IN THE UNITED STATES OF AMERICA

10 9 8 7 6 5 4 3 2 1

For Jerry and Ginger Kopp,
with friendship and appreciation

A CHRONOLOGICAL HISTORY OF THE TIME WARS

April 1, 2425: Dr. Wolfgang Mensinger invents the chronoplate at the age of 115, discovering time travel. Later, he would construct a small-scale working prototype for use in laboratory experiments specifically designed to avoid any possible creation of a temporal paradox. He is hailed as the "Father of Temporal Physics."

July 14, 2430: Mensinger publishes "There is No Future," in which he redefines relativity, proving there is no such thing as *the* future, but an infinite number of potential scenarios, which are absolute relative only to their present. He also announces the discovery of "nonspecific time," or temporal limbo, later known as "the dead zone."

October 21, 2440: Wolfgang Mensinger dies. His son, Albrecht, perfects the chronoplate and carries on the work, but loses control of the discovery to political interests.

June 15, 2460: Formation of the international Committee for Temporal Intelligence, with Albrecht Mensinger as director. Specially trained and conditioned "agents" of the committee begin to travel back through time in order to conduct research and field test the chronoplate apparatus. Many become lost in transition, trapped in the limbo of non-specific time known as "the dead zone." Those who return from successful temporal voyages often bring back startling information necessitating the revision of historical records.

March 22, 2461:   *The Consorti Affair*—Cardinal Ludovico Consorti is excommunicated from the Roman Catholic Church for proposing that agents travel back through time to obtain empirical evidence that Christ arose following his crucifixion. The Consorti Affair sparks extensive international negotiations amidst a volatile climate of public opinion concerning the proper uses for the new technology. Temporal excursions are severely curtailed. Concurrently, espionage operatives of several nations infiltrate the Committee for Temporal Intelligence.

May 1, 2461:   Dr. Albrecht Mensinger appears before a special international conference in Geneva, composed of political leaders and members of the scientific community. He attempts to alleviate fears about the possible misuses of time travel. He further refuses to cooperate with any attempts to militarize his father's discovery.

February 3, 2485:   The research facilities of the Committee for Temporal Intelligence are seized by troops of the TransAtlantic Treaty Organization.

January 25, 2492:   The Council of Nations meets in Buenos Aires, capital of the United Socialist States of South America, to discuss increasing international tensions and economic instability. A proposal for "an end to war in our time" is put forth by the chairman of the Nippon Conglomerate Empire. Dr. Albrecht Mensinger, appearing before the body as the nominal director of the Committee for Temporal Intelligence, argues passionately against using temporal technology to resolve international conflicts, but cannot present proof that the past can be affected by temporal voyagers. Prevailing scientific testimony reinforces the conventional wisdom that the past is an immutable absolute.

December 24, 2492: Formation of the Referee Corps, brought into being by the Council of Nations as an extranational arbitrating body with sole control over temporal technology and authority to stage temporal conflicts as "limited warfare" to resolve international disputes.

April 21, 2493: On the recommendation of the Referee Corps, a subordinate body named the Observer Corps is formed, taking over most of the functions of the Committee for Temporal Intelligence, which is redesignated as the Temporal Intelligence Agency. Under the aegis of the Council of Nations and the Referee Corps, the T.I.A. absorbs the intelligence agencies of the world's governments and is made solely answerable to the Referee Corps. Dr. Mensinger resigns his post to found the Temporal Preservation League, a group dedicated to the abolition of temporal conflict.

June, 2497–
March, 2502: Referee Corps presides over initial temporal confrontation campaigns, accepting "grievances" from disputing nations, selecting historical conflicts of the past as "staging grounds" and supervising the infiltration of modern troops into the so-called "cannon fodder" ranks of ancient warring armies. Initial numbers of temporal combatants are kept small, with infiltration facilitated by cosmetic surgery and implant conditioning of soldiers. The results

are calculated based upon successful return rate and a complicated "point spread." Soldiers are monitored via cerebral implants, enabling Search and Retrieve teams to follow their movements and monitor mortality rate. The media dubs temporal conflicts the "Time Wars."

2500–2510: Extremely rapid growth of massive support industry catering to the exacting art and science of temporal conflict. Rapid improvement in the international economic climate follows, with significant growth in productivity and rapid decline in unemployment and inflation rate. There is a gradual escalation of the Time Wars, with a majority of the world's armed services converting to temporal duty status.

Growth of the Temporal Preservation League as a peace movement with an intensive lobby effort and mass demonstrations against the Time Wars. Mensinger cautions against an imbalance in temporal continuity due to the increasing activity of the Time Wars.

September 2, 2514: Mensinger publishes his "Theories of Temporal Relativity," incorporating his solution to the Grandfather Paradox and calling once again for a ceasefire in the Time Wars. The result is an upheaval in the scientific community and a hastily reconvened Council of Nations to discuss his findings, leading to the Temporal Strategic Arms Limitations Talks of 2515.

March 15, 2515–
June 1, 2515: T-SALT held in New York City. Mensinger appears before the representatives at the sessions and petitions for an end

to the Time Wars. A ceasefire resolution is framed, but tabled due to lack of agreement among the members of the Council of Nations. Mensinger leaves the T-SALT a broken man.

November 18, 2516: Dr. Albrecht Mensinger experiences total nervous collapse shortly after being awarded the Benford Prize.

December 25, 2516: Dr. Albrecht Mensinger commits suicide. Violent demonstrations by members of the Temporal Preservation League.

January 1, 2517: Militant members of the Temporal Preservation League band together to form the Timekeepers, a terrorist offshoot of the League, dedicated to the complete destruction of the war machine. They announce their presence to the world by assassinating three members of the Referee Corps and bombing the Council of Nations meeting in Buenos Aires, killing several heads of state and injuring many others.

September 17, 2613: Formation of the First Division of the U.S. Army Temporal Corps as a crack commando unit following the successful completion of a "temporal adjustment" involving the first serious threat of a timestream split. The First Division, assigned exclusively to deal with threats to temporal continuity, is designated as "the Time Commandos."

October 10, 2615: Temporal physicist Dr. Robert Darkness disappears without a trace shortly after turning over to the army his new invention, the "warp grenade," a combination time machine and nuclear device. Establishing a secret research installation somewhere off Earth, Darkness experiments with temporal translocation based on the transmutation principle. He experiments upon himself and succeeds in translating his own body into tachyons, but an error in his calculations causes an irreversible change in his subatomic structure, rendering it unstable. Darkness becomes "the man who is faster than light."

November 3, 2620: The chronoplate is superseded by the temporal transponder. Dubbed the "warp disc," the temporal transponder was developed from work begun by Dr. Darkness and it drew on power tapped by Einstein-Rosen Generators (developed by Bell Laboratories in 2545) bridging to neutron stars.

March 15, 2625: *The Temporal Crisis:* The discovery of an alternate universe following an unsuccessful invasion by troops of the Special Operations Group, counterparts of the time commandos. Whether as a result of chronophysical instability caused by clocking tremendous amounts of energy through Einstein-Rosen Bridges or the cumulative effect of temporal disruptions, an alternate universe comes into congruence with our own, causing an instability in the timeflow of both universes and resulting in a "confluence effect," wherein the timestreams of both universes ripple and occasionally intersect, creating "confluence points" where crossover from one universe to another becomes possible.

Massive amounts of energy clocked through Einstein-Rosen Bridges has resulted in unintentional "warp bombardment" of the alternate universe, causing untold destruction. The Time

Wars escalate into a temporal war between two universes.

9 ⟰TIMEWARS

THE LILLIPUT LEGION

PROLOGUE ═══════════════

"Go on, ask him about the little people," said Pontack, grinning and nudging Addison in the side.

"The little people?" said Joseph Addison, taking a small pinch of snuff and then sneezing prodigiously into a Mechlin lace handkerchief. "You mean the leprechauns?"

"Leprechauns?" said Richard Steele, who together with Addison published *The Spectator*, a daily periodical of news, essays, philosophy and gossip that was very influential among the citizens of 18th century London. "What's this about leprechauns?"

Pontack, the proprietor of the fashionable French eating house that bore his name, shook his head and chuckled. "No, not quite leprechauns, exactly," he said. "Something a bit more original than that, near as I can tell. Something even smaller, on the order of six inches."

"Six inches?" Steele said, frowning. "What, you don't mean six inches tall, surely?"

"The very thing," said Pontack, as he conducted them to a table in the back around which a small crowd had gathered. "Six inches tall. Or so the man insists. And he swears that every word of it is true. I thought perhaps it might make for an interesting story for your paper."

"And a bit of free advertisement for your own establishment, is that it?" Steele said, with a wink at Pontack as they pressed through the crowd, "Very well, we shall ask this adventurer of yours about his leprechauns."

"Not leprechauns," said Pontack. "Little people."

"L'il pipils," slurred a disheveled-looking man slumped over at the table. "L'il pipils . . ."

His eyes were bloodshot and wild looking. His clothes were tattered and filthy and his hair stood out in all directions. His hands trembled.

"The poor man looks hopelessly demented," said Addison, with concern.

"The poor man looks hopelessly drunk," commented Steele, wryly.

"L'ilipipils . . ." the man stammered, having difficulty getting out the words.

"Lilliputians!" boomed a stentorian voice behind Addison and Steele. They turned around. "That's what we shall call them, gentlemen, lilliputians!"

"Swift," said Addison, rolling his eyes. "I might have known."

"Addison!" said Swift. "Pontack, you old poltroon, since when do you allow Whigs upon these premises?"

Addison turned to his friend and collaborator. "Richard, allow me to present Mr. Jonathan Swift, indefatigable champion of the Irish resistance, Tory politics, and any other lunacy that happens along. Oh, and he writes a bit, as well," he added, as an afterthought.

"Steele!" said Swift, as if it were an accusation. "I've read some of your essays."

"And I've read some of yours," said Steele. "Quite amusing. Are we witnessing another in the making?"

"Perhaps, perhaps," said Swift, evasively, elbowing some people aside and resuming his place at the table beside the drunken man. Having made room for some more wine, he immediately started to fill up again. He had, apparently, a capacity far greater than his friend.

"Gentlemen," he said, "allow me to present Dr. Lemuel Gulliver, late of the good ship *Antelope*, under Capt. William Prichard, which was tragically lost at sea while en route to the East Indies. Dr. Gulliver was the ship's surgeon and the only one to have survived the disastrous shipwreck somewhere in the waters off Van Diemen's Land."

He turned to Gulliver with an expansive gesture. "Dr. Gulliver, these two gentlemen are Messrs. Addison and Steele, late of that eminent journal of philosophical and political buffoonery, *The Tatler*, and currently publishing *The Spectator*, wherein one may find all manner of portentous nonsense concerning which nostril to stuff snuff in and the etiquette of breaking wind and whatnot. Perhaps you would care to repeat your fascinating tale for their benefit?"

Gulliver grunted and passed out, striking his forehead on the wooden table with a resounding thud.

"Brief, but effective," Steele said, wryly.

The people standing around the table laughed, all except for one young man who stood at the edge of the crowd. He was in his early twenties, tall and well built, light haired and fair complected. He looked like any other young London dandy, but there was something about him that was different. Just prior to the arrival of Addison and Steele, he had been listening intently to Dr. Gulliver pouring out his tale as Swift poured in the booze and continued to encourage him, occasionally adding editorial embellishments of his own.

It was difficult to separate fact from fancy when it came to the whimsical Swift, but it seemed that the satirist had encountered Dr. Gulliver in a pub somewhere not very far from Pontack's in Abchurch Lane, though one that attracted a considerably less-well-heeled clientele. Swift claimed to "hate and detest that animal called man," meaning he had little use for society as a whole, but he had an affection for the common individual, the ordinary working man, and he often frequented their watering holes, ever on the alert for inspiration. In Dr. Lemuel Gulliver, he had struck the motherlode.

"Dash it all, Swift, now look what you've done!" said Pontack, indicating the unconscious and throughly disreputable-looking Gulliver. "I simply cannot have this sort of thing in here!"

"Indeed?" Swift said. "My good Pontack, you have 'this sort of thing' in here all the time, only the patrons are generally better dressed and have bigger purses which you considerably lighten for them while they're resting. Here, you may lighten mine a bit if it will improve your disposition."

Everyone laughed once more and Pontack pretended to be outrageously affronted.

"Now see here, Swift, that is most egregiously unfair—"

"Egregiously?" Swift interrupted, raising his bushy eyebrows in mock astonishment. *"Egregiously?"* He glanced at Addison and Steele. "He *has* been reading your modest little journal, hasn't he? Egregiously, my buttocks!"

This elicited another burst of laughter as Pontack sputtered and turned red in the face. Addison and Steele merely smiled at one another, thinking that the incident might indeed make for an amusing bit of reportage in their paper. And it would serve Pontack right for raising the prices on his claret. Only the dapper young man who stood at the edge of the crowd seemed unamused. His expression remained alert and somber.

"Say what you will, Swift," Pontack said, "but I cannot have this . . . this sort of person lying about senseless on my tables as if this were some seaman's tavern! You brought him, now you must get him out of here. Take him outside and let him sleep it off in an alleyway somewhere, where his sort belongs."

"His sort?" said Swift, with an edge in his voice. "This man is a surgeon, Pontack, a learned physician. 'His sort,' as you so disingenuously put it, keeps you and your establishment in business. Under other circumstances, you'd be fawning over him like the servile dog you are, because he represents the medical profession, yet because he is in tattered clothing and drunk to numb the pain of his ordeal, you so harshly and unfairly—yes, even to the point of being *egregious*—judge a poor unfortunate survivor of a terrible shipwreck, who has gone through God only knows what manner of hardship. If it were not for me, you would throw this poor man into an alleyway like so much human refuse. Shame, Pontack! May you never find yourself in such a pitiable condition, lest you should encounter someone with as little heart as you."

"Hear, hear!" said someone in the crowd, and others joined in with similar supporting comments.

"He actually did that all in one breath, didn't he?" Steele said in an aside to Addision.

"Mmmm." Addison murmured. "You ought to hear him when he really gets his wind up."

"Oh, very well," Pontack said, relenting as he saw that the

prevailing opinion stood against him. "But can't you at least prop him up and wipe his chin or something? Tidy him up a bit, can't you?"

"No, I shan't," said Swift. "Dr. Gulliver should not, even in his unfortunate condition, stay a moment longer where his presence is not wanted. We shall take our leave and dine elsewhere."

This elicited a storm of protest, though Swift showed no sign of leaving.

"Perhaps, sir, I could offer a small compromise," said the fair-haired young man, stepping forward. "Surely Dr. Gulliver would be more comfortable sleeping it off—uh, taking his ease in a coach rather than atop a hard wooden table or in a refuse-strewn alleyway. I would be pleased to let him rest a while in mine."

"You, sir, are a gentleman," said Swift, rising to his feet to shake the young man's hand. "May I have the honor of knowing your name?"

"Steiger," said the fair-haired young man. "Alexander Steiger, at your service, sir."

"Well, Mr. Steiger, it is a genuine pleasure to meet you, sir," said Swift. "Allow me to buy you drink?"

"Thank you, that would be most kind," said Steiger. "I will join you as soon as I have seen to the comfort of your friend. Perhaps one of these gentlemen would be so kind as to assist me?"

A man stepped forward and together they took the unconscious Gulliver and lifted him up, holding his arms across their shoulders. They took him outside, dragging him along to Steiger's coach. The driver jumped down and opened the door, then moved to help Steiger with Gulliver, laying him out upon the cushioned seat.

"Thank you for your assistance," Steiger said to the man who'd helped him. "Please tell Mr. Swift that I will merely see to this man's comfort and then I will be back inside directly."

Steiger watched the man go back inside, then he turned to the driver and said, "Threadneedle Street, quickly." He got inside the coach and the driver whipped up the horses. The coachman drove quickly to Steiger's rooms in Threadneedle Street, and by the time they arrived, Dr. Gulliver had come around, though he was still groggy and hungover.

"What. . . . where am I? Who are you?"

"A friend," said Steiger, helping him inside and up the stairs. "A friend who believes your story, Dr. Gulliver."

"You. . . . you *believe* me?" Gulliver said, astonished.

"Yes," said Steiger, helping him into the bedroom and easing him down onto the bed. "Yes, I believe you. Here, lie down. Rest a moment."

He went over to his desk, sat down and started writing quickly.

"Wh— What are you doing?" Gulliver said.

"I'm making out a report," said Steiger, writing furiously.

"A report?" said Gulliver, frowning.

"Never mind, I'll explain later. I want to make certain that I have all this written down, and then I'm going to read it back to you and I want you to tell me if I've got it all right. Are you sober enough to do that?"

"I . . ." Gulliver sat up in bed, felt suddenly dizzy, leaned back and closed his eyes. "I am not very sober, I'm afraid, but I think I can manage."

"Good." Steiger tossed a tiny snuffbox to Gulliver. It landed on the bed. Gulliver picked it up.

"What's this? Snuff? No, thank you, I don't—"

"Just swallow two of them. It will make you feel better."

Gulliver opened the box and glanced inside. "What. . . . what is it?"

"Aspirin," Steiger said, distractedly, concentrating on his writing. He was trying to recall every element of Gulliver's story and note it down in shorthand.

"Ass-prin?" said Gulliver, staring at the pills dubiously. "What. . . . I don't understand. What manner of—"

"Just swallow two of them, all right? Don't chew, just swallow them quickly. Trust me, it'll make you feel better. It's . . . it's an old family remedy. It's quite safe, I promise you."

"Safe? Gulliver snorted. "No one is safe. Nothing and no one." He took two of the pills and swallowed them. He made a face. "Ugh. Bitter."

"You didn't chew them, did you? I told you not to chew them."

"Who are you? Are you an apothecary?"

"My name is Alexander Steiger," he said, still writing

quickly in the precise characters of shorthand. "My friends call me Sandy."

Gulliver leaned back against the headboard and closed his eyes once more. "Mine call me Lem. You are very kind, Sandy. I don't know why. Why should you believe me? Even *I* would never have believed it had I not seen it all with my own eyes. I would have thought anyone telling such a tale quite mad." He swallowed hard and brought his hands up to his face. "Ohh, my head is splitting. Sandy, tell me truthfully, do you think I'm mad?"

"No," said Sandy. "In fact, I'm certain that you are absolutely sane." He glanced up at Gulliver. "Whatever happens now, Lem," he said, emphatically, "you *must* promise me that you will not forget that. You are not insane. I have no doubt that you have seen some astonishing things that seem impossible to explain. You've been through a terrible ordeal. It took a great deal of courage to get through all that. You must hold on to that strength, resist the temptation to drown your memories in wine and keep telling yourself that you have *not* gone mad."

"How can you be so certain?" Gulliver said. "You have but my word!"

"And I'm sure it's the word of a gentleman," said Steiger, turning back to his report. "I must complete this, Lem. Please, be patient with me for a few moments and I will try to explain later, after I have—"

Gulliver cried out suddenly. The terror in his cry made Sandy spin around. He felt a sharp, searing pain across his cheek, as if an extremely fine filament of superheated wire had been drawn across it. As he cried out with pain and brought his hand up to his face, he saw his attacker firing once more—*a tiny man, no more than six or seven inches tall, firing a miniature laser pistol.*

The beam struck him in his left eye, and Sandy screamed in agony as his eyeball was cooked right out of its socket. More tiny people were materializing out of thin air. They were equipped with floater paks and firing tiny weapons. The air in the room was filled with a crisscrossing web work of brilliant light. Sandy grabbed his chair and hurled it at the miniature invaders, then grabbed his report and dove onto the bed, covering the terrified Gulliver's body with his own. He stuffed the report into Gulliver's pocket and then snapped a small metallic bracelet around his wrist.

"General Forrester!" he shouted. *"Get that report to General Moses Forrester!"*

He felt a barrage of tiny laser beams slicing through his flesh. Dozens upon dozens of them. He screamed in agony and activated the warp disc.

Gulliver disappeared.

1

As the first light of dawn washed over the jagged, snow-capped peaks of the Hindu Kush, General Blood gave the order to advance. The pipes and drums struck up and the main body of the expeditionary force moved off down the graded road in perfect fours formation. At the same time, an assault team of three hundred picked men, taking advantage of the dim light and the early morning mist, silently crept up the slopes toward the stone sangars, snipers' nests of piled rock that the Ghazis had erected on the cliffs above the fort. The Ghazi sentries were taken completely by surprise. They were busy watching the crazy British *firinghi* assembling below them and marching to their apparent doom when all of a sudden the assault team was upon them. The troopers charged, spreading out and moving in from opposing flanks, scrambling up the rocks and firing at will, engaging the Ghazis at bayonet point. Surprised, and with no one to direct their movements, the Ghazis gave ground before the furious assault and the ridge was captured completely without losses.

Andre Cross had seen it all before. She had experienced it all before, and she was reliving it again as she tossed in bed, moaning in her sleep. She had relived this scene countless times in the recurring nightmares that had plagued her ever since she had returned from that assignment. The year had been

9

1897, and the place was the Malakand Pass on the northwest
frontier of the British Raj, in the high country of Afghanistan.
The fanatic Ghazis, led by their insane holy man, Sadullah,
had risen up to drive the infidel *firinghi* (their word for
foreigner) out of their desolate land forever. The blood lust was
upon them as the tribes all joined in the jehad, the holy war
against the British. For the 19th Century British Raj, at stake
was the security of their northwest frontier. For the Time
Commandos from the 27th Century, at stake was the entire
future.

A young subaltern in the 4th Hussars had obtained tempo-
rary leave from his regiment to join the Malakand Field Force
and cover the uprising for the London *Daily Telegraph*. His
name was Winston Churchill.

Fate had brought him to that savage place at the top of the
world, where a British fort was under seige, surrounded on all
sides by screaming Ghazis, and fate had brought the Time
Commandos to there as well, to locate a temporal confluence
point where two separate timelines intersected and the direction
that the future took became as hazy as the mountain mist.

When the crossbow was invented, people had predicted that
the world would end, that civilization could never survive such
a devastating weapon. But the world survived and became even
more civilized. They said much the same thing with the advent
of the machine gun, and the atomic bomb, and plasma
weapons, and the warp grenade, yet still the world survived.
Somewhat the worse for wear, but it nevertheless survived.
And Prof. Albrecht Mensinger, whose father had invented time
travel, had predicted that the world would end if governments
insisted upon traveling through time to fight their wars, but the
world still managed to survive. Just barely. Only now the Time
Wars had escalated to unprecedented heights. The chronophysical alignment of the universe had shifted, Einstein somer-
saulted in his grave and two parallel universes had come into
congruence with each other, their timelines rippling like
undulating snakes—and, at times, they intersected.

Wherever such a confluence point occurred, it was possible
to cross over from one universe into another. And such a point
had occurred somewhere in the mountains of the Hindu Kush,
in the year 1897. Soldiers from the future of the other timeline
had crossed over, intending to interfere with history and create

a temporal split. The Time Commandos stopped them, but at a terrible cost. During the mission, their team leader, Col. Lucas Priest, had died.

Since she had returned from that mission, Andre had suffered from recurring nightmares in which she kept reliving that awful moment, when Lucas Priest had died before her very eyes, shot through the chest by a .50 caliber ball from a jezail rifle. She had borne her grief stoically, as a soldier should. She had never mentioned the nightmares to anyone, not even Finn Delaney, who was her closest friend. He had been Lucas's best friend as well, and he had understood her loss and shared her grief; yet still, she had never told him about the nightmares.

In time, she thought the dreams would go away. Time, it was said, could heal all wounds. Only this wound refused to heal. Instead, like a suppurating sore, it grew worse and worse. Nothing she did would make it go away. She could put it out of her mind for a time while she was on a mission. She could forget herself in the furious pace of her muscle-straining workouts and, on occasion, she could drink herself into oblivion and dull her mind to the point where she no longer felt anything. But it always came back afterwards. She dreaded the quiet times, alone at night, in bed. No amount of alcohol could keep away the nightmares. In dreams, it all came flooding back to her.

She and Lucas Priest standing once again with General Blood and his staff up on the newly captured ridge, watching from the heights as the British troops below pressed home their advantage. Watching the infantry fix bayonets and advance into the Ghazi ranks. The Ghazis panicking and fleeing, breaking ranks and running, their snipers scrambling down from the rocks where, with the sun coming up, they were suddenly vulnerable to fire from the British troops up on captured ridge. Ghazis taking flight down the graded road, running ahead of the infantry, fighting with one another to escape being trapped by their own numbers in the narrow mountain pass.

"We've done it, General!" cried Surgeon-Lieutenant Hugo, standing beside Blood and watching the enemy in full flight. "We've broken through! We can post pickets in the pass and reinforce our position. Now we can— "

"No," said General Blood, grimly. "I will not allow them to

escape so they can join with the rebel tribesmen at Chakdarra and warn them. We'll finish this here and now. They'll be on the plain once they have retreated through the pass. Fully exposed and on foot. Order forth the lancers. No prisoners. No survivors."

The signal was given and the four squadrons of calvary charged. Finn Delaney, leading the second squadron of Bengal Lancers, couched his lance and leaned forward slightly, bearing down upon the fleeing Ghazis before him. It was going to be a slaughter.

The tribesmen still trapped in the pass were run down and trampled by the lancers as they thundered through. Then the cavalry formed a line upon the plain and charged the fleeing enemy. There was no escape. The Ghazis died in the rice fields, run through by the lances and struck down by the cavalry sabres. Bodies fell everywhere as the lancers descended on the running Ghazis and butchered them.

"Christ," said Hugo, turning away from the carnage down below. "I'm sorry, General, but that's more than I can stand to watch. I've seen enough of death."

Churchill was riveted by the spectacle. "They shall not forget this," he said. "It's probably the first time any of them have seen what cavalry can do, given room to deploy their strength. Henceforth, the very words 'Bengal Lancers' shall strike terror into their hearts."

As he spoke, a lone Ghazi sniper, who had remained undiscovered, hidden behind the rocks of his crumbled sangar, rose to a kneeling position and brought his jezail rifle to bear upon the surgeon, Hugo, whom he mistakenly took to be the commander of the British forces. As he raised his rifle, Lucas spotted him.

He yelled, *"Hugo look out!"*

Instinctively, after so much time spent under enemy fire, Hugo reacted by throwing himself down flat upon the ground. In an instant, Lucas saw that Hugo's combat-quick response had placed Churchill directly in the line of fire. In an instant of white hot, adrenalin-charged clarity, he saw it all and made a running dive for Churchill, knocking him out of the way. And in that same moment, the Ghazi sniper fired. The .50 caliber ball slammed into Lucas's chest, ploughing through the thorax and tearing everything in its path. Too late, Andre fired her revolver, shooting the Ghazi sniper right between the eyes.

Churchill stood there, striken, staring at the limp body at their feet. Lucas Priest was face down on the ground, blood draining from the gaping hole in his chest.

"My God," said Churchill.

He crouched over the body and gently turned it over. The others gathered round.

"Doctor, can't you do something?" Churchill said in an agonized tone.

"I'm sorry, son," said Hugo, looking down and shaking his head. "There's nothing to be done."

Andre knelt over Lucas, staring down at him with shocked disbelief. His sightless eyes stared up at the sky.

"*Andre . . .*" someone said.

She reached out to close his eyes.

"*Andre . . .*"

Her hand came away wet with his blood.

"*Andre!*"

She awoke with a start. She took a deep breath and let it out in a weary sigh, running her fingers through her thick blond hair, brushing it back away from her face. Another nightmare. Would they never end?

"*Andre?*"

She sat up quickly, grabbing for her plasma pistol and thumbing off the safety as she aimed it—

There was a dark figure standing silhouetted by the window of her bedroom.

"Andre, don't shoot! It's me."

Her eyes went wide as she stared at the shadowy figure. "*Lucas?*"

It was impossible. She squeezed her eyes shut tightly and then opened them again. There was no one there. The window was bright with the reflected glare from the lights of Pendleton Base. No one was silhouetted against it. And no one could have come in through that window. It was on the forty-seventh floor and sealed so that it couldn't open.

She exhaled heavily and lowered the gun, being careful to put the safety back on. Sleeping with a plasma weapon under her pillow was hazardous to the point of being suicidal, especially after she'd been drinking. It wouldn't do to incinerate herself in the middle of the night or wake up and start blasting away at hallucinations left over from a nightmare, but she had never learned to be comfortable without having a weapon within easy reach, whether it was a plasma pistol or a broadsword. She was a temporal agent and, as such, she was an expert with a wide variety of weapons. Control was so firmly ingrained that it was a matter of instinct. Still, her hand was shaking as she put the pistol down.

She swallowed hard, took another deep breath and leaned back against the wall. *"Damn,"* she said to herself. "It's *got* to stop. I'm starting to lose it."

A soft red light suddenly came on above her comscreen and an electronic buzzer sounded three times in rapid succession, paused, then sounded again. General Forrester's face appeared upon the screen.

"Lt. Cross?"

"Here, sir," she said.

"Come up to my quarters, on the double."

"Sir!"

She rolled out of bed and quickly slipped into her black base fatigues. Moses Forrester was not in the habit of calling the people under his command in the middle of the night and summoning them "on the double" unless there was a damned good reason for it. She was dressed in moments and out the door, running down the corridor toward the lift tubes.

Brigadier General Moses Forrester was an unusual commander. He was entitled to a full complement of personal security and staff at his quarters and offices atop the Headquarters Building of Pendleton Base, but he had only four guards working two shifts, which meant that there were only two guards on duty at any one time, plus an orderly who doubled as a secretary. Rather than wear full dress uniforms or even the less formal duty greens, Forrester insisted that his guards dress in the infinitely less impressive and more comfortable black base fatigues, which he himself preferred. No ribbons, no decorations, no insignia other than division pin and rank. This gave him the impression, he said, that he was surrounded by soldiers, rather than hotel doormen.

Formerly the commander of the elite First Division, the Time Commandos, Forrester had been promoted and was now the director of the Temporal Intelligence Agency, which had absorbed the First Division. Although Forrester was entitled to wear civilian clothing if he chose to, he never did, except for the 19th century, green, brocade smoking jacket he liked wearing during evenings in his quarters, when he was fond of settling down with one of his cherished Dunhill or Upshall pipes and a good book. Forrester had been in the service all his life. He had enlisted straight out of high school and risen through the ranks, taking advantage of military benefits to secure an education for himself along the way. He had earned a doctorate in history, one in political science, and one in temporal physics, though he often professed to know less about the intricacies of what was more commonly called "zen physics" than he really did.

Few people knew his exact age. He never spoke of it and no one ever had the temerity to ask. He looked positively ancient. His face was deeply lined and his hair might have been white if he had any, but Moses Forrester had shaved his head for as long as anyone could remember. However old he looked, and he looked like an old grizzly bear with hemorrhoids, he was in remarkable physical condition. He was well over six feet tall and ramrod straight, with shoulders that filled a doorway. He had a chest like a bull and he could effortlessly curl an eighty pound dumbbell with one hand.

When he led the First Division, he knew every soldier under his command by name. He had handpicked them all. He had not had the same luxury with his new command, since he had inherited all the agents of the T.I.A. in a lump sum, but he was rapidly "weeding out the deadwood," as he put it, which had led to some resentment on the part of many of the T.I.A. personnel. Forrester didn't give a damn. The ones who would resent him were precisely the ones he wanted to get rid of. He'd get to all of them eventually.

When they had been two separate branches of government service, there had been no love lost between the First Division and the T.I.A.. There had been an intense rivalry between them. Now they were all together under one command, and it was an uneasy marriage. Forrester allowed the former soldiers of the First Division to wear their old commando insignia, a stylized number one bisected by the symbol for infinity, while the agents of the T.I.A. continued to wear their own official insignia, which consisted of the symbol for pi. (Forrester himself wore both, one on each side of his collar.) The T.I.A. insignia had always been something of an agency in-joke, as it represented a transcendental number, infinitely repeating, therefore suggesting the true nature of the Temporal Intelligence Agency—an organization whose reach and whose agents were infinite. However, it wasn't until recently that Forrester had realized the true nature of that sly "Company" joke.

A former agency director had once requested complete data on all agency personnel and he'd been told that his request was impossible to grant. When the director had asked why, he was told that it was because no one in the agency knew exactly how many T.I.A. agents there were. Headquarters staff was one thing, but section chiefs out in the field had virtually complete autonomy to function on their own, to pick and choose their own personnel, either recruiting from other units or from civilians in the field, and they had literal carte blanche in their budgets, requesting whatever they thought they needed to maintain their sections. Usually, they got their allocations with no questions asked.

When Forrester reviewed the budget of the T.I.A., which was among the agency's most closely guarded secrets, he had been absolutely staggered. Not only did the T.I.A. command the single largest budget among all the government services, but it appeared that many of its operatives generated their own supplementary budget on the side, as well. A large number of individual field agents, section chiefs and even department heads were covertly involved in everything from legitimate businesses to organized crime, including such unsavory pursuits as gambling, prostitution, drug trafficking, contract assassination and using time travel to conduct stock manipulations.

Forrester was aghast. He had previously encountered the Temporal Underground, a loosely connected organization of deserters from the future who had managed to set up a sort of transtemporal underground society, but now it turned out that the T.I.A. had its own version of the Underground, known as the "Network," and that over the years, these renegade covert field agents had set up an entire transtemporal economy. Forrester's investigations had only revealed the very tip of the iceberg.

There was even a rumor that an entire 21st century American crime family was, in fact, a Network operation, funneling profits into the past in what had to be the most elaborate laundering scheme in history. Wealth generated by organzied crime in one time period financed complex operations in earlier centuries that were aimed at placing Network agents in key positions in governments and in the private sector, thereby enabling them to skim profits and set up complicated secret trust funds and numbered accounts that would, over the years, mature and be passed on to individuals designated as "Network affiliates"—people in the past who looked after Network interests in exchange for wealth and power. The end result was a cyclical economy that fed upon itself and grew by exponential leaps and bounds.

Forrester had used some of his crack commando units to infiltrate his own agency and so far he had managed to establish T.I.A. involvement in Al Capone's Chicago crime syndicate, as well as certain clandestine branches of American, Soviet and Israeli intelligence services in the 20th century, a time before advanced mind scanning techniques became available. Over the years, Network agents had been skimming profits from such diverse sources as the British East India Co., United Fruit, 19th century Moroccan slave trade operations, IBM, Bell Telephone, various South African diamond mines, Roman tax collectors—one section chief had even managed to become appointed the Roman governor of Antioch—casinos in both Las Vegas and Monte Carlo, and a host of other businesses in a wide variety of time periods into which they had infiltrated.

The money itself was virtually impossible to trace. It was difficult enough to conduct a modern paper chase in an attempt to untangle the complicated finances of corporate bandits, how was it possible to trace money laundering operations that transcended the boundaries of time? Swiss bank accounts? Perhaps, only in which time period? Liquid assets? Maybe, only in what form? Gold dust taken out of Colorado mine shipments in the 19th century? Jewels pirated from a Spanish treasure fleet in the 1700's? 20th century bearer bonds hijacked from a messenger on Wall Street, which were then converted into cash, transferred to a Panamanian account, wired to Brussels and used to purchase weapons at a discount from an arms dealer who was a Network front operation to begin with, which meant simply taking money from one pocket and putting it right back into another, increasing it along the way? It was absolutely mindboggling and it had been going on for years.

Corrupt T.I.A. section chiefs affiliated with the Network often lived better than heads of state. They had become so involved in their own transtemporal private enterprises that they looked upon the T.I.A. as a sort of part-time job, their official duties merely the cost of doing business.

Forrester had taken it upon himself to put them *out* of business, every last one of them, but it was a mighty tall order. In the first sweep operation conducted by the newly organized Internal Security Division, no less than twenty-seven section chiefs were clocked back from their posts, ostensibly for "orientation conferences," and placed under arrest. The first attempt on Moses Forrester's life was made the very next day.

There had been several more attempts since then, despite the dramatically increased security. Forrester did not like to be crowded and refused to accept having any more guards around him in his private quarters, so elaborate measures had been taken to protect him without his being aware of the increased protection. Security throughout the entire Headquarters Complex had been beefed up. Scanning devices and automated defense mechanisms had been installed in all the corridors and lift tubes leading to Forrester's offices and private quarters. Enough security and antipersonnel devices had been installed to hold off an entire battalion, but Forrester had found out about them and ordered them removed, saying that he didn't much care for the idea of computer-controlled autopulsers tracking everybody's movements through the hallways. What would happen if there was a glitch? The antipersonnel devices were removed, but Security had clandestinely re-installed the scanners.

The whole thing had led to a great deal of friction within the agency. Not only had two rival commands been united into one, with all the attendent complications that imposed, but commandos were being used to round up renegade field agents, which only served to exacerbate the problems. What it all came down to was the fact that there was another T.I.A. within the T.I.A., and as if it wasn't bad enough that they were faced with opposition from a parallel timeline, the agency now had to do battle with itself. The urgent summons to Forrester's quarters could have meant anything from another attempt on his life to a new temporal crisis, so Andre wasted no time in getting up there.

Finn Delaney met Andre in the corridor leading to the lift tubes. A bullish, muscular man with dark red hair and wide, good looking, typically Irish features, Delaney was, after Forrester, the most decorated soldier in the Temporal Corps. He might have been command staff rank himself by now if he hadn't been reduced in grade so many times for various infractions, ranging from direct disobedience to specific orders to striking superior officers. He had little patience for such trivialities as hand salutes and uniform regulations and expecting a veteran with his record to adhere to such things was an invitation to have one's teeth loosened. Delaney took no orders from anybody except his commanding officer, for whom he had boundless respect and admiration. Aside from which, for all his years, Forrester was the one man Delaney was not sure he could take. As a major, Forrester had been their training officer on their first temporal adjustment mission and Finn remembered all too well what the old man was capable of dishing out.

Currently, Delaney held the rank of captain, but there was a pool going to see how long he'd keep his bars. Delaney didn't care. The only thing rank meant to him was a slight boost in pay grade, but the only thing he ever spent his money on was Irish whiskey, so it didn't make much difference to him one way or another. A private could get drunk just as cheaply as an officer in the First Division Lounge. And Delaney was a simple man; the service provided all his other needs. He wasn't a parade ground soldier. He was an adventurer at heart. He was a man who had been born too late and so he lived chiefly in the past. Quite literally. The present was just something he barely tolerated. He and Andre both got into the tube and punched for the top floor.

"He say anything to you?" said Finn.

Andre shook her head. "No, just said to get up there on the double."

They were both tense, not knowing what it could be, but

knowing that Forrester would never have summoned them like that unless it were something serious.

Col. Creed Steiger was already there when they arrived, having responded to a similar summons. Large-framed and well-muscled, though smaller in stature than Delaney, Steiger was very blond, with pale gray eyes and a sharp, hooked nose, like the beak of an eagle. It gave him a cruel look. He moved with the casual, relaxed-yet-controlled bearing of the seasoned soldier. He was Forrester's exec, formerly the senior covert field agent of the T.I.A. Given recent developments, his position was somewhat uncomfortable, if not acutely precarious.

For years, he had gone simply by the codename of "Phoenix," working mostly on his own, changing his entire physical appearance from one covert assignment to the next, assuming a different personality with each role he was required to play. Even within the agency, he had been known as a maverick. Finn and Andre first met him when one of his covert assignments coincided with one of their temporal adjustment missions. With the merging of the First Division and the T.I.A., Forrester chose Steiger as his executive officer and assigned him as a partner to Finn and Andre, to replace the late Lucas Priest as the third member of his top temporal adjustment team.

When Forrester's investigations had uncovered the extent of the corruption within the T.I.A. organization he had inherited, he had called in Steiger and asked him point blank, "Did you know about any of this?"

"Yes, sir, I did," Steiger had replied. "Some of it, anyway. And to anticipate your next question, no, I wasn't involved. I had a job to do and I had to look the other way a lot."

"I see," Forrester had said. " Dammit, why didn't you tell me?"

"With all due respect, sir, I didn't see what in hell would be the point," Steiger had said. "You couldn't really do anything about it and with the temporal crisis that we're facing with the other timeline, I figured you already had plenty on your mind. It was a question of priorities."

"Indeed? Are *you* making command decisions for me now, Colonel?" Forrester had said, an edge to his voice. "What the hell made you think I couldn't do anything about it?"

"No offense, sir, but I don't think you have any idea what you'd be going up against if you took on the Network. You'd be taking on an entrenched clandestine bureacracy that's been in operation for years. For *centuries*. A bureacracy that has its own heirarchy, its own funds, its own supply and communications network and its own agents, all of which means that it can function completely independent of the agency. And it often does. The agency, on the other hand, cannot function completely independent of the Network, because the Network is an integral part of the agency, infesting it like a cancer. You can never really know for sure who's in and who's out."

"I could issue an order to scan all personnel," said Forrester.

"Yes, sir, you could do that. It would tend to make things a little rough on your new command, but even so, you'd still never get them all. Not by a long shot. There are covert field agents out there, hell, there are entire *sections* out there that have been operating off the books for years. They're so deep, nobody knows about 'em anymore. But the single biggest problem is that you don't know who they are or where they are, while they know who you are and how to get to you, believe me."

"Is that supposed to scare me?" Forrester said, wryly.

"I don't think you understand, sir. These people play hardball and if you went up against them, you'd have to throw the book right out the window and play twice as hard and three times as nasty. It would be a war, sir. And frankly, I think you'd get your ass shot off."

"Then you think that I should just look the other way and get on with business, is that it?" said Forrester, in a level tone.

"I guess it doesn't matter what I think, sir, because you're not going to do that, are you?" Steiger had said.

"No, Colonel, I'm not. I can't. I'm just not built that way."

"Then with your permission, sir, I'd like to take charge of the operation. I know at least a few people in the agency that I could count on and who might just be crazy enough to take on something like this."

"No, Colonel," said Forrester. "I appreciate the offer, but I want you to remain on standby status with Cross and Delaney. With the current crisis, I need my best temporal mission teams available on a moment's notice. I intend to assemble a special strike force to deal with this so-called Network. It will be composed of former members of the First Division, people I know the Network hasn't got its hooks into. And most of them have some experience with 'throwing the book right out the window and playing hardball,' as you put it. I intend to clean house, Colonel. Make no mistake about it, I'm prepared to do whatever it takes to get the job done. *I'm* the one running this outfit, not a bunch of underground profiteers and scam artists."

"I think you'll find that they're a little more than just profiteers and scam artists, sir," said Steiger. "At least let me help organize the strike force while I remain on standby. I have some idea of what they'll be going up against. I can point them in the right direction, maybe keep them from making some mistakes. And it might create less friction in the agency if the former senior covert field agent was officially heading up the strike force, rather than having it all be a First Division show."

"All right," said Forrester. "I see your point. But I don't want you going out on any field operations, is that understood? I need you available, on standby with your team."

"Understood, sir. May I have your security detail take me into custody now for immediate scanning?"

Forrester frowned. "What for?"

"I want to have myself scanned so that you can be absolutely certain that I'm not involved with the Network. And I'd like to be taken into custody at once so that you'd be certain I'd have no time to warn them if I were," said Steiger.

Forrester shook his head. "That won't be necessary, Colonel. I'd be a damned sorry commanding officer if I couldn't pick an exec that I knew I could trust."

"I appreciate that, sir," said Steiger, "but just the same, I'd like to insist. I want to be able to say that I did it, that I didn't get any preferential treatment, that I got on the machines and passed. I can't expect to ask anybody else to do it if I don't."

"I see," said Forrester, nodding. He summoned his security detail. "Sergeant, place Col. Steiger under arrest."

Finn and Andre hadn't seen much of him since he'd taken command of the Internal Security Division, but they had sure heard a lot about him. In a matter of weeks, Steiger had organized the I.S.D., composed largely of handpicked commandos from the First Division, some headbusters borrowed from the M.P.'s and a few trusted T.I.A. agents. He had whipped them into shape as a tight, well-coordinated unit and brought down twenty-seven section chiefs who were functioning as cell commanders in the Network. Steiger had hit hard and fast and he had made his presence known. He, along with Forrester, was a marked man now.

"Creed, what's going on?" said Finn.

"I don't know," said Steiger. "I only just got here. I got the call a few minutes ago and hurried right up."

"The general will see you now," the sergeant of the guard said, beckoning them to follow him. He conducted them down the hall to Forrester's private quarters, then left them. Forrester was waiting for them, fully dressed in his black base fatigues. It was three o'clock in the morning and he looked wide awake.

"At ease," said Forrester, tensely. "Bar's open. Delaney, do the honors."

They exchanged quick glances, then Delaney went over to the bar and poured a couple of neat Scotches for Andre and Creed, and an Irish for himself. He saw that Forrester already had a glass on the end table.

"To those who fell," said Forrester, after they all had their drinks. They all stiffened slightly, then tossed back their drinks, emptying their glasses. Forrester sighed. "Your brother's dead, Creed," he said, flatly.

Steiger paled. "Sandy?" He blinked twice, his breath caught and then he swallowed hard and stiffened, getting control of himself. "How did it happen?" he said, softly.

"Sit down," Forrester said. They all sat. Forrester took a folded sheet of paper out of his pocket and handed it to Steiger. "That is your brother's handwriting, isn't it?" he said.

Steiger unfolded the paper and glanced at the shorthand notation. He nodded.

"Read it out loud," said Forrester.

"Field Observer Report, Cpl. Steiger, A.P., T.O. #617079972, Post 17-259, 29 April 1702, 1930 hours, Post Headquarters." Steiger took a deep breath, cleared his throat and continued. "At approximately 1800 hours, encountered Dr. Lemuel Gulliver in the company of Mr. Jonathan Swift at Pontack's eating house in Abchurch Lane."

Delaney frowned. "*What* were those names again?" he said.

"As you were, Delaney," Forrester said. "Hold the thought." He turned to Steiger. "Go on."

"Dr. Gulliver claimed to be the sole survivor of a shipwreck," Steiger read, "the *Antelope*, under Capt. William Prichard, reportedly lost at sea somewhere off Van Diemen's Land. The man was in a state of near nervous collapse. He had been drinking heavily, but his report of encountering miniature people, approximately six inches in height—"

"What?" said Andre.

Forrester silenced her with a look. Steiger continued.

" . . . approximately six inches in height, created quite a stir. Most people hearing this reacted as if he were demented, but certain elements of his fascinating story drew this particular observer's attention. Dr. Gulliver described, in great detail, some of the weapons used by these little people, or lilliputians, as his companion, Mr. Swift, referred to them. From the lucid description of these miniature weapons and their function, they were unquestionably miniature lasers and autopulsers."

Steiger stopped for a moment and glanced up at Forrester with astonishment, then continued reading the report.

"From the description of their uniforms and tactics, these so-called 'lilliputians' sounded exactly like modern commandos, only on an incredible, miniature scale. The story sounds unbelievable, until one asks himself how a man of Gulliver's time could possibly imagine weapons such as lasers and autopulsers and describe their function in such accurate detail, right down to reporting the extremely high-pitched, staccato, whooping sound made by a cycling autopulser—the extremely high pitch possibly accounted for by the scale of the weapon. Taking into account the fantastic genetically engineered creatures from the alternate timeline previously encountered by temporal adjustment agents on—"

The expression on Steiger's face abruptly changed.

"What is it?" Andre said.

Steiger looked up. "It stops there." He glanced at Forrester. "Do we have a confirmation on this?"

Forrester nodded. "Your brother was very thorough in noting the time and the location. I had an S & R team clock back. I took special care to instruct them not to risk arriving any earlier than an hour after the stated time in the report. You understand, of course."

Steiger nodded.

"Search and Retrieve clocked back with your brother's body

about half an hour ago," said Forrester. "We have full confirmation."

"I'd like to see him, sir."

"I'm told he looks pretty bad, Creed," said Forrester.

"I don't give a damn. Sir."

Forrester nodded. "I understand. But you're to report directly back here when you're through. I have a security detail standing by to escort you."

"I don't need a goddamn—"

"As you were, Colonel," Forrester said, quietly, and Steiger immediately shut up. "I'm not insensitive to your feelings at the moment. However, there have been threats against your life and you are understandably distracted. You will accompany the detail and return here when you're through. Is that clear?"

Steiger licked his lips and took a deep breath. "Yes, sir."

"Good. You are dismissed."

Steiger stood, snapped to attention and saluted smartly. As he turned to leave, Forrester stopped him.

"Creed?"

"Sir?"

"I'm sorry as hell, my friend."

Steiger grimaced and nodded curtly. "Thank you, sir."

As he left, Delaney said, "I think I'd like another drink, sir."

Forrester nodded. "Get me one, too," he said.

"What killed him, sir?" asked Andre.

Forrester hesitated. "Laser rifles," he said, softly. "Miniature laser rifles."

2

It was Sandy. There was no question of it, though there was not much left of him to recognize. His body looked as if a dozen psychopathic surgeons had been at work on it with laser scalpels. Sandy had fought before he died. He had fought hard, but it hadn't helped him any. Steiger turned away, struggling to control his emotions. Sandy had been all the family he had left. The white-coated pathologist slid the long drawer holding Sandy's body back into the freezer.

Steiger blamed himself. When they were children, Sandy had always been the weaker one, smaller and more delicate. He was much more sensitive to things and much less aggressive. He had always been more naturally empathic and more thoughtful than his older brother. His strengths, Creed knew, lay in different areas than his own, but unfortunately, that was something that their father never understood. Victor Steiger had been a lumbering ox of a man, with all the inner sensitivity of a tree trunk. He had valued Creed's obvious gifts over Sandy's more subtle ones. Consequently, Creed was always held up as a model to his younger brother and Sandy was often mercilessly taunted by their father for not being able to match Creed's athletic abilities. Privately, Creed always sought to reassure his younger brother, trying to minimize the hurt caused by their father's scorn of him, but the damage had been irrevocable. Sandy had always felt, deep down inside, that he simply didn't measure up.

Creed had been against his entering the service. Not because he didn't think that Sandy would make a good soldier, but because he knew that making a soldier out of Sandy would be like trying to hammer a square peg into a round hole. A scientist, perhaps, or better still, an artist; some sort of creative profession would have suited Sandy perfectly and given him more joy, but Sandy had insisted on following in his older brother's footsteps. It was as if the shade of their dead father still loomed over them and Sandy felt he had to prove that he could measure up. And now he was dead.

Steiger shut his eyes and struggled to get his emotions back under control. If only he could travel back through time and change things, save his brother's life or get to him even earlier, when he was still only a small boy, and explain to him that those things which their father saw as weaknesses were not weaknesses at all, but simply different strengths their father couldn't recognize for what they were. If only he had known then what he knew now, he could have done ever so much more than merely reassure his younger brother each time he failed to live up to their father's expectations.

And the hardest part of it all was knowing that he had the ability to do just that—he had the ability to travel back in time. But he would not. He *could* not. Something like that was against all regulations and for damned good reasons. It was far too dangerous. There was no telling what could happen if you went back into the past and confronted your own relatives or even yourself when you were younger. To do that meant to risk creating a temporal paradox, one that might not be severe enough to split the timeline, but one that could create profound changes in your own life, changes that would be completely unpredictable, changes that could set off a chain of circumstances that would lead to even greater temporal contamination.

"Come on," Steiger said to his security escort, two armed M.P.'s who had been waiting at a respectful distance while he viewed his brother's remains. "Let's get the hell out of here."

As the M.P.'s turned to go out through the doors, Steiger heard several sharp, rapid, chuffing sounds and something whizzed past his left ear. The bullet took one of the M.P.'s in the back of the head and exited through his forehead, splattering brains, blood and bone fragments all over the door. As Steiger threw himself to one side and clawed for his sidearm, he felt the second bullet graze the lower part of his lat muscle on the left side. The second M.P. went down before his weapon had a chance to clear its holster. Steiger rolled and fired. The low intensity plasma charge struck the pathologist in the chest, burned a fist-sized hole right through him and dissipated on the wall behind him in a brief, incandescent burst of flame and smoke.

Steiger slowly got to his feet and winced with pain. He was bleeding from the side. He ripped open his shirt and checked the wound. Luckily, it was only superficial. The amount of blood always made a flesh wound look much worse than it really was. The M.P.'s, unfortunately, hadn't been so lucky. Both of them were dead.

"Damn!" Steiger swore through clenched teeth.

A young doctor dressed in surgical greens came through the door abruptly. Steiger, his nerves ragged, almost shot him.

"What the hell . . ." the doctor's eyes grew wide at the sight of Steiger's plasma pistol, then he saw the dead bodies on the floor. "Oh, my God!"

"Who're you?" said Steiger.

"What happened here?"

"Answer my damn question!"

"I . . . I'm Dr. Philip Torvalt, pathology resident."

"You know that man?" Steiger asked the young doctor, indicating the dead assailant in the lab coat. "He one of your people?"

Torvalt glanced again at the slain M.P.'s, then approached the assassin's corpse, glanced down at him, swallowed hard and shook his head. "No. No, I've never seen this man before." He looked back up at Steiger. "What the hell happened here? I was . . . Colonel, you're wounded!"

"It's only a scratch." Steiger glanced down at the two dead M.P.'s, his lips compressed onto a thin line. "They got the worst of it."

"You're bleeding profusely," Torvalt said, frowning. "You'd better let me see that. It could be serious. I've never seen a laser wound that didn't cauterize."

"It wasn't a laser," Steiger said. "Bring me that man's weapon."

Dr. Torvalt started to reach for the pistol, then hesitated. "Should I be touching this?"

"Why not?"

"Well . . . I don't know, I mean . . . it's evidence, isn't it?"

"Were you planning on arresting him? Come on, snap out of it, Doctor. You act as if you've never seen a dead body before. What the hell kind of a pathologist are you?"

"There's no need to be sarcastic, Colonel," Torvalt said, stiffly. He wrenched the pistol loose from the dead man's grip. "After all, it isn't every day I walk into the middle of a war."

"War?" Steiger snorted. "Hell, this wasn't a war, Doctor. This wasn't even a small skirmish. This was merely murder."

"Merely?" said the doctor.

Steiger winced. "Sorry. I tend to get a little testy when people try to kill me."

"Here." Torvalt handed Steiger the gun, handling it gingerly.

"Well, I'll be damned," said Steiger, examining it.

"What kind of weapon is that?" Torvalt said, fascinated in spite of himself. "I've never seen anything like it."

"That's because it's a bit before your time, Doctor. It's a true collector's item. A Semiautomatic lead projectile pistol fitted with a custom silencer. A 10-mm Colt Delta Elite, circa the late 20th century."

"The *20th century*?" said Torvalt, with astonishment.

Alarmed faces were looking in through the windows in the doors. Several hospital staff people started to come in.

"Stay out!" snapped Steiger. They quickly backed out once again. "Doctor, I want this place secured. I'll have I.S.D. coordinate with you. Get those men up off the floor and then I want a full workup on that one," he pointed at the assailant's corpse. "Retinal patterns, finger and palm prints, dental analysis, genetic mapping, the works. I want to know who he was before the night is out."

"Colonel, that's impossible! There's no way I can do all that in—"

"Then get someone who can. This is top priority. I'm holding you personally responsible."

There was a knock at the door.

"What is it? Steiger shouted, angrily.

"I.S.D., Colonel."

"That you, Danelli?"

"Yes, sir."

"Come on in."

Three commandos in black base fatigues entered, their sidearms held ready. Steiger recognized them and lowered his pistol.

"You all right, sir?" Sgt. Danelli said, holstering his pistol.

"Yeah. You got here quick."

"Responding to a report of a dead body, sir. One of the hospital cleaning staff found one of the doctors murdered." He bent down and pulled the nametag off the dead man's lab coat. "Now we know why. What are your orders, sir?"

"First of all, get some more people down here and secure the area." Steiger winced, holding his arm up as Torvalt staunched the flow of blood and examined the wound. "Nobody comes in, nobody leaves. Nobody goes off duty. I want all hospital personnel questioned. *Everybody.* We probably won't learn anything, but do it anyway. Delegate someone to take charge of that. I want you personally to get on the com right now and call the old man. Alert his security detail, tell him we've got two men down, both dead, and I've got a superficial flesh wound. Pure dumb luck. The hitter was a pro. It was the Network, no doubt about it. Find out how many people knew about my brother's body being brought in. Then get on to the S & R team that actually brought him in. I want to know how that hitter knew to be here. Then have someone call Archives Section and tell them to stand by for a download. Dr. Torvalt here is going to feed them everything they need for an I.D. check on the hitter. I want to know who the son of a bitch was. You got all that?"

"Yes, sir?"

"Right. Go to it." Steiger winced again as Torvalt probed the wound. *"Christ!* You having fun, Doctor?"

"Sorry, Colonel," Torvalt said. "It's just that I've never seen a wound like this before. I wanted to make certain that there were no lead projectile fragments remaining in the wound. There could be a danger of lead poisoning—"

Steiger laughed. "Hell, Doc, if that had been a fragmentation round, I wouldn't be sitting here. The bullet went clean through. Just spray on some disinfectant, slap a graft patch on and let me out of here. I've got work to do."

Forrester glanced at the nervous-looking man who'd just entered the room. "With the security situation the way it is, I wanted Dr. Gulliver close by, where I could personally keep an eye on him."

"Forgive me, gentlemen," Gulliver said, hesitantly. "I did not mean to intrude, but I . . ." he stared at Andre. "Good Lord! You're a woman!"

"I was last time I checked," said Andre.

Gulliver turned to Forrester with a befuddled look. "But . . . a *female* military officer?"

And as he turned, he noticed the far wall of Forrester's penthouse quarters. The entire wall was a window looking out over the lights and illuminated towers of Pendleton Base sprawled out below, a panoramic view that even included the sulferous glow of Los Angeles off in the distance, to the north, Gulliver gasped.

"Merciful heavens! Where in God's name *am* I?" He approached the window slowly. "I could have sworn there was a wall here when I came in!"

Forrester picked up his remote ambience control from the coffee table and opaqued the window, switching to the holographic slide. Gulliver caught his breath as he suddenly found himself staring at what appeared to be a solid wall, painted a deep maroon, with paintings hanging on it. The effect was completely three dimensional.

"It's done with this, Dr. Gulliver," said Forrester, showing him the remote control unit. "It isn't a real wall, you see. It's only a projection . . . uh, an illusion. A sort of trick. See, I can change the color of the wall in an instant if I choose to."

He clicked another button on the unit and the wall became dark green.

"However, in actuality, the entire wall is really a large window," Forrester said, canceling the projection.

Gulliver stared out at the view, mesmerized. "I am not insane," he mumbled. "I am *not* insane. I am *not.*"

"No, Dr. Gulliver, you're not," said Forrester, coming up to the man and putting his hand on his shoulder. "You have simply found yourself in a situation that taxes all your beliefs. However, I remind you of the things that you have already experienced and seen and known without a shadow of a doubt to be absolutely real. And as difficult to believe as this may seem, this too is real. You have been transported almost a thousand years into the future, to the 27th century, where the advances in our technology make your society seem as primitive as Norman England would seem to Londoners in the year 1702."

Gulliver slowly approached the window, then recoiled with a small cry.

"Don't worry, it's quite safe," said Forrester.

Gulliver shook his head. "At first I thought that we were in a house atop some mountain, but . . . dear Lord, this building must be . . ." his voice trailed off in incomprehension.

"A hundred and fifty stories tall," said Forrester. "And it's not even a very tall building by the standards of this time."

Gulliver continued to stare raptly out the window at the panoramic view. Delaney came up to him and offered him a glass of whiskey.

"Here, Doctor," he said. "For medicinal purposes."

Gulliver sniffed the glass and smiled. "Good malt whiskey," he said, with a weak smile. "Thank God for something familiar."

He drained the glass.

"I think I had better sit down, if I may," he said.

"Please do," said Forrester. "I know things have been very confusing for you since you arrived here, Dr. Gulliver. One moment, you were in 18th century London, and the next, you were somehow magically transported to a sort of prison cell and held there without explanation for twenty-four hours. In fact, it was not really a prison cell at all, but something we call a 'secure transport coordinate zone.' We maintain a number of such secure areas and one of their functions is to handle unusual cases such as yours, where it becomes necessary to transport someone from the past without adequate preparation or warning. It was necessary to hold you for that time so that we could take certain precautions."

"I know you must have many questions," Forrester continued. "So do we. Alexander Steiger was a soldier, a Temporal Observer . . . a sort of spy, if you will. Since Cpl. Steiger had no time to send us a complete report, he sent you, instead. Whatever it was that attacked you and killed Cpl. Steiger located you by means of this."

Forrester held up a little plastic envelope containing what looked like a tiny, bright blue seed.

"By means of *that* little thing? What is it?" Gulliver said.

"It is a highly sophisticated signalling device," said Forrester. "It's been deactivated. It was implanted under your skin, behind your left ear."

Gulliver's hand went to the spot behind his ear. "What? But . . . *how?* There is nothing . . ."

"You were rendered unconscious for a time," said Forrester. He held up his hand as Gulliver was about to speak. "Yes, I know you don't remember. And there is no point in feeling around behind your ear, Doctor. You will find no evidence of surgery, I assure you. Not even the faintest scar. Please, try to understand, we have the ability to do things that someone from your time could not even begin to understand. It is unavoidable that you will be exposed to some of them, and I will attempt to explain whatever I can if there is time; but in many cases, the explanation itself would require a complex explanation, and it would involve a challenge to your systems of belief. I know it is difficult, but please try to bear with me and accept that what I tell you is the truth. We need your help, Dr. Gulliver. Millions of lives could be at stake. Will you help us?"

"I do not understand any of this, General," said Gulliver, nervously, "and I must admit that I am frightened, but somewhat less frightened now then when I first arrived here. You have been most considerate. And as you have pointed out, I have already seen things that defy belief on the island of the little people and somehow I have managed to accept them and survive. There is much here that I don't understand. I cannot comprehend how it is possible that I have been somehow transported a thousand years into the future, but I cannot deny the evidence of my senses."

He gestured at the window. "That is unquestionably *not* the world I came from. Sandy . . . or Cpl. Steiger, as you call him, accepted my tale when everyone else believed me to be mad. And now, because of me, he is dead. That, General, is something I can comprehend only too well. Yes, of course, I will do whatever I can to help."

"Good," said Forrester. "Then if you will bear with me, I'll attempt to answer some of your questions and explain who Sandy was and why he sent you here. . . ."

"Excuse me, sir," said Forrester's orderly, interrupting them.

"Yes, Roberts, what is it?"

"Sgt. Danelli of the I.S.D. just called from the base hospital. There's been an attempt on Col. Steiger's life."

Delaney was out of his chair like a shot. "Is he all right?"

"He's been wounded, sir," said Roberts, "but I'm assured it's only superficial. In fact, I was told he'll be on his way up here momentarily. Unfortunately, both men on his security escort were killed. Sgt. Danelli said Col. Steiger is certain the Network was responsible. Obviously, someone knew he was going to be in that hospital morgue."

"Hell, he only left here less than twenty minutes ago!" said Forrester.

"It's seems likely that someone affiliated with the Network reported that his brother's body was being brought in," said Sgt. Roberts. "Sgt. Danelli is going to be checking with the S & R team that brought Cpl. Steiger back and working back from there to see how many people knew about it. Along the line, someone must have leaked the information and an assassin was sent to the hospital morgue on the theory that Col. Steiger would be bound to go there. I.S.D. found one of the pathologists murdered and stuffed into a supply closet. Col. Steiger felt, however, that there was another possibility."

"That this place is bugged," said Andre.

"What, my own quarters?" Forrester said, with disbelief.

"An I.S.D. unit is on its way to sweep for surveillance devices," Roberts said. "However, Sgt. Danelli seemed to think it was an unlikely possibility. If they could get in here to plant a bug, then why not go ahead and plant a bomb?"

"We'd better get you out of here, sir," said Delaney.

"Well, now where the hell am I supposed to go?" said Forrester. "You think it's any safer out there? Forget it. I'm not going to run from these people. I'm much better off being where they can make a try for me. That'll at least give us an opportunity to tackle them. Hiding won't solve anything. Besides, if they wanted to, they could take out this entire building with a small guided missle."

"I.S.D. has already anticipated that, sir," said Roberts. "There's been an S.D. battery emplaced upon the roof."

Forrester stared at him. "Are you serious? Somebody installed a Strategic Defense battery on my roof? *When?*"

"Last week, sir," Roberts said. "It was air lifted into place and—"

"On *whose* orders?"

"Col. Steiger's, sir."

"Well, it's sure as hell nice of somebody to tell me!" Forrester said.

"I . . . I'm sorry, sir, I thought you knew," said Roberts.

"Well, it's a fine goddamn thing when the Director of Temporal Intelligence doesn't even know there's an autopulser battery up on his own roof! What the hell *else* has Col. Steiger authorized that I don't know about?"

"I've ordered your personnal security increased, for one thing," Steiger said, walking in on the tail end of the conversation. He hadn't even stopped to change his torn and bloodied shirt. "And I don't want to hear any arguments about it, either. These people aren't playing around."

"Colonel, you're insubordinate!"

"Fine, you want my damn birds, you can have 'em anytime you want," Steiger snapped back, ripping off his insignia and tossing them on the floor at Forrester's feet. "I only know one way to do my job and that's not to take any halfass measures! You're not out in the field facing soldiers anymore; it isn't that straightforward. You're up against intelligence pros who make the Timekeepers look like a smalltime inner city street gang. The Network wants you dead and if I was a betting man, my money'd be on them. However, since *I'm* one of their targets too, I'd kinda like to make it a little harder for them to score a hit. They came pretty damn close just now and I almost bought it. I'm not about to let them get that close to you. So either let me do my job or relieve me of command!"

There was a moment of shocked silence following his outburst, then Forrester softly cleared his throat.

"Are you finished?" he said.

"Yes *sir*, I'm finished, *sir!*"

"Fine. Pick up your eagles. When and if I want them, I'll tear them off you myself, is that understood?"

"Yes, sir."

"I didn't hear you."

"Yes, *sir*!" said Steiger, snapping to attention.

"Oh, stand at ease, for God's sake. Roberts, get the colonel one of my fresh shirts. He seems to have torn his."

"You okay?" Delaney said. Steiger was wired so tight, he seemed to be vibrating.

Steiger took a deep breath and let it out slowly. "Yeah, I guess I'll live." Then he seemed to notice Gulliver for the first time. He looked at him and blinked twice, taken aback at not having realized there was a stranger in the room with them. "Who the hell is *that*?"

Gulliver had followed the preceeding conversation with incomprehension and alarm. Now he rose uncertainly to his feet and hesitantly extended his hand.

"Dr. Lemuel Gulliver, at your service, sir."

"Col. Creed Steiger." They shook hands.

"I perceive you have been wounded. I do not have my instruments with me, but . . ."

Steiger shook his head. "Thank you, but it wasn't very serious. I've already had it seen to." He frowned. "*What* did you say your name was?"

"Dr. Gulliver is the man mentioned in your brother's report," said Forrester.

Steiger stared at him. Gulliver had been given a suit of disposable green transit fatigues to wear, so there had been nothing to mark him externally as a T.D.P., a temporally displaced person.

"Sandy was your brother?" Gulliver said. "There is a strong family resemblance. He was very kind to me." There was a pained expression on his face. "If not for me, he might have . . . I . . . I wish . . . it really should have been me, instead."

Steiger stared at him for a moment, then nodded sympathetically. "No one's blaming you, Doctor." He glanced at Forrester. "Sandy sent him through?"

"Yes, to tell us what he couldn't," said Forrester, with a tight grimace. "You saw him?"

Steiger nodded. The tension had started to go out of him, though he was still wired from the news of his brother's death and the attempt on his life. Roberts brought him one of

Forrester's black fatigue shirts and Steiger accepted it grate-
fully, wincing as he removed his own torn and bloodied
one.

"They homed in on him with this," said Forrester, handing
Steiger the plastic envelope containing the implant transmitter.

Steiger examined it, frowning. "It doesn't make sense. If
they had him long enough to surgically install a cybernetic
implant, they had him long enough to kill him. Why fit him
with an implant, let him go, and then track him down and kill
him?"

"Maneuvers?" said Delaney.

They all turned to look at him.

"What?" said Steiger.

"I was just thinking out loud," Delaney said. "Maybe they
installed the implant and let him go so they could practice
long-range assault tactics. Track the target, home in on the
target's coordinates, clock in, hit hard, take out the target and
clock out again. Suppose you had a target area that was hard to
get to, maybe you could only get one man in or you had the
coordinates, but a full-scale assault would be impractical for
whatever reason. Too well defended, not enough room to
maneuver . . . but if you could clock in a miniaturized
assault force . . ."

"Jesus," Steiger said. "That could be a bloody nightmare!"

"It *is* a bloody nightmare," Forrester said, grimly. "What's
more, we're not even sure who's responsible for it. Is this some
new wrinkle from the Special Operations Group in the parallel
universe or has the Network somehow managed to come up
with this?"

"Either way, we've only got one lead," Delaney said. He
looked at Gulliver.

"You're not going to ask me to go back there, are you?"
Gulliver said, in a hollow voice.

"Our Archives Section has been unable to find any record of
such an island, Dr. Gulliver," said Forrester. "I realize you've
already been through a great deal, but perhaps if you could help
us to locate this island, or at least show us its location on a
chart, then we'd require nothing further from you."

"And what shall become of me then?" Gulliver stared at
them all anxiously.

"Have no fear. You'll be returned to your own time," said Forrester. "And we shall arrange it so that you have no memory of this experience."

"You could do that? You could actually take away my memory?"

"Yes," said Forrester. "But there's no need to be concerned. The procedure is quite safe and painless, I assure you."

Gulliver shook his head vehemently. "No! No, absolutely not! I cannot allow that."

"I'm afraid you have no choice in the matter, Dr. Gulliver," said Forrester. "You have seen entirely too much."

"And who in their right mind would believe me?" Gulliver responded. "They ridiculed me for my story of the lilliputians, as Mr. Swift called them, can you imagine how they would react if I told them about *this*? They would undoubtedly put me in a madhouse. I suppose that I could not prevent your using force against me, but in that case, I would refuse to help you. I would tell you nothing."

"Dr. Gulliver," said Forrester, "please try to understand—"

"No, General, *you* try to understand. A man's life is but the sum of his experience. How can I forget what's happened to me? How can I forget that gallant young man who gave his life to save my own? I said that I would help you, but it must be in my own way. If I were to tell you all I know and show you the island's location on a chart, then there would be nothing to prevent you from doing as you will with me. No, sir. If you are going back there, then much as I dread it, I fear that I must go as well."

Forrester glanced at Gulliver, his mouth set in a tight grimace.

"Dr. Gulliver, you're putting me in a very difficult position. We could easily get the information that we need from you, even without your consent. And yes, it would involve using a form of force, though not what you might think. You would feel no pain whatsoever. In fact, you would feel mildly euphoric and be happy to tell us whatever we wanted to know. However, I would prefer to have your voluntary cooperation. And I'm not unsympathetic to your feelings in this matter. I'll have to give it some thought."

Suddenly Andre gasped and dropped her glass.

"What is it?" Steiger said.

She was staring at the window behind them. For a moment, only the briefest instant, she had seen Lucas standing in front of it, but there was nothing there now. She blinked and shook her head.

"Nothing," she said, swallowing hard. "It was nothing. I just thought . . . for a moment, I thought . . ."

Delaney was watching her with concern. "Andre, you all right?"

"You didn't see anything?" she said. "Over there, by the window? You didn't see?"

Delaney shook his head, frowning. "No, I was looking at Dr. Gulliver."

"What did you see?" said Steiger, frowning.

Andre shook her head. "Nothing," she said, nervously. "It must have been my imagination, a trick of the light . . . I don't know."

"What do you *think* you saw?" Delaney said.

"*Nothing*! It was nothing, just *drop* it, all right?"

"Lieutenant?" said Forrester.

"I'm sorry, sir," she said, sheepishly. "It wasn't anything. I . . . I guess I'm a little jumpy, what with everything that's happened tonight."

"Well, we've all been under a strain," said Forrester. "And I'm afraid it's going to get a lot worse before it gets much better." He glanced at his watch. "It's almost dawn. Why don't you all go freshen up and grab some chow and coffee? Dr. Gulliver will stay here with me. Be back here for a briefing at oh-six-hundred hours."

As they left, Finn Delaney grabbed Andre by the arm. "You're not the type to jump at shadows," he said. "You want to tell me about it?"

"I've already told you—"

He interrupted her. "Something's bothering you, Andre. I know you too damn well. You saw something back there or you *thought* you saw something. What was it?"

"Okay, you're right, I thought I saw something. I guess I'm seeing things. That makes me a liability, right? Maybe I should go to the division shrink and get myself checked out."

"Hell, you're saner than anyone I know," Delaney said.

"And we've known each other too long to keep things from each other. Now tell me what you saw."

Andre licked her lips nervously. "A ghost, all right? I just saw a ghost."

3

"You should've let me stay dead," said Lucas Priest, sighing and wearily running his hand through his dark brown hair. "I simply can't seem to control it."

Dr. Robert Darkness turned a steely gaze on Priest. "You *will* control it. You will *learn*. You have become the living embodiment of my life's work, Priest. I brought you back from death for this and I'll be damned if I'm going to allow you to give up!"

"It doesn't look as if I have much choice, does it?" Lucas said, rubbing his aching head.

He lit up a cigarette and inhaled deeply. The simple act of smoking helped to keep his mind occupied. It was excruciatingly difficult trying to control his thoughts. It had never before occurred to him just how exhausting it could be. Random thoughts were taken for granted by most people, but unlike most people—in fact, unlike anyone else in the entire universe—Lucas Priest could no longer afford to take random thoughts for granted. A random thought could mean disaster for him now. And his thoughts were becoming increasingly harder to control. A person could concentrate only for so long and then something had to give. Lucas was tired. And he was afraid.

He had always thought of Dr. Darkness as a brilliant

scientist, eccentric, highly idiosyncratic and unpredictable, but it went beyond that. Dr. Darkness was a madman. Not a raving lunatic, but a madman just the same. It was often said that there was an exceedingly fine line between genius and insanity. When had Darkness slipped over the edge? Was it after his invention of the warp grenade, the most devastating weapon known to man? Perhaps his sanity had been derailed by the knowledge that his invention had been responsible for the loss of billions of lives, when the surplus nuclear energy of exploding warp grenades was mistakenly clocked into a parallel universe, setting off the war between the timelines. Or maybe he lost it after the disastrous experiment in which his atomic structure became permanently tachyonized, turning him into the man who was faster than light. There were so many cataclysmic upheavals in the life of Dr. Darkness, so much pressure brought to bear upon his fragile genius that it was a wonder he had not snapped completely.

Dr. Darkness never spoke about his past. Lucas knew nothing about it whatsoever prior to the event that gave him both his fame and infamy. After years of laboring as an obscure research scientist in the Temporal Army Ordnance Division, Darkness had invented the terrifying warp grenade purely as an accidental by-product of his own independent work in temporal translocation.

He had begun by working on voice and image communication by tachyon radio transmission. He eventually achieved a method of communication at six hundred times the speed of light, but that still wasn't good enough. He wanted it to be instantaneous, even over distances measured in hundreds of light years. Working from the obscure zen mathematics based upon Georg Cantor's theory of transfinite numbers, Darkness found a way to make his tachyon beam move more quickly by sending it through an Einstein-Rosen Bridge, more commonly known as a "space warp." The result was instantaneous transmission, going from point A to point B without having to cover the distance in between. The warp grenade was merely an incidental by-product of this discovery.

It occurred to Darkness one day that his method of translocation through an Einstein-Rosen Bridge could be applied to nuclear devices, allowing unprecedented control of nuclear explosions and drastically limiting fallout, in some cases almost eliminating it entirely. Having explored this idea merely as an intellectual exercise in abstract theory, Darkness lost all interest in it. However, since the Temporal Army Ordnance Division took control of all the paperwork and computer data generated by its scientists, from complex equations down to incidental doodles done on Temporal Army time and in Temporal Army facilities, the end result of this "intellectual exercise in abstract theory" was the warp grenade, a combination nuclear device and time machine, small enough to be held in one hand and capable of adjustable, transtemporal detonation.

The principles behind the function of the warp grenade led Darkness to the development of the warp disc, which had rendered Prof. Mensinger's chronoplate obsolete. It had also led him to the development of the disruptor, or the "warp gun" as it was sometimes called by those few who knew of its existence. It was the first true disintegrator ray. Yet as frightening a weapon as the disruptor was, the warp grenade made it seem tame by comparison. It could be set to destroy a city, or a city block, or one house within that block, or a room within that house, or a space within that room no larger than a breadbox. The surplus energy of the explosion, whatever was not required to accomplish the designated task, was then clocked instantaneously through an Einstein-Rosen Bridge, to explode harmlessly in the Orion Nebula—or so it was believed.

The problem was that so much devastating energy clocked through Einstein-Rosen Bridges eventually shifted the chronophysical alignment of the universe. The result was that every time a warp grenade was detonated, instead of the surplus energy being teleported to the Orion Nebula, a parallel universe was nuked. Millions of lives were lost and though Darkness had never detonated a single warp grenade, he had to live with the knowledge of what his work had led to. That alone, thought Lucas, could easily destroy a man.

Shortly after the Temporal Army had conducted its first test detonation of a warp grenade, Dr. Darkness disappeared. No one knew where he had gone. He had wanted to get as far away from people as it was possible to get, so he took off for some remote part of the galaxy, to carry on his work in an environment where he could keep complete control of it. From time to time, he would release some new discovery through one of several Earth-based conglomerates he controlled, thereby financing his further experiments in tachyon translation, a process no one else alive could even begin to understand. And, as it turned out, even Dr. Darkness hadn't fully understood it.

He had been obsessed with the idea of perfecting a process whereby the human body could be translated into tachyons, which would then depart at six hundred times the speed of light along the direction of a tachyon beam through an Einstein-Rosen Bridge.

On paper, he believed that he had solved the problems, but what was mathematically real and what was *really* real were often two very different things. His main concerns had to do with the reassembly process, ensuring that the organs and the tissues were reassembled in the appropriate order at the appropriate time and place. Because there would be no "receiver," Darkness had incorporated a timing mechanism into the tachyon conversion, so that the tachyonized body could be reassembled at the instant of arrival based on the time/space coordinates of the transition. And when he was certain that he had the process finally perfected, he became his own first human test subject. His ego would never have allowed anyone else to be the first to experience direct translation into tachyons.

Unfortunately, Dr. Darkness had neglected one small element of the equation. His "taching" process was ultimately restrained by a little known principle of physics called the law of baryon conservation. Lucas was never quite able to follow the scientific explanation, but it had something to do with the idea that objects with mass could not be translated into particles with "zero rest mass." Or, as Darkness had sarcastically put it, "you can't roller skate in a buffalo herd." When Lucas questioned that enigmatic analogy, Darkness lost his patience and told him to look up the works of a 20th century philosopher named Roger Miller.

In nonabstract terms, what the principle meant to Darkness in the real world was a glitch in the translation process that resulted in his body being permanently tachyonized. He became "the man who was faster than light." He could travel from his secret laboratory headquarters somewhere in the far reaches of the universe to Earth or anywhere else in the blink of an eye— much quicker, actually—but once he had arrived, he was incapable of normal movement, appearing much like a holographic projection or a ghost seen underwater, frozen in time, trapped by the immutable laws of the universe.

Unlike a holographic projection, he was not insubstantial, although being faster than light, he *could* be if he wanted to. However, like a holographic projection, he could not move so much as one step. At least, not normally. He needed to project himself from one place to another. "Taching," as he called it. His atomic structure had become unstable. His tachyonization had rendered him immune to aging or disease. No bacteria could latch onto him because they simply were not fast enough. In a sense, Darkness had become immortal, yet due to the increasingly unstable nature of his atomic structure, he knew a time would one day come when his body would literally discorporate, departing at multiples of light speed in all directions of the universe.

It seemed incredible to Lucas that anyone could maintain even a semblance of sanity under such conditions; yet on the surface, Darkness was completely lucid, brilliant, and controlled . . . albeit in a thoroughly skewed manner. He was a driven man, obsessed, not knowing how much time he had before he flew apart in all directions. It could be centuries or it could be only seconds and he did not want to leave his work undone. And that was where Lucas had come in.

During their mission to destroy Nikolai Drakov's pirate submarine, *The Nautilus*, Darkness had "terminaled" Lucas with a tachyon symbiotracer that bonded to certain protein molecules in the cells of his nervous system. The device, which operated on the particle level, represented a technology which Darkness had pioneered and which only he fully understood. The purpose of the symbiotracer was to allow Darkness to "home in" on Lucas no matter where he was in space and time. However, unknown to Lucas, the symbiotracer had built into it a prototype of the particle-level chronocircuitry that Darkness was experimenting with— essentially, a particle-level warp disc, organic and completely thought controlled.

The device had become a permanent part of Lucas Priest's atomic structure. He could no more get rid of it than he could get a body transplant. When the symbiotracer had first been given to him in the medium of a graft patch from a medikit, he had believed that minor surgery would be able to remove it. He had never suspected that the device would fuse with his very atoms. He was even more dismayed when he realized that the symbiotracer function was only *part* of what Darkness had designed the chronocircuitry to do. But by the time he knew that, he had already died.

At least, he had been *meant* to die. And in some parallel timeframe that wound its way about him like a double helix strand of DNA, Lucas thought he must have realized that fate and *had*, in fact, died. He did not remember dying, of course, because that event had been in his future, relative to the moment in which Darkness had snatched him away, and that future had been changed. His death was now an irrevocable fact of Finn and Andre's past, yet it was only an alternate future for himself, a potential future he had bypassed. It happened . . . and it didn't happen.

It was the sort of zen koan puzzle that was taught in advanced temporal physics classes, a hypothetical set of temporal conditions that zen physics professors referred to as "problem modules," situations that were mind-boggling, defying any application of conventional science or logic, capable of inducing nervous breakdowns in even the most gifted students who attempted to relate them to conventional reality or solve them with conventional reasoning. Only this was not a classroom problem module. This was real.

Ever since he had learned what happened, Lucas had been trying desperately to figure it all out, to assess the implications, both for himself and for the timeline. It was driving him to the brink of a nervous collapse. And he knew that now, of all times, he had to keep his cool, his mental discipline focused, and yet it was impossible. Thanks to Dr. Darkness filling in the blanks for him, he knew what the original scenario had been, *before* Dr. Darkness had effected his unique temporal adjustment. It was, of course, a scenario that Lucas had never personally experienced—not from where he stood right now. He remembered only part of it. But from the vantage point of another time frame, he *had* experienced it. And it had killed him.

The tribesmen still trapped in the pass were run down and trampled by the lancers as they thundered through. Then the cavalry formed a line upon the plain and charged the fleeing enemy. There was no escape. The Ghazis died in the rice fields, run through by the lances and struck down by the cavalry sabres. Bodies fell everywhere as the lancers descended on the fleeing Ghazis and butchered them.

"Christ," said Hugo, turning away from the carnage down below. "I'm sorry, General, but that's more than I can stand to watch. I've seen enough of death."

Churchill was riveted by the spectacle. "They shall not forget this," he said. "It's probably the first time any of them have seen what cavalry can do, given room to deploy their strength. Henceforth, the very words, 'Bengal Lancers' shall strike terror into their hearts."

As he spoke, a lone Ghazi sniper, who had remained undiscovered, hidden behind the rocks of his crumbled sangar, rose to a kneeling position and brought his jezail rifle to bear upon the surgeon, Hugo, whom he mistakenly took to be the commander of the British forces. As he raised his rifle, Lucas spotted him.

He yelled, "Hugo, look out!"

Instinctively, after so much time spent under enemy fire, Hugo reacted by throwing himself down flat upon the ground. In an instant, Lucas saw that Hugo's combat-quick response had placed Churchill directly in the line of fire. In an instant of white hot, adrenaline charged clarity, he saw it all and made a running dive for Churchill—

—and landed on a hand woven carpet of Chinese silk.

For a moment, he lay stunned, unable to move. All he could see were the colors of the carpet, brilliant red, metallic gold and indigo, a richly complex pattern, figured with dragons and stylized lions. Slowly, he pushed himself up and looked around.

He was in a large, circular room with a domed, observatory ceiling. The most dominant object in the room was a huge radio telescope. All around him were banks of computers and other electronic instruments he could not identify, with rows upon rows of blinking lights and dials and digital and video displays. Laboratory equipment vied for space with exquisite Victorian antiques and bronze sculptures and impressionistic oil paintings. Books were everywhere, crammed to overflowing in tall bookcases, stacked upon tables and piled high upon the floor. As Lucas slowly stood, he turned and saw a huge, curved bay window behind him. The landscape outside was rocky and desolate. And red-orange. The vermilion sands stretched out for as far as the eye could see, nothing but an unbroken vista of rock-strewn, reddish-orange desert. And there were three moons in the sky.

"What the *hell*?" said Lucas.

"It does rather look like hell, doesn't it?" said a deep, vaguely continental voice from behind him.

Lucas turned to see a tall and slender man, with dark, unruly hair that came down to his collar in the back and a neatly trimmed moustache. He was gaunt, with dark, penetrating eyes and a sharp, prominent nose. He was dressed in a button-down white shirt, a silk tie with a regimental stripe, a dark brown waistcoat with a gold watch chain and a brown, tweed Norfolk jacket with dark wool trousers and expensive, handmade Italian shoes. He carried a hickory walking stick and wore a brown fedora. One moment, he seemed solid and the next, he was semitransparent. He seemed to flicker like a faulty hologram.

"Darkness!" Lucas said. "What the hell is going on? Where *am* I? What happened to the others? Where's Churchill? Is he all right?"

Dr. Darkness raised his eyebrows. "Which of that plethora of questions would you like me to answer first?"

"How about where am I?"

"You are a guest in my home," said Darkness.

"Your . . . home?" said Lucas, feeling totally bewildered. Darkness put the walking stick down on a table and then moved across the room toward a sideboard where he kept several bottles of whiskey, a gasogene and a decanter.

Lucas stared at him with astonishment. He had never before seen Dr. Darkness walk. However, what he was doing wasn't exactly walking. Darkness seemed to be moving in a series of extremely rapid, stop-motion frames, as if he were illuminated by a strobe light. As he made his way across the room, he left behind a series of blurred, ghostly afterimages of himself that faded out like contrails.

"I was once able to walk normally while I was here in my unprojected state," he explained when he noticed Lucas staring. "However, it appears that the stability of my atomic structure is gradually degenerating. I'm having some anxiety over it, since there doesn't seem to be anything that I can do about it."

He poured himself a glass of single malt Scotch and then started to pour one for Lucas. He was at least twenty feet across the room when he held the glass out to Lucas, but in the next split second, he was standing right in front of him, close enough for him to take the glass. Lucas blinked. He never could get used to the way the man could project himself through time and space. It was . . . unsettling, to say the least.

Lucas accepted the whiskey and took a hearty swallow from the glass. It felt good going down. "Why am I here? What happened, Doc?" he said.

"Nothing much," Darkness replied. "I've only saved your life."

Lucas stared at him. He felt confused. "But what about . . . God, what about Churchill?"

"Rest assured that Winston Churchill is perfectly all right," Darkness said.

"But . . . how? He was right in the line of fire!" Lucas said. "I jumped to shove him out of the way and . . . and the Ghazi fired and . . ." His voice trailed off. He had a horrible feeling that something was very, very wrong. "Doc, tell me what happened back there!"

"I simply tached you out of harm's way," said Darkness. "Otherwise that bullet would have struck you and you would have found it decidedly unpleasant."

"But . . . then what kept it from hitting Churchill?"

"I merely interposed another mass between Churchill and the bullet."

"What are you talking about? What mass?"

"Your twin."

"My *what*?"

"Your twin from the parallel universe," said Darkness. "He was already dead, you see. Your friend Delaney killed him, which was quite convenient. All I did was move at multiples of light speed, take your twin's body and switch it with yours, taching you back here while I positioned your double's corpse in such a way that the ball from the Ghazi's rifle would enter at the exact same spot as Delaney's bayonet had when he killed your twin. It was actually rather complicated and it took some careful timing, but— "

"Wait a minute, wait a minute!" Lucas said, staring wide-eyed at the scientist. "What the *hell* are you talking about? *What* twin from the parallel universe? And what's this about Delaney killing him? When did all this happen? I don't remember *any* of this!"

"Well, naturally. That's because it all happened in a slightly different timeframe," Darkness explained. He hesitated. "After you . . . uh . . . died."

"After I *what*?" Lucas suddenly felt as if his stomach were trying to turn itself inside out.

"Died," said Darkness. He cleared his throat. "After you died. Here, perhaps you'd better have another drink. Settle your nerves."

He handed Lucas another glass of Scotch. Lucas never saw him go back to the bar and pour it. It didn't even look as if he'd moved. He felt dizzy and there was an aching pressure in his chest.

"I think you'd better sit down," said Dr. Darkness.

Lucas half sat, half collapsed into a large, leather uphol-stered reading chair.

"Jesus, Doc . . . what have you done?"

"Well, I saved your life, for one thing. You might at least say thank you."

"No," said Lucas, softly. He swallowed hard and shook his head. "No, I won't thank you. I can't." He closed his eyes. "Oh, Jesus, I'm dead. Or I should be dead. That Ghazi fired his rifle a split second after I leaped and . . . and that bullet should have hit me. It *did* hit me! My God, Doc, don't you realize what you've done? *You've caused a timestream split!*"

"I've done no such thing," said Darkness. "I have been monitoring the situation assiduously and my instruments have detected absolutely no evidence of a timestream split. I rather thought there wouldn't be, but I couldn't be absolutely certain." He shrugged. "Occasionally, one must take some risks in order to gain knowledge. Actually, it was quite an interesting experiment. You see, I could easily have deflected that bullet. It wouldn't have taken much, merely matching its speed and giving it a slight nudge would have accomplished the desired result. However, in that event, I would have altered the conditions of the past in a manner that might have affected the entire scenario, not only yourself.

"For one thing, a number of people had already seen you die," Darkness continued as Lucas listened with stunned disbelief. "That in itself might not have been all that significant from a temporal standpoint, but unfortunately, by the time I learned about your untimely demise, you had already been buried and certain significant events had already proceeded from that point, taking the factor of your death into account."

Lucas listened to it with a sort of shocked detachment. He simply couldn't take it in. Darkness was calmly talking about his death, *about his having been buried,* and yet, incredibly, despite having died, he was alive. His mind reeled as he tried to assimilate it all. The more Darkness told him, the crazier it sounded.

"I recall standing over your grave and feeling absolutely furious," said Darkness. "You were to have been the vehicle for my greatest achievement, the living prototype of my ultimate invention, and you were dead! Well, granted, I always knew there was some risk of that, considering the highly dangerous nature of your occupation, but that was precisely what made you such an ideal candidate. You routinely traveled throughout different time periods and were exposed to a wide variety of environments, all of which made for excellent field testing conditions. Being a temporal agent, you were equipped with a warp disc, which provided a perfect failsafe system. And finally, I don't think that anyone but a temporal agent would have possessed the necessary abilities to deal with the stresses the field testing would have generated. You were perfect. However, to be on the safe side, I also terminaled Andre Cross and Finn Delaney, in case anything should have happened to you. Just my luck, Cross and Delaney's terminals malfunctioned. The symbiotracer functions continue to work just fine, but the telempathic chronocircuitry embedded in the particle chips burned out during the process of molecular bonding. I still haven't entirely licked that problem. In any case, that left me with only you. Your telempathic chronocircuitry survived the bonding process. And then, like an idiot, you had to go and get yourself killed. Which meant that my project, the end result of my life's work, was also dead. And *that,* my friend, was simply unacceptable!

"I didn't see how I could possibly do anything about it, though," Darkness continued, "until I discovered that among the enemy soldiers who had crossed over from the parallel universe was your alternate self, your mirror image from the other timeline. He was an officer in the Special Operations Group—their counterpart to the Time Commandos. His name was also Lucas Priest and he was indistinguisable from you in virtually all respects, right down to his DNA. And that's when inspiration struck! The perfect opportunity presented itself when the twin Lucas Priest attempted to kill Andre Cross and Finn Delaney saved her life by bayoneting him.

"All this occurred after you'd already died, you see," Darkness explained, "shot down saving Winston Churchill's life. I theorized that there would be little danger of temporal interference if I merely switched the bodies. Lucas Priest had died in front of witnesses, saving Winston Churchill's life. After the switch was made, a Lucas Priest would still be dead. It would be a *different* Lucas Priest, but no one would be the wiser. And if the switch did not affect the outcome of events in any way, then the danger of temporal interference seemed minimal, if not nonexistent. It required only that I dress the corpse of the twin Priest in clothing identical to that which you'd been wearing, use the terminal to tach you out of the bullet's path an instant before impact, then position the corpse of the twin Priest in such a manner that the bullet would impact precisely upon the bayonet wound, allowing the corpse to then fall to the ground an infinitessimal fraction of a second later, all of it occurring at a speed faster than the eye could follow or a bullet could travel. True, a close examination would have disclosed that the body had been stabbed first, and then shot in the exact same place, but there would never be such an examination. There would be no reason for it. They had all seen what had happened, after all. They would have no reason to suspect that anything else other than what they had seen might have happened at faster than light speeds. The result of it all would not only be a fascinating experiment in temporal physics, but it would also save the invention that I'd worked my whole life to perfect."

"This thing you keep referring to," said Lucas, trying to keep up. "This terminal . . . you said something about *telempathic* chronocircuitry?"

"Correct," said Darkness. "I haven't really given it an official designation yet. It more or less functions as a sort of terminal, or at least it makes *you* function as one, so that's how I've been thinking of it. Essentially, it is a particle-level, thought-controlled warp disc employing telempathic chrono-circuitry. It had to be initially triggered by a remote-controlled, tachyon signal, which is to say that I had to turn it on, but after that it became permanently armed, so to speak, controlled exclusively by the thought waves of the recipient. That's you."

"You mean . . ." Lucas felt his voice break momentarily and he cleared his throat. "You mean to tell me that this thing enables the recipient to clock through time merely by *thinking* about it?"

"Well, it would entail a great deal of control and mental discipline on the part of the recipient," said Darkness, "but essentially, yes, that's quite correct. So it helps to pay close attention to what you're thinking about, otherwise you might just 'tach off' somewhere, if you'll excuse the pun."

Lucas stared at him with horror. "Are you telling me that you've turned me into a *living time machine*?"

"Well, that's a rather colorful way of putting it," said Darkness, "but it's more or less correct. Now that the telempathic function of your molecular-bonded chronocircuitry has been triggered, you can travel anywhere you want, instantaneously, merely by thinking about it."

There followed months of carefully controlled experiments in which Darkness used hypnosis to place Lucas into a trance state and then, through the medium of hypnotic suggestion, programmed him with specific translocation coordinates, from one side of the room to the other, for example. This sort of testing procedure, under rigidly controlled conditions, eliminated much of the danger, but the conditions could not remain so rigidly controlled forever. Lucas had to learn how to develop amazing mental discipline in order to control his telempathic chronocircuitry, otherwise a random thought could translocate him across time and space.

He had already accidentally "tached" or translocated back to Earth on several separate occasions, when he had found himself thinking about Andre and wishing he could be with her, explain to her what happened. And afterwards, each time,

he had felt ill. There was something about the process that
produced aftereffects, a pounding headache, pressure in the
chest, profound dizziness and nausea. She must think she's
losing it, he thought, seeing ghosts. He quickly pushed the
thought away with alarm. Lucas needed to maintain his mental
discipline in order to keep from 'taching off,' as Darkness had
put it. The man's got to be crazy, he thought. How the hell
could he have done this? He had changed Lucas's life—and
death—merely to safeguard an experiment. And as if that were
not enough, there was still the question of what effect his being
brought back to life would have upon the timestream.

Darkness seemed to believe that there would be no effect at
all, or else it would be a negligible one. Lucas was not so
certain. Without question, Darkness was more versed in the
mysteries of zen physics than Lucas was, but then Darkness
wasn't exactly normal anymore and hadn't been for quite some
time. In his own bizarre way, Darkness was reordering his own
reality and now he'd pulled Lucas into it, as well. He hadn't
done it out of any altruistic motive; he had merely wanted to
have his prototype telempathic translocator back. But regardless of what Darkness had said, there was no denying the fact
that *something* had occurred to "bump" the timeflow when he
had snatched Lucas out of that bullet's path.

If, in fact, there had been no temporal interference as a
result, then did that mean that nothing had changed at all? If
Lucas went back to 19th century Afghanistan and dug up his
own grave, would he find his *own* body mouldering inside it?
Or if the Search & Retrieve teams had already brought it back,
would they have cremated it according to the instructions in his
will and scattered the ashes throughout time? Would he be able
to walk into the headquarters building of the Temporal Army
Command and see his own name engraved upon the Wall of
Honor?

But then the fact of his survival meant that there *had* been a
change. Perhaps, since Darkness claimed his sophisticated
instruments had not detected any significant temporal fluctua-
tions, the event hadn't been temporally significant, but there
was a "ripple" in the timestream now—a timeframe in which
Lucas had died and a timeframe in which he hadn't—and those
two timeframes had to somehow become reconciled with each
other if there was to be no timestream split. Lucas knew there

was no guarantee at all that the temporal ripple which Darkness had set in motion by altering his fate would not somehow build momentum in the current of the timestream, setting off a series of seemingly insignificant events that could eventually result in a massive temporal disruption—perhaps even the timestream split that everybody feared. There was only one way that he would ever know for sure. And it didn't matter if he wasn't ready. There was too much at stake and there wasn't any choice. He simply had to risk it.

He had to go back.

4

Capt. Reese Hunter had become separated from his unit. In fact, he was about as far separated from his unit as it was possible to get. They were an entire universe apart and Reese Hunter was in the wrong one. The planet he was on was known as Earth, but it was not the Earth he came from. He was as thoroughly alien here as if he'd been a creature from another galaxy. Which, in fact, he was. His was a mirror-image galaxy, a parallel universe in a congruent timeline. The same, and yet, profoundly different. Hunter was behind enemy lines . . . and there was no way back.

He had been taken prisoner by a team of temporal agents who had crossed over into his universe. He had been unconscious when Andre Cross, Creed Steiger and Finn Delaney had brought him through the confluence point. When he had escaped from them, using a stolen warp disc, he hadn't realized that they had brought him back into their own timeline. It was only after he had clocked in at Pendleton Base, at the preset transition coordinates the warp disc had been programmed with, that he suddenly realized, as Dorothy would have said, that he was not in Kansas anymore. Fortunately for him, no one at Pendleton Base had expected an escaped prisoner with a stolen warp disc to be clocking in, least of all an officer of the S. O. G.'s Counter Insurgency Section. As a result, he'd been able to bluff his way through, buying himself just enough time to program a new set of transition coordinates into the stolen disc. It had been one hell of a big risk. The discs used by his people were not quite the same and he hadn't really been sure of what he was doing.

He didn't know if they'd be able to trace him through the disc or not, but he had known that he could not afford to wait around and find out. It would have been only a matter of time, perhaps only moments, before the alarm was given and they'd be looking for him. He had no intention of being anywhere near Pendleton Base when that happened. So he had clocked out once again. Unfortunately, now he had no idea where he was. Which was rather ironic, since he knew exactly where he was.

He knew he was in New York City, but that really wasn't much help at all because *this* New York City did not correspond exactly to the one in the universe from which he came. He had learned, from picking up a copy of the *Daily News*, that it was the 20th century, but he could take no comfort in that knowledge, either. Events in this timeline did not correspond exactly with the events in his. The president of the United States in 1989 was not a woman, as in his timeline. The mayor of New York City wasn't black. And the citizens were apparently not allowed to carry weapons.

Hunter had, at best, only a sketchy knowledge of the history of this timeline, supplied by S.O.G. agents who had crossed over and infiltrated the Temporal Army Archives Section. Their mission had been sabotage and intelligence gathering and they had managed to get a great deal of information through before they had been caught, among which was a detailed explanation of the failsafe systems the Temporal Corps used on their warp discs. Hunter had benefited from all that, but still, it was nowhere near enough, not when even one slight misstep could get him into trouble. Paranoia had welled up within him. He felt like a bleeding swimmer treading water in the middle of a school of sharks.

There was only one way for Hunter to get home. Somewhere, he had to find a confluence point. The trouble was, he didn't even know how to begin to look for one. A confluence point wasn't something you could see. When they were found, they were usually discovered by accident. You simply turned a corner and you were in another universe. If you could keep your head about you and retrace your steps exactly, you could get back home. But Hunter didn't even know where the corner was in this case. Because he had been unconscious when he was brought through, he had no idea *where* they had crossed over, not even in what country or what time period. Instinctively, the first thing he had done when he had regained his senses was to attempt escape. The attempt had been successful. The only trouble was, now he was trapped in the wrong universe and he had no idea how to get back home.

Part of the problem was that confluence points were completely unpredictable. There were no scientific principles governing their behavior that anybody knew of, much less understood. With sophisticated instruments, it was possible to detect the energy field of a confluence, but you had to be practically on top of it. And there was no way of knowing where a confluence point would lead to. They did not correspond in space and time. Hunter knew that a confluence point located in his own universe in the 27th century could intersect with this timeline in such a manner that crossing over would result in entering a completely different century in a completely different geographical location. Conceivably, a confluence point located in Paris, France in one universe could open onto the middle of the Atlantic Ocean in the other. Theoretically, it was entirely possible for a confluence point occurring on Earth in one timeline to open onto deep space in the other, although the vacuum on one side would probably act as a miniature black hole, sucking through everything from the other side where there was an atmosphere, resulting in a devastating temporal whirlpool that would last until the confluence point shifted. And there was no way of telling when that could occur.

Hunter didn't even want to think about what would happen if he were to cross over at the moment a confluence point shifted. He still remembered the disaster that occurred when S.O.G. troops had launched an invasion of this timeline through a confluence point located in the Khyber Pass. At the crucial moment, the confluence point had shifted without warning in a rippling effect that had continued down the timelines as temporal stability had been restored to that location. An entire battalion of soldiers had been caught in the middle of the shift. None of them were ever seen again. They had been trapped forever in the limbo of nonspecific time known as the dead zone. Or at least that was the theory. No one really knew for sure what happened to them.

The average person, in either universe, had no conception of the danger, no real understanding of the instability brought about by the congruence of two universes, instability that was magnified by the confluence of two separate timelines that intersected at various points in time and space because of the increasing chronophysical imbalance. It occurred to Hunter that most people had never really understood the fragility of their existence anyway, largely because they didn't want to.

The generation that had grown up with atomic weapons had clung to the idea that atomic warfare was "unthinkable," not so much because no one could win such a war (which was debatable), but because a "nuclear exchange" (how much more sanitized a term than nuclear war!) was, in reality, simply too horrifying to comprehend. So most people tried not to think about it. That was what the word "unthinkable" really meant. In the same manner, they had chosen not to think about the irreparable damage they were doing to their ecosystem through the pollution of their air and water and the abuse of their resources. They clung to a lunatic philosophy that held that there was no limit to growth. All criminal foolishness. Someone had to pay the piper in the long run, but most people never considered the long run. They took the short view, looking to their wallets at the expense of their legacy.

It had been the same with time travel, an idea that had seemed quite harmless, even quaint, alongside the specters of nuclear missiles and orbital beam particle weapons platforms. And yet, it was a thousand times more dangerous. If people ever really took the time to think about the sort of world they lived in now, thought Hunter, it would reduce them to hysteria and raving paranoia. Nothing was certain anymore. Perhaps it never had been.

With the advent of the Time Wars, it all became a tightrope walk without a net. By far the largest percentage of troops in both timelines were now essentially noncombative Temporal Observers, assigned to lonely posts scattered throughout time—their duty to monitor historical continuity and be on the alert for temporal anomalies. And there was a temporal Underground in Hunter's universe as well as in this one, each a loosely organized society of deserters from the future who had become frightened or disaffected and had dropped out, fled to the past on the theory that disaster was imminent, and that when it came, the worst effects would be felt further up the timeline.

The Underground, with its black market chronoplates and warp discs and its complex system of transtemporal contacts, offered a tempting mode of life. In a sense, these people had achieved the ultimate in freedom. All of time was at their beck and call. Hunter had once found himself temporarily separated from his unit, stranded in time, and the temptation to seek out the Underground had been very strong. He had held out and waited until rescue came, but his twin in this universe had succumbed to the temptation and gone over to the Underground. Delaney, Cross and Steiger had said that he was dead now, murdered in 17th century France. It had been a blow for Hunter to learn that, in this timeline, "he" had died—or at least a version of himself had—just as it had been a shock to encounter Finn Delaney and Andre Cross, mirror-image twins of those he had known back in his own timeline. In Hunter's timeline, Finn and Andre had been killed. In theirs, he had been the one to die. It was madness.

In both timelines, the boundaries between reality and metaphysics were being blurred. Nothing was certain anymore. How many people in the past were really people from the future? How dependable was history when, at any moment, a person from the future could clock back in time and change it, altering—perhaps irrevocably—the flow of the timestream? And with the confluence phenomenon, how could anyone hope to lead anything even resembling a normal life if they knew that at any given moment, they could slip through a wrinkle in time and wind up in another universe, in another timestream, in an alternate reality?

No, it was better not to think about such things. It was easier to go through life taking the short view and passing the buck, ignoring that Sword of Damocles suspended over your head and hoping it would fall on someone else. Preferably someone you didn't know too well. Like your great, great grandchildren, for instance.

However, Hunter did not have the dubious luxury of self-deception. He was in the same position as his counterparts in this universe; he knew all too well how fragile the continuity of both timelines had become. And the war between them was only making matters worse.

It had come very close to being an all out war, especially after the scientists in Hunter's universe finally figured out where all those devastating nuclear explosions were coming from, but it didn't take long for leaders in both timelines to realize that all-out warfare between them would be equally devastating to both. Quite possibly, no one would survive. So a form of limited temporal warfare was being waged. The military scientists in Hunter's timeline believed the only way to end the confluence effect was to cross over into the congruent universe and create a temporal disruption of sufficient magnitude to bring about a timestream split. The resulting creation of another parallel timeline would then act as a sort of chronophysical "wedge" driven between the two parallel universes, forcing them apart and ending the confluence phenomenon. In theory, it would constitute a temporal buffer zone between them. In theory.

There was, however, another theory that held that a temporal disruption resulting in a timestream split in either timeline would only compound the problem by creating yet a *third* timeline, another parallel universe in confluence with the previous two. And such a magnification of the confluence effect could only serve to introduce further temporal disruption into all three timelines, which could then result in even more timestream splits, creating yet a *fourth* parallel universe in confluence with the other three, and perhaps a *fifth* and *sixth* and so on, exponentially, in a chronophysical chain reaction that would be impossible to stop. But the proponents of that theory were very much in the minority because such an event, their fellow scientists insisted, would simply be "unthinkable." There was that word again. And in any case, they said, the confluence effect was already introducing temporal disruption into both timelines. Sooner or later, the scientists insisted, something had to give. Far better that it give in *their* universe than ours.

Hunter no longer knew whom to believe. If he stopped to think about it for very long, he started to get the shakes. Perhaps it was only combat fatigue. Or maybe it was the desperate fear of a rational man confronting his own ephemeral existence in a totally irrational world. Either way, there didn't seem to be anything that he could do about it. For now, his one imperative was to survive.

It had occurred to him that, purely by accident, he had been placed in a unique situation. Ironically, he was now in a position to become the C.I.S.'s most effective deep cover operative. Even in the event of a penetration of his counter insurgency unit by the T.I.A., nobody could blow his cover because no one knew where he was or how to get in touch with him. They didn't even know that he was still alive. Not even he knew exactly where he was, relative to historical continuity in this timeline. However, he could learn. It would not be very difficult. All he'd have to do was clock forward a few centuries in time, purchase a microcomputer or even an cybernetic implant, and then buy himself an education—download some history and world affairs. There would be some risk of getting caught if they were expecting him to try something like that, but the risk would be extremely small. The T.I.A. had no idea where he was, or where he might pop up or when, so the risk was slight and well within acceptable parameters. With his captured warp disc and a detailed knowledge of this timeline's history, he could become a virtually untraceable saboteur. He might easily bring about a timestamp split in this timeline all by himself and, if the scientists back home were right, he'd single-handedly end the confluence effect and be a hero.

Of course, no one back home would ever know he'd done it, because in that event, he would undoubtedly become forever trapped within the timestream split he had created. That was something he had been resigned to from the very start, when he'd become an agent of the C.I.S., yet on the other hand, what if the scientists were wrong? What if the minority view held by the so-called "lunatic fringe" academicians was the correct one? What if the creation of a timestream split served only to *compound* the crisis, setting off a chain reaction of temporal disruptions on a cataclysmic scale? In the absence of direct orders, Hunter had to rely upon his own initiative. And what if he made the wrong decision?

Still, there *were* other choices. He could do as his twin in this timeline had done and join the Temporal Underground, assuming he could find a way to get in touch with them. Or perhaps, better still, he could opt out and do it on his own. Did he really need the Underground? Even if he decided to function as a deep cover C.I.S. saboteur within this timeline, what better way to do it than from within the Underground? But did he really owe that much to the C.I.S., who certainly would not be supporting him in any way and who would undoubtedly have already listed him as killed or missing in action? What about patriotism? Well, what about it? Would anyone care about his patriotic motivations if the choice he made only served to make the situation worse? And what did the concept of patriotism mean, anyway, when ripples in two congruent timestreams resulted in a confluence effect that rendered even boundaries in time and space irrelevant?

He needed time to think and plan. And in order to do that, he needed money and a place to stay. Once again, it came down to bare essentials. Survival.

Fortunately, he did not look too out of place in the simple green transit fatigues he had picked up at Pendleton Base before he had clocked out again, but he needed other clothing and, most of all, he needed money. And when a soldier was trapped behind enemy lines, he had to improvise as best he could.

He picked out a likely looking prospect and mugged him in the subway, knocking him out with a sharp chop to the neck. It was a quick and efficient hit-and-run. The robbery netted him a brown eel skin wallet containing a driver's license, some credit cards, and forty-five dollars in cash. Not very much, but it would do for a start. He went up the stairs to Pennsylvania Station, sat down at a bar, drank some coffee and perused a copy of the *Daily News*. After a while, he went to the men's room, locked himself up inside a stall and clocked ahead several hours. Then he left the stall, walked out of the bar with the paper folded up under his arm and headed toward the Off Track Betting counter he had spotted earlier inside the station. He spent a short while there, noted the racing results, went back to the bar, entered the men's room once again and clocked back once more. Then he returned to the Off Track Betting counter and placed several bets. Needless to say, he did very well indeed.

His winnings enabled him to purchase a new suit of clothes and have a satisfying dinner in a Chinese restaurant. He then found a different Off Track Betting parlour and repeated the performance, placing larger bets and spreading them out more.

He slept that night in the Waldorf Astoria Hotel, using the name—but not the credit cards—of the man whose wallet he had stolen. The next morning, he had room service send up breakfast and a copy of *The Wall Street Journal*.

He spent several hours looking over the stock market and commodities reports, then without leaving the room, clocked ahead one day and went out to pick up that day's copy of *The Wall Street Journal*, taking care to note the time so that he could avoid encountering himself the following morning. Having picked up the paper, he clocked back to the previous day and spent another several hours in the hotel comparing the performance of the various stocks and commodities. Then he took a cab to a brokerage firm on Wall Street and opened an account with twenty thousand dollars in cash, using the identity of his mugging victim, Charles Forman. He then took a cab to the public library and spent the rest of the day reading historical survey texts. It was not as efficient as computer learning, but it would do for a beginning.

He returned to the hotel that evening, had dinner, went to bed, and left a wake-up call for seven A.M., early enough to ensure that he could leave the room before he was due to clock in from the previous day. He had breakfast in a coffee shop, then went back and checked out of the hotel. By now, Charles Forman would probably have reported the theft of his credit cards and cash, and if he had the time, he might possibly have gotten around to getting a new driver's license, but it would never have occurred to him that someone might use his name and social security number to open an account. He'd be more concerned with fraudulent charges on his credit cards, which Hunter had avoided doing, merely using the cards to reinforce his position, by allowing the broker to catch a glimpse of the gold American Express card while he was filling out his account application.

By the end of the week, Hunter was living in a suite at the Plaza Hotel. He had purchased a conservative wardrobe at Brooks Brothers (for visits to the brokerage firm and lunch at '21') and somewhat sleeker, more fashionable suits at Barney's (for the track and dinners in Little Italy). He made daily trips to Belmont Park by rented limousine, increasing his cash flow dramatically each time and attracting attention with his unerring instinct and ostentatious style. Some people started to approach him and he made his choices carefully after some initial probing conversation on both sides. He traded tips for information. And for certain services and introductions.

His disbelieving stockbroker had about a million questions, but wouldn't dare to ask a single one so long as he could make the same investments as his apparently clairvoyant client. The broker didn't want to scare him off. And in order to be helpful, the broker fell all over himself when Hunter requested a few favors, such as certain introductions to certain types of people.

By the end of the month, Hunter had become a multimillionaire with bank accounts in Switzerland and the Bahamas. He had also established a number of different identities for himself, each fully documented and backed up by impeccably forged credentials, enabling him to drop the identity of his mugging victim, leaving the unfortunate Mr. Forman with an interesting tax problem. Hunter was soon on a first name basis with some of the most influential citizens of New York City, Miami and Geneva, as well as some of the most powerful figures in organized crime. He was moving fast, establishing connections, putting out feelers, making inroads. Surviving. Doing business. And, as the old saying went, sooner or later, everyone does business with everyone. Though Hunter didn't know it, through one of his connections, he had started doing business with the Network.

"What do you mean, you lost him? How the devil could you lose him? Explain yourself!"

The officer in the black beret and combat fatigues stood stiffly at attention atop the mahogany writing table, all six and a half inches of him. His fatigues were crisply pressed and his combat boots were spit shined to a glass-smooth gloss. He looked like a toy soldier, except that this toy soldier was alive.

"It wasn't anything we could have foreseen, sir," he said, his voice as formally correct as his stiff, military bearing. "The mission plan was followed to the letter. Gulliver was released in a manner that allowed him to think he had escaped. We tracked him until he returned to England and then the assault team was clocked out to make the strike. It turned out that Gulliver was not alone at the time of the engagement, a contingency we had prepared for, but there was no way we could have prepared for the target employing a warp disc to escape, sir."

"He did *what*?"

The officer winced from the volume of the full-sized voice. "Used a warp disc to escape, sir."

"*Gulliver*? Impossible! Where the hell would he obtain a warp disc? And how would he know how to use one?"

"As I've already stated, sir," the lilliputian officer continued, "Gulliver was not alone. The advance scouts clocked in first, according to the mission plan, and they established that there was another man with Gulliver. The mission plan called for them to wait until the target was alone before calling in the strike. However, the scouts were able to establish that the man Gulliver was with was a Temporal Observer and they decided to go ahead and call in the strike."

"An Observer? Are you sure? How did they know?"

"Gulliver was apparently suffering from a hangover. The man gave him some aspirin. The scouts also observed that he was writing a report. In shorthand, with a ballpoint pen."

"Go on."

"Based on what they saw, the scouts called in the strike and the field commander made the decision to go in. Because the Observer was deemed the greater threat, he was designated the priority target. The intention was to take him out quickly and then take care of Gulliver, but the man was a good soldier. He kept his cool under fire and used his own body to shield Gulliver while he put the warp disc on him and clocked him out. The transition coordinates must have been preset; he didn't have time to reprogram the disc. The Observer could have escaped himself, but Gulliver had all the information. It was an unexpected move, although a tactically sound one, assuming you don't mind committing suicide."

"What did they do with the body?"

"The field commander determined that with the target clocked out, presumably back to the Observer's base, a Search and Retrieve team could be coming through at any time, so they left the body, clocked out the dead and wounded and got the hell out of there. With Gulliver clocked ahead to tell them what happened, destroying the body would have been pointless in any case. And too time consuming. The risk was deemed unjustifiable."

"Unjustifiable, indeed! All they did was leave behind incontrovertible evidence to confirm what happened."

"Even using lasers to dismember the corpse, disposing of a full-sized human body would have taken hours," said the colonel. "And with Gulliver in their hands, they'd already know what happened."

"Assuming the shock of the experience didn't make him take leave of his senses. According to your report, he was already disoriented and drinking heavily. Either way, the T.I.A. will be investigating for certain now. Allowing Gulliver to escape was a serious mistake. Your team bungled the entire mission and jeopardized our security."

The lilliput colonel drew himself up to his full height, but since his full height was only six and a half inches, the effect was negligible.

"I lost *fifteen* men on that mission," he said, through gritted teeth. "And six seriously wounded, four of them critically. Twenty-five men went out on what was supposed to be a routine training exercise and only *four* returned in one piece!"

"And what does that tell you, Colonel? Your assault team was almost completely wiped out by *one* man, and a mere Observer, at that! What do you think would have happened if he had been a Time Commando?"

"Sir, those men were green," the colonel said. "Only their commander and their sergeant had any field experience at all. It was supposed to be a routine training exercise. How were they supposed to expect—"

"They're supposed to expect *anything*! Anything at all! And be ready for it! *Nothing* is routine! Those fifteen men were lost because they were not good enough! And that was *your* responsibility, Colonel! It's *your* command! Don't come to me with excuses! I am not concerned with excuses, only with results! Is that clear?"

"Yes, *sir*."

"The entire operation has been jeopardized as a result of this fiasco. I want you to Execute Plan Delta immediately."

Sandy Steiger's apartment on Threadneedle Street had been thoroughly cleaned up by the S & R team. There was no sign of the battle that had taken place there, nothing to indicate that it had been used as an Observer outpost.

Temporal Observers were trained to become completely assimilated into the time periods to which they were assigned. With the sole exception of the warp discs that they carried on their persons at all times, they were under strict orders to have nothing else that could not be obtained within their assigned time zone. In practice, however, this regulation proved difficult to enforce. Observer postings were long term and often entailed hardship. It was difficult to resist smuggling back some seemingly inconsequential items.

Such things as deodorant, or toothpaste or even toilet paper were easily concealed and served to make the posting a bit more pleasant. A carefully doled out ration of cigarettes served to remind one of home just as much as they satisfied the cravings of a habit. A favorite paperback novel reread over and over by candlelight was a harmless way of maintaining contact with the world one came from, so long as precautions were taken to ensure that no one else would ever see the book, especially if the posting was in a time period when the only writing to be found was in the form of scrolls or illuminated manuscripts or cuneiform.

In the early days, a number of Observers became a bit too casual about following such regulations and, having gotten away with a few seemingly inconsequential items, they took to accumulating more. Miniature portable stereos with headphones began appearing in the 14th century. Minicomputers and microwave ovens were brought back to Victorian London. In one celebrated case, a tiny, portable holographic projection system smuggled back to 17th century America led to the burning of an Observer as a witch when she was seen (by a peeping tom) "consorting" with demons in her bedroom, demons who were, in actuality, merely holograms of actors in an entertainment feature. The Army finally clamped down and instituted the practice of surprise inspections with stiff penalties for the slightest infractions. Still, in many cases, Observers continued to smuggle back some small conveniences.

The S & R team had gone over Sandy Steiger's apartment with a fine tooth comb and, according to their report, they had found nothing more esoteric than some aspirin tablets, a ballpoint pen, some timed-release decongestant pills, a modern tooth brush and nine cartons of cigarettes concealed beneath a loose floor board. Their report stated that Sandy had clearly broken regulations, but the few items he had smuggled back had not seemed very significant. They had no way of knowing that the contraband had been enough to cost Sandy his life. The S & R team had been quite thorough. Nevertheless, the commandos conducted their own search.

Gulliver stood by the door and watched them anxiously. He was clearly uncomfortable at being back in the same room where Sandy had been killed and where he had almost met the same fate.

"One thing puzzles me," he said, as Creed Steiger, Finn Delaney, and Andre Cross carefully searched through the apartment once again. "Since you have this astonishing ability to travel back and forth through time, is it not possible that you could go back and prevent Sandy from being killed by those horrible lilliputians?"

"You think I wouldn't save my own brother if I could?" said Steiger, grimly.

"Why can't you?"

"It's difficult to explain, Doctor, but the fact is it would be too dangerous. What's done is done. There's nothing we can do about it."

"Can you not tell me why?" said Gulliver.

"Go ahead," Delaney said. "We'll check out the sitting room."

Steiger sighed and sat down on the bed. "Very well, Doctor. I'll see if I can explain it in a way that you can understand. Think of time as a river. A very swiftly flowing river. The current of that river is the timestream, specifically, the inertial flow of the timeline."

Furrows appeared in Gulliver's forehead as he frowned, trying to follow it. Steiger grunted and shook his head.

"Look, just imagine that the current of our river of time is the force that impels events, all right? And the length of the river itself is all of history, the timeline. Got that?"

Gulliver nodded. "Yes, I think I understand."

"Good," said Steiger. "Now, when someone from the future, someone like myself, goes back into the past, he risks doing something that would somehow interfere with the flow of events. Actually, everything I do back here constitutes a form of interference. Even my presence in this room is a form of interference, because after all, there was a point in time at which, in this particular moment, I was never *in* this room at this particular moment, do you understand?"

Gulliver was frowning once again.

Steiger grimaced. "Hell, I told you it was complicated. Look, as we sit here right now, this very moment, I won't even be born for about another thousand years. And yet, here I am, sitting here and talking to you, a man who lived almost a thousand years before my time. That's an example of what we call temporal interference." He picked up a pillow. "Even an action as insignificant as my picking up this pillow is an example of temporal interference, because there was a point in time, before we came back here, when this moment passed and I was not *here* to pick up this pillow and the action of this pillow being picked up didn't happen, see?"

"I . . . I believe I do see, yes," said Gulliver. "You were right, it *is* rather complicated, isn't it? Much like these circular arguments philosophers are always having."

"Yes, very much like that, in a way," said Steiger. "Now, take the fact that I've picked up this pillow." He dropped it back down onto the bed. "It's an insignificant action. It doesn't really change anything, does it? In fact, it's so insignificant that it doesn't have any effect upon our river of time at all. The fact that I have picked up a pillow in this room has had no discernable effect upon events in this time period, even though it was an event that did not originally take place. You follow?"

Gulliver nodded once again, though he looked a bit uncertain.

"Good. Now imagine that you and I go out tonight and have a few drinks. On the way back, as we're passing a dark alley, a thief confronts us at knifepoint and demands all of our money. He lunges at me with the knife and in the struggle, I manage to get the knife away from him and kill him. Now, that act is obviously much more significant than merely picking up a pillow, and I don't mean merely for its moral implications. Suppose the man I've killed had no wife or children. Perhaps he never would have had a wife and children. It's possible that he would have lived out the remainder of his life alone, in insignificance, doing nothing of any importance whatsoever. And it's also possible that if I hadn't been there, *you* would have been the one to struggle with him, get the knife away and kill him. In that case, his death, in and of itself, has not significantly altered events in this time period. My temporal interference in causing his death is neglible in terms of the grand scheme of things. You with me so far?"

"Yes, I think so," said Gulliver, listening intently.

"All right," said Steiger, "now let's examine another possibility in that same hypothetical situation. Suppose that if it wasn't for my interference, that thief would have attacked somebody else. After all, it was my idea that we go out for a drink; if I hadn't come back here and interfered, you would have stayed home and the thief would have attacked another victim. And in that event, he would *not* have died. He would have killed his victim, prospered from his ill-gotten gains, married and had children. Except, now that I have gone back into the past and killed him, obviously those children will never be born. And that victim will not die, at least not at that particular time. So by my interference, I have altered history. I have changed the past. I have disrupted the flow of events. Now let's take it a bit further. What if that thief had been my ancestor, my great, great grandfather about a dozen times removed?"

"Good lord!" said Gulliver. "Then by killing him, you've prevented the birth of his children, which means that . . . that *you* could never have been born!"

"Precisely," Steiger said.

"But . . . but if you could never have been born," said Gulliver, frowning, "then . . . then how . . . how is it possible that you could have . . ." his voice trailed off and he stared at Steiger with an expression of utter confusion.

"That, my friend, is what's known as a temporal paradox," said Steiger. "If you went back into the past and killed your grandfather before your father had been born, then *you* wouldn't have been born, so how could you have gone back and killed your grandfather in the first place?"

"It makes no sense," said Gulliver. "How is it possible?"

"Well, for years, scientists believed it *wasn't* possible," Steiger replied. "They believed that the past was an immutable absolute. It had already happened, therefore it could not be changed. According to their thinking, if I went back into the past and tried to kill my grandfather, something would have prevented me from doing it, otherwise I couldn't have gone back to try it in the first place because the very fact that I was alive to do it meant that my grandfather had survived my attempt on his life. You see.?"

Gulliver knitted his brows as he ran through it once more in his mind and nodded slowly. "Yes, I think I understand. It all seems very logical now that you've explained it."

"Except it doesn't work that way," said Steiger.

"Oh, dear," said Gulliver. "And I thought I was beginning to understand it."

"Don't worry," Steiger said. "All the scientists were wrong as well and they had the advantage of having a lot more knowledge than you do. Or perhaps I should say they *will* have that advantage . . . in about another 950 years or so."

"What is the answer, then?" Gulliver said, anxiously.

"Let's go back to our river," Steiger said. "Remember that I said the current of the river is the timestream and that the river itself represents history, the timeline? If a person travels back in time and does something relatively insignificant—my picking up the pillow, for example—then that would be like tossing a very small pebble into a swiftly flowing stream. It wouldn't even make a ripple. A more significant form of interference— the killing of our hypothetically childless thief, for example— might be compared to tossing a rather large rock into the river. It would make a splash, but unless the interference was significant enough to alter the flow of events, the ripples would be dissipated by the force of the current. Still with me?"

"Yes, I think so," Gulliver said, paying very close attention.

"Now," said Steiger, "an act of interference that was significant enough to actually alter the flow of events and cause a severe temporal disruption—something like my killing my great grandfather, in other words—could be compared to our throwing a gigantic boulder into the river, something huge, big enough to make the river overflow its banks on both sides and flow *around* it. And that is what we call a timestream split. For a short period of time, you would have *two* rivers, one flowing around each side of the giant boulder. One fork of the river would represent the past as it had happened before the act of disruption. The other would represent the creation of a *second* past, a parallel timeline, in which the act of disruption had been taken into account. A live grandfather in one, a dead grandfather in the other. And the person causing the disruption which created the split would wind up in that second timeline, because there would have to be an original timeline in which his past, up to the moment he disrupted it, was preserved intact. And at some point, unless the disruption was of sufficient magnitude to keep both timelines apart indefinitely, those two separate timelines must rejoin and the results could be disastrous."

Gulliver gaped at him, slack jawed.

"And that's only the *simplified* explanation," Steiger said. "It can get a great deal more complicated than that. Even if it wasn't against all regulations for me to attempt to save my brother's life—and I've never been all that religious about following regulations to begin with—there would still be no guarantee that I could do it. And even if I could, there would still have to be a past in which my brother died, because it's already happened, do you see? If I tried to change it, I'd risk creating a timestream split. Or at the very least, I would bring about what's known as a 'ripple' in the timestream, sort of a miniature timestream split of short duration, one that would also have completely unforeseeable results."

"The place is clean," Delaney said, coming back into the bedroom. "Well, did he explain it to you, Doctor?"

Gulliver looked up at him and the bewildered expression on his face said it all.

"Yep, I guess he did," Delaney said.

Then Andre screamed.

Delaney and Steiger both drew their weapons and ran into the sitting room.

"Don't shoot, it's only me," said Lucas Priest.

5 _____

"It can't be," said Andre, after a moment of stunned silence.

Delaney had his plasma pistol aimed directly at Priest's chest. "I don't know who you are, mister," he said, "but don't you move a muscle."

Lucas stood motionless with his hands raised. "Come on, Finn, it's me, for chrissake. Lucas. Your old partner, remember?"

"Try again. I buried my old partner."

"Yeah, I know," said Lucas, with a grimace. He kept his hands raised and carefully avoided making any sudden moves. "I figured this wasn't going to be easy. Look, I can explain. I realize this is going to be bit hard to believe, but—"

"It's gotta be his twin," said Steiger, interrupting him. "From the congruent universe."

Delaney shook his head. "No, he's dead, too. I ought to know, I killed him."

"Maybe in the congruent universe, Lucas Priest had a twin brother," Steiger said, keeping his gun trained on Lucas.

"Yeah, and maybe I was triplets," said Lucas, wryly, "but I'm not. Finn, remember that time we took some R & R and went down to that Mexican border town and got in—"

"That was all in the arrest report the Federales filed," said

Delaney. "You could have seen that when the S.O.G. swiped data from the Archives Section."

"Oh, Right. I forgot about that. Okay, wait a minute, what about that time we got drunk and you told me that when you were fourteen, that sexy young high school English teacher you had made you stay after school one day and—"

"I've been drunk lots of time," Delaney said, hastily, with a quick glance at the others. He swallowed nervously and moistened his lips. "It's entirely possible I might've told that story to somebody else."

"Priest had a bionic eye," said Steiger.

"If they knew about our arrest in Mexico and . . . that other thing, they could've duplicated that, as well," Delaney said. "Hell, Creed, he *can't possibly* be Lucas! Lucas is dead! It's some kind of trick."

Andre hadn't taken her eyes off him for an instant. She stared at him as if he were a ghost. "Who was the Red Knight's squire?" she said, softly.

"His name was Marcel," said Lucas. "He was murdered by the Templar, Brian de Bois-Guilbert, and you avenged his death. He was your brother, Andre. You were the Red Knight. Remember our first meeting, in the lists at Ashby? You damned near killed me."

"My God," she said, turning to Delaney with a wide-eyed look. "Finn, besides you, no other living person could have known that."

"Can I put my hands down now?" said Lucas.

"Not just yet," said Steiger. "I'm still not convinced. I gave you something once and you can't give it back. If you're really Lucas Priest, then you'll know what I'm talking about."

"Boy, do I ever," Lucas said. "Your favorite mad scientist and mine, Dr. Darkness, had you give me a particle-level symbiotracer. It was a top secret prototype, not even the army knows about it. Each of you have one, as well. Only there's something about them you don't know, something Darkness didn't tell you. They weren't just symbiotracers, as it turns out. They also contained something he calls telempathic chronocircuitry, a cute little experimental device he whipped up in his lab back on that red planet with the three moons."

Steiger's jaw dropped. The only way he could have known that Darkness had his lab on a red planet with three moons would be if he had been there. Darkness kept the location of his base a closely guarded secret. So far as he knew, Steiger had been the only one who'd ever been there besides Darkness himself.

"It seems this telempathic chronocircuitry is extremely delicate," Lucas continued. "Yours didn't survive the molecular-bonding process, but mine did, which is why I can do this."

He disappeared. A second later, he reappeared, standing on the opposite side of the room.

"Look, ma, no hands!" he said, his hands still raised to show he wasn't operating a warp disc.

As they spun around to face him, he disappeared again, to reappear an instant later on the same spot where he'd stood initially.

"It's a fugue sequence," Steiger said. "He had it preprogrammed in his warp disc."

"Look again, Creed," Lucas said, trying to ignore the headache and the dizziness. "I'm not wearing one. You see, this is the process that Darkness had been trying to perfect. Time travel by *thought*. And since these little molecular-bonding gizmos of his are apparently extremely hard to make and I had the only one that worked right, rather than lose his only working prototype, he decided to effect a little temporal adjustment of his own. He went back and translocated me out of that bullet's path while at the same time taking the corpse of my dead twin moments after you killed him, Finn, and interposing his body between Churchill and that bullet. Essentially, he had me switch places with a dead man. My twin from the parallel universe. The result was that I sidestepped my death and wound up as a living time machine, which makes things a little troublesome. See, if my mind happens to wander, so do I."

"Then I wasn't seeing things!" said Andre. "That really *was* you in my room?"

Lucas nodded. "That was sort of a brief glitch. An unintentional translocation. The telempathic chronocircuitry was designed to analyze and compute transition coordinates from a built-in encyclopedic *database* as well as my own memory. Unfortunately, I'm not too great at controlling it and it seems that Darkness didn't quite get all the bugs out. All I had to do was think about you, Andre, and I wound up in your room. And it happened again when I started thinking about the old man and suddenly found myself in his quarters. There were times when I'd fall asleep and dream about a place and the next thing I knew, I'd wake up there. The first few times that happened, Darkness had to home in one me through the symbiotracer so that he could come and get me, because I absolutely froze. The truly frightening part of it all is that there's no way to turn the damn thing off. Once Darkness activated it with a special coded tachyon signal to the symbiotracer, the telempathic chronocircuitry kicked in and now I can't turn it off anymore than I can turn *myself* off. It's part of me, permanently bonded to my atomic structure. You'd think the great genius would have thought to build in some kind of 'off' switch, but noooo. . . ."

Steiger and Delaney slowly lowered their weapons. Lucas sighed with relief and put his hands down. "You know, for a minute there, I thought you were never going to believe me." He looked past them and frowned. "Who's your friend?"

Gulliver had entered the room and now he came forward hesitantly and held out his hand. "Dr. Lemuel Gulliver, at your service, sir."

Lucas shook hands with him. "Col. Lucas Priest," he said. "You were at General Forrester's quarters, weren't you?"

"Yes, that's quite true," said Gulliver. "however, I—"

He never got to finish his sentence as Andre, unable to restrain herself any longer, suddenly slammed into Lucas and threw her arms around him, hugging him hard enough to take his breath away.

"You're alive!" she said, her voice breaking. "God, I can't believe it! You're alive!"

She kissed him long and hard.

Steiger and Delaney were still staring at him with dazed expressions. Gulliver looked uncomfortable and confused.

"I thought I'd lost you," Andre said, fighting back tears. "And I never . . . and I never got around to telling you I—"

Lucas put his finger to her lips. "I know," he said, softly.

"Then you never really died!" said Delaney. "Dr. Darkness saved your life and what we thought was you was the body of your twin!"

"Well, no, not exactly," said Lucas. "In a sense, I *did* die, but then Darkness went back and altered that scenario. I guess you might say he brought me back to life by altering my past. Or, from where I stand right now, a potential future that I never realized."

For a moment, nobody said anything as they stared at him with astonishment, then Gulliver was the first to break the stunned silence.

"Col. Steiger," he said, "I realize that I don't really comprehend your science of the future, but isn't that what we were just discussing moments ago in regards to your brother? Altering the past so that someone who died might live?"

"That's exactly what we were discussing," Steiger said, slowly, "and it's simply not possible! Not unless . . ." He swallowed hard, a cold fist squeezing his insides. "Not unless Darkness brought about a timestream split!"

"No," said Delaney, shaking his head. "That can't be. If a timestream split had occurred, then we wouldn't have remembered Lucas's death."

"But you would have," Lucas said, "because you *saw* it. You were there. Or at least Andre was. Only what you saw, Andre, was my twin's corpse, not me."

"Except that I *did* see you," said Andre. "If what you're saying is true, then I saw you die and it was only *afterward* that Dr. Darkness went back and changed the past, after you'd already died the first time!"

"This is most confusing," Gulliver said, scratching his head. "How can someone die and yet still be alive? It sounds like one of these paradoxes you were telling me about."

"That's exactly what it is," said Steiger, "a temporal paradox. And that's impossible."

"Then how can I be here?" said Lucas. "Darkness says there hasn't been a timestream split. He claims his instruments have not detected one."

"Only if there was a timestream split, then maybe his instruments *couldn't* detect it," said Delaney, "because it's possible that they could then be a function of that split, part of the newly created matter that would comprise the parallel timeline. For that matter, we all might be part of a newly created parallel timeline and not know it."

"No, that can't be," said Lucas, shaking his head. "Darkness said that no significant events were changed. What's the only thing that's different as a result of what Darkness has done? The fact that I'm alive. And that's it. Otherwise, there was no disruption of events at all."

"There *had* to have been some kind of disruption," Steiger insisted. "The past *was* changed!"

"But only my past," Lucas said. "Or, to be technically correct, my past from your point of view, and my potential future from mine, since I obviously never died. My death occurred in some sort of alternate timeframe for me."

"Is that what Darkness told you?" said Delaney.

Lucas glanced him with a frown. "Yes. Why?"

Delaney shook his head. "Because I don't think it works that way, old friend. Granted, I haven't had as much training in temporal physics as Darkness must've had, but unless everything that we were taught in R.C.S. was wrong, there had to have been some kind of a disruption. Creed is right. The past *was* changed."

"Only it's not *my* past," insisted Lucas. "It didn't *happen* to me! I'm obviously still very much alive!"

"Then either there's been a timestream split," Delaney said, "or *you're* the split yourself, a parallel Lucas Priest. *Something* had to give. Either a another timeline was created or another Lucas Priest was." He glanced uneasily at the others. "Only how do we tell which one?"

Gulliver sighed and rubbed his temples. "Colonel," he said to Steiger, "I don't suppose you would have any ass-prin, would you?"

"There are times I'd like to kill that man," the lilliput colonel said, clenching his fists. "You know, maybe one of these days I will."

"Maybe one of these days, I'll help you," his lieutenant said, as he absently sharpened a commando knife the size of a pin on a tiny whetstone. "I wouldn't mind seeing that son of a bitch bleed a little."

The two men were very different in appearance. The colonel was slim, solidly built, with a square jaw, steely blue eyes and close-cropped sandy hair. His manner and his speech were as crisp as his freshly pressed fatigues, which he kept sharply creased by carefully folding them every night and placing them beneath a brick. The lieutenant was, by contrast, something of a slob. His fatigues were wrinkled and stained and his shirt was usually worn unbuttoned, revealing an extremely muscular upper torso. He had a bodybuilder's physique, strong and sharply defined. His black, wavy hair hung down to his shoulders, and he habitually kept it held down with a cloth headband. Once in a while, he remembered to shave, which he did with his razor-sharp commando knife and water. Unlike the fair-skinned colonel, he was dark complected and his large brown eyes had a sleepy cast to them. He looked less like a soldier than a circus roustabout, but appearances could be deceiving, especially in the case of these two men. The colonel was six and half inches tall; the lieutenant stood all of five and three-quarters.

They were in the lieutenant's tent, which was made from a man's white cotton handkerchief. It was supported by tent poles made out of quarter-inch wooden dowling rod and staked to the floor by thumbtacks. All around them were dozens of similar tents housing the remainder of the regiment, all of which was billeted within a small loft in a warehouse building near the docks off Washington Street on New York City's Lower West Side.

"I liked the island better," the lieutenant said, putting down the knife and unwrapping a chunk of jerky that was lying on the plastic table. The table was toy furniture out of a doll's house, as were the chairs. "I don't like the city. I miss the fresh air." He cut up the piece of jerky with his knife and started chewing on a slice.

"How the hell can you eat that stuff?" the colonel said, with a look of disgust. "Rat meat, for God's sake!"

The lieutenant shrugged. "Meat is meat," he said, masticating furiously. "The hunting is a little limited around here, y'know? Like I said, I liked the island better."

"He does bring us food, you know," said the colonel.

"That shit he brings us isn't food," responded the lieutenant, irately. "Why'nt you tell him to go to a market and get a couple decent cuts of steak and some fresh vegetables? He thinks he can feed us all on a bag of quarter pounders and some fries. He's just fuckin' cheap, that's all. Half the regiment has got gas and the other half has got the runs. We can't eat that garbage."

"I'll talk to him," said the colonel.

"He expects us to fight for him, tell him to bring us some decent food, for cryin' out loud."

"I *said* I'll talk to him!"

"Yo, I'm on your side, remember?"

The colonel sighed. "I'm sorry. I guess the whole thing is just getting to me. He was furious about the practice strike. He said we failed."

"Yeah, well, fuck him," said the lieutenant, bitterly. "I lost sixteen men on that damn 'practice' mission!"

The colonel glanced at him sharply. "Sixteen?"

"Yeah. My sergeant didn't make it. He died this morning."

"Oh, damn."

"What the hell is going to happen to us, sir?" said the lieutenant. "What the hell kind of life have we got to look forward to?"

The tiny colonel stared out at a shaft of sunlight coming down from the skylight of the loft. "I don't know, Lieutenant," he said. "I honestly don't know. How are the men doing?"

"About as well as could be expected. They're getting a little wired. I try to keep the tension down by running the hell out of 'em all day, setting up obstacle courses and practice maneuvers. Lord knows we've got enough damn room here, but there's a limit, y'know? They don't like it here anymore than I do. And losin' sixteen of the boys on what was supposed to be a training exercise didn't exactly boost moral."

The lieutenant threw the knife down angrily and it stuck, quivering, in the wooden floor of the loft.

"I never should've called the strike in," he said, bitterly. "I should've waited."

"The presence of the Observer changed everything," said the colonel. "You did what you had to do. You might have lost him if you held off."

"Hell, we lost him anyway. And you know something? I'm not sorry. It eats my guts out that my boys had to die, but I'm not sorry that Gulliver got away. After all we put him through, that poor bastard deserved a decent break. At least somebody got out of this damn nightmare in one piece."

"I wonder if we will," the colonel said.

"We will. Count on it. We'll make it."

"I wish I could be so sure," said the colonel. "Tell the men there's a briefing scheduled for 0600. A target's been selected. We're going out tomorrow night."

I could sure get used to this, thought Hunter, toying with the stem of his wineglass as he stared at the beautiful, elegant blonde sitting across the table from him. She was dressed in a simple, low cut black dress, an expensive designer original that clung to her lush figure, accentuating it with every move she made. The table top was glass, allowing him to appreciate her gorgeous legs, which were crossed in a calculated manner so that the dress would ride up high. Throughout the meal, she'd been leaning forward slightly, inconspicuously matching her physical attitude to his, making little, almost unnoticeable movements, speaking a subtle body language that was almost as blatant in its effect as if she had torn off all her clothes and sprawled out naked on the table. She smiled and her sea green eyes whispered promises. She was good. She was very, very good.

Yes, sir, thought Hunter, I could sure get used to this. Fine clothes, expensive cars, beautiful women . . . becoming stranded in this timeline could be the best thing that ever happened to him. In a matter of months, he had effortlessly parlayed the few dollars he had stolen into a multimillion dollar fortune. And that money had opened many doors. And the more doors the money opened, the more money came in. And as more money came in, more doors were opened for him. After a while, it seemed as if the entire process had started to become completely self-sustaining. The warp disc and a little common sense was all it took. I should have done this years ago, he thought.

"Penny for your thoughts," the blonde said. Her voice had the rich, low contralto tones of a cello by Stradivarius.

"Hmm?"

She smiled a dazzling, slightly crooked smile. "It doesn't exactly do wonders for a girl's ego when you drift off like that, you know," she said.

"I'm sorry," he said, with an apologetic smile.

"You seemed so far away. What were you thinking just now?"

"I was just thinking about something I had started out to do." He gazed out the bay window of her penthouse apartment with the view of Central Park. "At one point, not so very long ago, it seemed terribly important." He smiled. "I guess I was just trying to remember why."

The compact disc player automatically segued from Pat Metheny to some mellow, soulful blues by Carlos Santana. The dinner she had cooked for him had been exquisite, the wine was an excellent vintage white Margaux, and there was something very tantalyzing about the subtle scent of her perfume. This woman was trouble, Hunter thought, but it was the kind of trouble a man usually walked into with both eyes wide open.

Her name was Krista and they had met at a party hosted by Domenico Manelli, a man who described himself as an investor and a financier. He did invest quite heavily, but not all of his investments were in blue chip stocks. He also dealt in some commodities that did not appear on the big board. And as for being a financier, well, he did finance certain politicians, a few judges, several entertainers, and a battery of lawyers.

It hadn't taken Hunter very long to figure out that Krista was on Domenico Manelli's payroll. She undoubtedly did not think of herself as a hooker, Hunter thought, because there was a world of difference between Krista and a common prostitute. She was much more than an exclusive call girl, too. Men did not call Krista and pay her exorbitantly for her favors. Few men would have been able to afford the price, either financially or psychologically. Besides, she couldn't be bought that way. No, Krista was a much more interesting creature. She was a weapon that Domenico Manelli used with careful judgement and restraint. And a weapon like Krista was worth an entire team of intelligence agents, Hunter thought.

The fact that Krista had approached him meant that Manelli had become interested in him and Hunter had been trying to decide how to react to that. He didn't quite know what to make of Domenico Manelli. In some ways, the man was astonishingly obvious, while in others he was as complex and devious as a Medici prince. He had taken the twofold path, as all really smart criminals did, establishing himself as a solid, taxpaying citizen with a wide variety of legitimate business interests and community activities while at the same time cleverly furthering his illegal operations, which had provided the seed capital for him to become a respected pillar of the community to begin with.

Manelli functioned on the principle that it was never very smart to become too visibly successful, but that if one did, the thing to do was to create an economic smokescreen. The moment the money became significant—and at the same time, inconveniently inexplicable—he invested it. He invested it legitimately in a manner that allowed for a reasonable return that could then be used to grease the wheels. He used the dirty money to create clean funds that were then used for paying taxes, contributing to various charities and political campaigns, supporting popular causes, starting businesses, creating jobs . . . in other words, buying his way to indispensability to as many people as possible.

In the meantime, he erected barriers between himself and the criminal activities that had financed the whole thing to begin with. He carefully selected subordinates who did not appear to be subordinates and who could be trusted to keep their mouths shut and take the fall if it became necessary, knowing they'd be taken care of for their loyalty. And along the way, the campaign contributions and the community activity gave him access to important people and allowed him to determine which ones to stay away from, which ones could be manipulated, and which ones could be bought outright.

Hunter's instincts told him to stay away. Getting involved with a man like Manelli could be dangerous, but then if he had wanted to play it safe, he would never have joined the C.I.S. in the first place. The trouble was, Hunter was having a hard time deciding what to do. The odds against his stumbling upon a confluence point all on his own were astronomical, not even worth considering seriously. The odds of his finding a way to contact the Underground were somewhat better, but he had no idea where to start or even if it was what he really wanted to do.

If his goal was to create a significant disruption in this timeline, then the Underground was an ideal place for him to be. He could convince them that he'd deserted from the Temporal Army and infiltrate their organization, using their contacts and their information to achieve his ends, although they'd kill him if they suspected what his plans were. Only *were* those still his plans?

Why not simply accept things as they were? He was trapped in this universe and chances were that he'd never find his way back home. But then, why should he even try? The life he had created for himself here was infinitely better than the one he had as an agent for the C.I.S. Why fight it? Back home, he never would have dared to try anything like what he had accomplished here. Even if the idea had occurred to him, he'd have resisted partly out of fear of getting caught and partly out of concern that he might somehow disrupt the timestream. Here, what did it matter? It made no difference what he did here, there would always be the fear of getting caught, so why not make the most of his opportunities? And if he did do something that created a disruption further up the timeline, then it would not affect him here and he'd be doing no more than his duty. The warp disc was his protection. He could always escape further into the past. The temptation to do exactly as his twin in this timeline had done and simply opt out was tremendous and Hunter was seeing less and less reason to resist it. The last thing he needed was to bother with someone like Manelli.

The problem was, Manelli was bothering with him. Hunter did not flatter himself that Krista had been coming on to him simply because he was so undeniably attractive. He'd been playing cat and mouse with her, knowing that she was subtly trying to draw him out and pump him, while at the same time he was purposely obscure about his background and tried to do the same to her, about both herself and her relationship with Domenico Manelli and his crowd. Prudence would have dictated that he break it off, but Hunter found himself unable to resist her and they had reached an impasse where both of them fully understood the game that they were playing, though neither would admit it to the other. They were both getting a perverse enjoyment out of it, though Krista was starting to exhibit some signs of frustration.

"I sometimes have the feeling that you're not really who you seem to be at all," she said, taking a gold cigarette case out of her purse. "It's almost as if you're playing a role."

With playful mockery, she took two cigarettes from the case and stuck them both between her lips, then handed him her Dunhill lighter. Hunter grinned and lit the cigarettes for her. She took a drag or two to get them going, then took one from her mouth and reached forward to place it between his lips. If she had done so seriously, it would have been extremely comical, but with her slightly exaggerated humor playing on the role reversal, she somehow made it very sexy.

He took a deep drag on the cigarette and leaned back in his chair. "Everyone plays roles," he said. "Mine just happens to be a bit more subtle than most people's. I don't really believe in going around baring your breast to everyone you meet, that's all. People who do that are insecure."

"You're definitely not insecure," she said, smiling. "Most men would go to a great deal of trouble to impress a woman. But you're not like that. You seem very comfortable with yourself. No need to prove a thing."

Hunter shrugged. "It takes too damn much energy to run around always trying to prove things to yourself and other people. I haven't really got anything to prove. But maybe that's because I don't have much imagination. I'm just an ordinary guy."

She shook her head. "I wouldn't say that at all. You're the most elusive man I've ever met. You really don't reveal very much at all, do you?"

"Well, I thought they said that a little mystery was supposed to add a bit of spice to a relationship."

"Is that what we're doing?" she said, arching her eyebrows. "Having a relationship?"

"I don't really know," said Hunter, loosening his collar slightly. It was getting warm. "What *are* we doing? You invite me up here, cook me a world class meal and ply me with vintage wine in an atmosphere of mellow, romantic jazz, soft lighting, a dazzling view—both through the window *and* the tabletop . . ." he grinned. "One would almost think that you were setting a trap for me."

She smiled. "You're absolutely right. I confess. It *is* a trap."

"Ha! I knew it all the time! The wine was drugged!"

She pursed her lips and watched him over the rim of her wineglass. "No, not the wine," she said, softly.

He suddenly felt dizzy as he stared at her, his vision blurred. She took her cigarette, which after the initial puff to get it going, she hadn't smoked at all, and stubbed it out in the ashtray.

The cigarettes!

He lurched to his feet and the room started to spin. She got up quickly and backed away. He grabbed the table for support and abruptly lost his balance, bringing the glass-topped table crashing to the floor. It shattered and he fell in a spray of glass. He heard a door open and footsteps come across the floor. He tried, but he could not make out their faces as they stood over him. He couldn't move. One of them bent down and pulled up his sleeve.

"That's it," someone said.

He felt the warp disc being removed and then everything went black.

6 _____

"There's nothing there," said Steiger, bending over the charts and studying them closely.

"Dr. Gulliver, are you sure that was the correct position?" said Delaney, glancing over his shoulder at Gulliver, who stood behind them, looking down at the charts spread out on the table.

"I'm absolutely certain of it," Gulliver said. "I've sailed as a ship's surgeon long enough to know my navigation, gentlemen. I took a reading with my sextant on the day of my escape. Longitude 110 degrees, 4 minutes east; latitude 30 degrees, 2 minutes south."

"That would put it approximately 200 miles to the northwest of Perth, Australia," said Steiger. "And there's nothing there."

"Quite so," said Gulliver. "I have already told you that the island does not appear on any charts."

"If that was the case only with the charts available in this time period," said Steiger, tossing aside the charts that Gulliver had obtained for them, "then that would be understandable. However," he tapped the modern maps spread out before him on the table, "it doesn't appear on any of *our* charts, either, and that's impossible. You must have made a mistake in calculating the position."

"I don't mean to argue with you, Colonel," Gulliver replied, "but had that been the case, then I would certainly have noticed it when I escaped, for I would have found myself off course. However, the course I had plotted turned out to be correct, which meant that my original reading had to be correct, as well. Lilliput Island lies exactly there." He stabbed his forefinger down at the map on a spot that showed nothing but open sea.

Steiger glanced up at Delaney and shook his head. "There's nothing there, Finn."

"Well, there's only one way to find out for sure," Delaney said.

"Wait a minute," Andre said, grabbing his arm. "You're not seriously suggesting clocking out there blind? What if Gulliver's wrong?"

"We'll wind up very wet," said Steiger. "And those are shark-infested waters."

"Look, I may be a little reckless sometimes," said Delaney, "but I'm not crazy. I'm suggesting that a couple of us clock ahead to base and pick up some floater paks so we can do an air reconnaisance. We can fly a search pattern within a fifty mile radius of Gulliver's coordinates, or a hundred mile radius if that's what it takes, but we're obviously not going to get anywhere sitting around here and arguing about what is or isn't on the map. We're simply going to have to go out there and look."

Gulliver cleared his throat. "Excuse me, Captain . . ."

"Yes?"

"Did . . . did I hear correctly? Did you just say that you were going to . . . to *fly*?"

"Don't worry, Lem," Delaney said, "no one's going to make you fly. Besides, it takes a bit of training to learn how to use a floater pak. You'll be staying here with Andre and Lucas while Creed and I clock out and fly our search pattern. And if we find your island, we'll come back for the rest of you and see if there are any little people on it."

"Six-inch commandos," Lucas said, shaking his head. "Incredible. If I didn't know better, I'd say we'd run into a bizarre new generation of Drakov's hominoids."

"You *know* General Drakov?" Gulliver said.

They all spun around and stared at him with amazement.

"*What did you say?*" said Andre.

"General Nikolai Drakov," Gulliver said. "He is the leader of the lilliput legion."

"But that's impossible!" Delaney said. "Drakov is dead!"

"Yes, that's right," said Andre, slowly. "And so was Lucas."

Nikolai Drakov stood in Central Park with his hands in the pockets of his elegant, dark wool velour topcoat. A cool autumn breeze ruffled his thick, wavy black hair as he watched a young mother and her small boy from a distance as they fed the ducks with bread crumbs. The dark-haired boy bore a startling resemblance to Drakov. In fact, he *was* Nikolai Drakov, or more precisely, a clone being raised under controlled conditions and carefully monitored from time to time by his creator/father.

This was the end result of Drakov's experiments with the hominoids, a subspecies of genetically engineered, human-based lifeforms that were first created under the auspices of Project Infiltrator, headed by Dr. Moreau and funded by the Special Operations Group. Drakov had deceived the S.O.G. and spirited Moreau away from the parallel universe with promises of generous funding and unrestricted research, the opportunity of developing his hominoids to their fullest potential. Instead, Drakov had taken control and carefully observed Moreau, studying the process until he had mastered it, and then he took the hominoids in directions Moreau had never dreamed of. Now, this was the crowning touch, the *pièce de résistance*. He had replicated himself.

The young boy he was watching along with his "mother," an earlier generation hominoid, had been part of the first run, a dozen versions of himself born out of petri dishes and artificial wombs, then clocked back to various periods in the past, each to be raised in different environments, but under highly controlled conditions with predetermined key stages of development, the first occurring when they received their cerebral implants in early childhood, enabling them to be programmed at specific points throughout their lives, and the last when they received the scars that matched his own, a diagonal knife slash that ran from beneath his left eye to just above the corner of his mouth.

The first of these secondary versions of himself had already been subjected to this process that Drakov called "time lapse maturation" and had been killed in an encounter with the temporal agents. They now believed him to be dead. Drakov smiled as he anticipated their rude awakening.

He turned and started walking back toward Fifth Avenue. Gulliver's escape had been a minor setback, but it didn't really matter. The temporal agents were alerted to the threat now, but it was far too late. Even as they prepared to seek the secret island base of the lilliput legion, the lilliputians would find them. And this time, his little soldiers would know what to expect.

"Wake up! C'mon, wake up!"

Hunter felt his face being slapped. His head rocked back and forth with the blows as if it were somehow a thing apart from himself and he tried to ignore it all, to retreat back into the warm, thick mist of unconsciousness, but they weren't having any of it.

"Come on, wake up, dammit!"

Whack!

"He's still out of it."

"The hell he is, he's playing possum, only I ain't buyin' it. Wake up, you bum!"

Whack!

An involuntary groan escaped him.

"Ah, there we go! Come on, baby, you can make it! Wakee, wakee!"

WHACK!

"Stop . . ." Hunter mumbled, his voice thick and slurred.

He felt someone take hold of his chin and steady his head.

"Open your eyes."

His eyes blinked open.

He was tied to a straight-backed wooden chair. There was a blurred face close in front of him and several people standing in the background. He tried to focus in. It came slowly. The blurry images gradually resolved themselves into a sharp-featured, hatchetlike face surmounted by thick, elaborately styled black hair and a custom-tailored, dark silk suit filled out well with muscle. The tie was incongruous. Bright canary yellow. Silk. The breath smelled of cigarette smoke.

Cigarettes.

Right. The cigarettes.

Behind the hatchet-faced, tough guy in the expensive, raw silk suit was another man cut from the same cloth, a smoothly styled sharpie in a mauve suit with a purple silk shirt and a purple tie the same shade as the shirt. And beside him stood the lovely, treacherous Krista, staring down at him as though he were some interesting new bug she hadn't seen before.

"Who are you?" asked the hatchet-faced man.

"George Palmer," Hunter mumbled, giving the name that he'd been using.

Whack!

"Wrong. Try again."

"My name is George Palmer. I don't—"

WHACK!

The force of the blow split his lip and he felt blood trickle down his chin.

"Look, my friend," hatchet-face said softly, bringing his face up close to Hunter's, "we know who you're *not*, okay? What we'd like to know is who you are. And where you got this pretty bracelet."

Hunter's gaze was riveted on the warp disc being dangled before him.

"I don't understand," said Hunter. "Why are you doing this? If you want money—"

WHACK!

"Okay, now listen to me, all right? That was the last time with the open hand. I'm getting impatient. Next one's a closed fist. And if losing a few teeth doesn't loosen you up . . ."

Snik. The six-inch blade sprang out of the handle.

"That will do, Vincent. Take Krista and go make some coffee in the kitchen. I'll call you if I need you."

Hatchet-faced Vincent gave Hunter a long look and then left the room with Krista. Domenico Manelli came around from somewhere behind Hunter to stand in front of him, looking like an investment banker in his tailored pin stripes and rep tie. So far as Hunter could tell, there were only three of them in the room now—himself, Manelli, and the smoothie in the mauve suit.

Manelli loosened his tie and took out a pack of cigarettes. He shook one out and offered it to Hunter. "Cigarette? These aren't drugged, by the way." While Hunter watched, he took one himself, lit up and inhaled deeply. "I have no need of playing tricks," he said. He shrugged. "Now that you're tied to that chair, I could shoot you up to my heart's content. A little Pentothol to make you talk, some uncut heroin to make you stop . . . or I could call Vincent back in for some of your more basic persuasion. I'd really rather not, though. You strike me as a reasonable man. I think we could discuss things like intelligent human beings."

He shook out another cigarette and offered it to Hunter. Hunter nodded and Manelli held the pack out so that Hunter could take the protruding cigarette between his lips. Manelli lit it for him with his gold lighter. The man in the mauve suit hadn't said a word. He hadn't even moved. He simply watched Hunter expressionlessly. Hunter decided that this man worried him even more than Vincent.

"The reason I sent the others out of the room is because they don't know what this is," said Manelli, holding up the warp disc, dangling the bracelet in front of him as Vincent had. "However, I do. And so does the gentleman behind me. In fact, he has one just like yours. Now isn't that an interesting coincidence?"

Suddenly, it was a brand new ball game. Hunter stared hard at the man in the mauve suit, but his face gave nothing away.

"I see we have your full attention," said Manelli, with a smile.

"All right, what do you want?" said Hunter.

"Let's start with your name."

"Hunter. Reese Hunter."

It was pointless to lie. If they did administer drugs, he'd tell them the truth anyway. The thing was to convince them that he was already telling them the truth and at the same time withhold some of it.

Manelli smiled. "There, you see? I knew we could discuss things in a reasonable manner. And how about your rank, Mr. Hunter?"

"Captain."

Manelli looked impressed. "A captain, no less. And your unit?"

Hunter hesitated, his mind racing. Should he risk a bluff? They could easily find out, but how much time would it buy him? Fortunately, Manelli misinterpreted his hesitation.

"Ah, I think I understand," he said. "You're a deserter, aren't you?"

Hunter chose not to reply, implying assent by his silence.

"Yes, I do believe you are," Manelli said, with a smile. "That would explain your rather interesting and somewhat reckless behavior. Actually, you've proven to be quite resourceful, Capt. Hunter. Your one mistake was that you moved too quickly. You got greedy."

"Am I under arrest?" said Hunter.

Manelli raised his eyebrows. "Why, Capt. Hunter, do I look like a policeman?"

Hunter frowned. "I don't understand. You're not . . ." And then it came to him. "You're the Underground?"

Manelli smiled. "No. Not exactly." He reached out and removed the cigarette butt from between Hunter's lips before he burned himself. "We'll be back soon, Capt. Hunter," he said. "Regretably, we're going to have to leave you tied up for the moment. I'll instruct Krista and Vincent to see to your comfort as much as possible under the circumstances. If you've been completely honest with us, you have nothing to be concerned about. In fact, we might even have a proposition for you. But if you have not been completely honest with us, then it won't be your comfort that Vincent will be seeing to."

"He was a gentleman. A very large man, built like a bull," said Gulliver, "with black hair and the most disquieting eyes I'd ever seen. A bright, emerald green, they were. At times, they almost seemed to glow. He was quite a handsome figure of a man, except for the disfiguring scar upon his face, from here to here." Gulliver ran his forefinger along his cheek, from beneath his left eye to the corner of his mouth. "A wound made with a sabre, I should think, or perhaps a knife."

"That's a perfect description of Drakov, all right," said Lucas.

They sat at the table in the house on Threadneedle Street, sharing a light meal of bread, smoked sausage and cheese along with a bottle of red wine. Finn poured himself another glass and shook his head.

"I can't understand it," he said. "Forrester shot Drakov. I was *there*. I *saw* it."

"I saw Lucas get shot, too," said Andre.

"What are you saying?" said Steiger, sarcastically. "That Drakov had a twin in the parallel universe too, and that Dr. Darkness switched the two of them, as well?"

"I wouldn't put it past him," Lucas said, "but maybe what we're facing here is a result of what Darkness did with me. If there was some sort of temporal disruption that came about from his changing my past, maybe it resulted in Drakov's past being changed, as well."

"I can't see how," said Finn. "As you said, Lucas, nothing was changed by Darkness altering your past. Nothing, that is, except that you survived. I don't mean to downplay that, obviously, but the circumstances were unique. Your being alive instead of dead hasn't altered any of the events that took place since your death."

"Excuse me . . ." said Gulliver. "Uh, Finn, would you mind—"

"Don't ask me to repeat it, Lem," said Delaney, wryly. "I'm not even sure *I* understand what I just said. The point is, either Darkness was right and the uniqueness of this situation hasn't resulted in any disruption at all or you're the disruption yourself, Lucas. Or all of us are."

"I'm very confused," said Gulliver.

"Brother, you're not alone," said Lucas.

"Either way, we're not going to solve anything by sitting around here," Steiger said. "Lucas, you sure you don't want to—"

"No, I don't think so," Lucas said. "It would only cause one hell of a commotion if I went back with you now and I'd never get away from them. They'd want to debrief me, put me in for observation . . ." He shook his head. "No, I could do more good here."

"Right," said Delaney. They got up from the table. "We'll clock back and pick up a couple of floater paks. And while we're at it," he said to Lucas, "we'll report your miraculous survival. Or rather, your nondeath. Or rebirth or whatever. Hell, we'll just report you as being alive and let them work it out."

"Uh . . . on second thought, Finn, maybe you shouldn't mention me just yet," said Lucas.

Delaney frowned. "Why not?"

"Partly because it would cause one hell of a commotion,"

Lucas said, "and I still don't fully understand what's happened to me. Nor can I predict how Dr. Darkness will react when he finds out that the one working prototype of his greatest invention has walked out on him. And I can think of one more reason. With this Network situation that you've described to me, it couldn't hurt to have an ace up your sleeve that no one knows about."

"Good point," said Steiger, nodding. "All right, then, we'll leave you officially dead for the time being. But we should let the old man know."

"I agree," Delaney said.

"All right," said Lucas. "You can tell Forrester, but no one else. Oh, and one more thing. Don't mention anything to him about Nikolai Drakov. At least not until we know for sure."

"I'll go along with that," said Steiger. "We'll leave directly from base to check out Gulliver's coordinates. If there's an island out there, we'll come right back here and pick up the rest of you. Meanwhile, sit tight." He checked his disc. "We'll be clocking back here in about two minutes, your time." He glanced at Gulliver. "That means don't move around the room much till we get back, Lem. I'd hate to materialize in the same spot where you were standing."

"Goodness. What would happen if you did?" asked Gulliver.

"Believe me, you wouldn't want to know," said Steiger.

The two men went over to the far side of the room, locked in the transition coordinates on their warp discs and clocked out. Gulliver stared at the spot where they had stood a second ago and shook his head with amazement.

"It truly is astonishing what one can become accustomed to," he said. "I've just seen two people vanish into thin air and here I sit, calm as you please, eating bread and cheese and drinking wine."

"You've certainly had your share of interesting experiences," Andre said. "All things considered, you're bearing up extremely well."

"What else is one to do?" Gulliver replied. "A man can't go jumping out of his skin every time something—*Great merciful Heavens!*"

He leaped out of his chair, sending it crashing to the floor and spilling wine all over the table as Dr. Darkness suddenly appeared sitting in the chair next to him, one leg casually crossed over the other.

"The Japanese have an old saying," Darkness said, playing with his walking stick. "When one saves another's life, that person becomes responsible for the life he saved." He grunted. "The Japanese can be a very irritating people." He glanced at Gulliver, standing back away from the table and staring at him open mouthed. "What are *you* goggling at?"

"I . . . that is, I . . . I . . . ai-yi-yi," said Gulliver, holding his head with both hands.

"Articulate chap, isn't he?" said Darkness.

"Now listen, Doc," Lucas began, but Darkness interrupted him.

"No, *you* listen," he said. "Did you think that I went to all that trouble simply so that you could come back here and continue playing soldier, perhaps get yourself killed again? Is that what comes of all my efforts on your behalf?"

"Doc, I didn't *ask* you to make any efforts on my behalf! I never asked you to do anything!"

"Indeed? And where would you be right now if I hadn't done anything?"

"Well, dead, presumably, but—"

"*Presumably*?" said Darkness, arching his eyebrows. "Nothing presumable about it. You would have been stiff as a carp." He grunted. "I saved your blasted life for you and what do I get in return? You simply walk out on me, without so much as a by your leave. Would it have been too much trouble to leave a note, at least? 'Dear Dr. Darkness, thank you for saving my life. I am off to make an asshole of myself and perhaps get killed again. Yours in perpetual confusion, Lucas Priest.' It would have taken less than a minute to dash that off. You couldn't be bothered?"

"Doc, you're starting to sound like my mother," Lucas said.

"I *am* your mother, for God's sake! I am both your mother and your father. I gave you life! Life and an opportunity such as no man has ever had before—"

"Doc, I didn't *want* it!"

"Well, who *asked* you?"

"Nobody did, that's just the point!"

"Wait a minute," Andre said. She turned to Lucas. "What do you mean, you didn't want it? You'd rather be dead?"

"You stay out of this!"

"I'd listen to her if I were you," said Darkness.

"Well, you're *not* me!" Lucas shouted. "What am I supposed to do, spend the rest of my life like some kind of laboratory animal on that cockamamie desert planet of yours, waiting around for you to perfect your telempathic terminal or whatever the hell it is before you discorporate?"

"I should think that most people would have found it a small enough price to pay for being brought back from the dead," said Darkness.

"And what happens if you *don't* perfect it?"

"Don't be absurd. It's already been perfected. It simply requires some fine tuning, a certain amount of training and adaptation on the part of the subject. Granted, it isn't exactly user friendly, but—"

"*User friendly?* Are you out of your tree? This damn thing is a time bomb ticking away inside me and I'm stuck with it for rest of my unnatural life, thanks to you! Did it ever occur to you that I might actually *resent* being your guinea pig?" He threw his hands up and rolled his eyes. "God, why am I even bothering trying to explain anything to you? You act as if I had to ask your permission to come back to Earth!"

"You certainly should have," Darkness said. "You're a fool, Priest. An astonishingly lucky fool, but a fool nevertheless. It's one thing to lose your concentration and accidentally translocate to Earth during an idle lapse or while you're dreaming, because in that event, the chronocircuitry computes the coordinates from your subconscious and its own inherent database, but to *consciously* attempt to program a translocation of such magnitude when you're not even certain of the distance was foolhardy in the extreme! Suppose you had mentally tried to program specific transit coordinates and overriden the telempathic database function?"

"Well, actually I thought of that, but you said that the telempathic chronocircuitry had a built-in, automatic trip computer or whatever and—"

"My *God!*" said Darkness. "And so you blithely flung yourself across two million light years when the furthest you'd ever consciously translocated before was *across the room*?"

Lucas merely gaped at him.

"Two *million* light years?" Andre said, in a voice barely above a whisper.

"What . . . what, pray tell, is a light year?" Gulliver asked, hesitantly.

"A unit of distance, determined by the velocity of the speed of light in a vacuum, which is approximately 186,000 miles per second, measured in miles per hour and multiplied by the number of hours in a year, which yields the distance that light travels in one year, which is approximately six trillion miles," Darkness said, impatiently. "I thought everyone knew that."

Gulliver tried—and failed—to comprehend the explanation he'd been given. He gave up and took a small flask from his pocket, unstoppered it and slugged down some whiskey in the hope that it would settle his nerves, so that the stranger who had just appeared would stop fading in and out like some ghostly apparition.

Only instead of Darkness becoming more substantial, Lucas disappeared.

"Lucas!" Andre cried.

"Oh, hell," said Darkness, irritably. "His bloody concentration slipped again."

"Where did he go?" said Andre, alarmed.

"I haven't the foggiest," said Darkness. "Who knows *what* he was thinking?" He sighed. "Now I'll have to track him through the symbiotracer. With any luck, I'll find him before he panics and thinks himself into a jam. Science would be ever so much more rewarding if one didn't have to deal with people!"

And he vanished.

Gulliver tossed the flask over his shoulder and put his head down on the table. "I give up," he said. "Wake me when this dream is over."

As the uniformed courier stepped out of the lift tube and approached the security station, the two armed guards posted at the lift tube entrance fell in on either side of him. He glanced at them briefly, but didn't pause. He was carrying a briefcase that was fastened to his wrist by a chain. He set the case down on the desk in front of the sergeant of the guard and reached into his inside jacket pocket for his I.D.

"Lt. Stroud, Council of Nations attaché," he said. "I have priority classified dispatches for General Forrester."

The sergeant of the guard carefully examined the credentials. "I have nothing on my log concerning dispatches from the Council of Nations, sir."

"They're priority dispatches, Sergeant," said Lt. Stroud. "This isn't a regular delivery. It wouldn't appear on your log."

The sergeant of the guard maintained direct eye contact with the courier. "I see. Would you open the case, please, sir?"

"I'm afraid I can't do that, Sergeant. Orders."

"I'm sorry, sir, but I have my orders, as well. And I do possess an A-6 level clearance."

"That doesn't help me, Sergeant. I have specific instructions to open this case only in General Forrester's presence."

"I'm afraid I'm going to have to insist, sir," said the sergeant of the guard. "That case isn't going anywhere until I've seen what's inside it."

Stroud's eyes widened. "Are you serious? Do you realize what you're doing, Sergeant?"

"I'm following orders, sir," the sergeant said, resting his hand on the butt of his weapon. "Open the case, please."

Stroud shook his head with resignation and reached into his pocket. The sergeant of the guard's gun leaped out if its holster. The men on either side of the courier instantly grabbed his arms.

"Easy, easy!" said Stroud. "Jesus, what *is* it with you people? I was only getting the key for this bracelet."

The sergeant of the guard nodded and the men released him. He kept the courier covered with his gun. "Just bring it out slowly, sir, if you don't mind," he said, his voice even and polite.

Moving carefully and deliberately, Lt. Stroud removed the key from his pocket and showed it to the sergeant of the guard.

"Take the bracelet off him," the sergeant of the guard said. One of the men took the key away from him and unlocked the courier's bracelet, removing it from his wrist.

"I've heard of tight security, but you guys are really something," said Stroud. "What the hell do you think I've got in here, a bomb?"

"We'll find out as soon as we scan it, sir," said the sergeant of the guard, reaching down and bringing out a portable scanner gun with a built-in screen. It hummed faintly when he turned it on. "All right, let's see what's in here. If these are nothing but dispatches, sir, you'll have my sincere apologies and—what the *hell*?"

The lid of the briefcase suddenly sprang open and a filament-thin beam of bright, coherent light lanced up out of the case. The sergeant of the guard screamed and recoiled, clapping his hand to his right eye, which the tiny laser had melted right out of its socket.

Stroud elbowed the guard on his right in the solar plexus, then back fisted the other one in the face, breaking his nose. He brought his right hand down in a sharp, chopping motion and the blow broke the neck of the first guard, then he hit the second guard again with a strike to the throat, collapsing his trachea. The sergeant of the guard hit the alarm button on the console as more laser fire hit him and he sagged down to the floor. As the alarm klaxon sounded, tiny, black-garbed commandos started rising rapidly up out of the case, carried aloft on miniature floater paks.

"Go! *Go!*" shouted Stroud, running around the counter and stabbing at the console, trying to find the switch to cut off the alarm.

In his office suite, across the hall from his private quarters, Forrester heard the alarm and glanced at the security monitor mounted in the corner, just below the ceiling. What he saw was a platoon of armed lilliput commandos wearing floater paks, hurtling down the corridor. A bright ball of blue-white fire from a miniature autopulser flew at the lens. The image on the monitor broke up and the screen went blank.

"Jesus Christ!" said Forrester, yanking open his desk drawer and pulling out an antique, ivory-stocked, Colt Python .357 Magnum with a six-inch, vent-ribbed barrel. As he bolted toward the door, he heard screams and autopulser fire coming from the front office.

He stuck his head out the door and almost ran right into a wire-thin laser beam. He brought up his gun and the Colt Python roared and bucked, sending a copper-jacketed, hollow-point .357 magnum round slamming into the oncoming lilliput commando, obliterating his entire upper torso and penetrating the miniature floater pak, which exploded in a tiny fireball.

Another laser beam singed Forrester's earlobe and one

autopulser blast narrowly missed his head as he fired twice more, two handed, then hit the floor and rolled as two little exploding fireballs passed over his head. He came up on one knee and fired again, then cried out with pain as he took a direct hit on his kneecap. The lilliput commandos had disposed of the security detail and were now swooping down on him like angry hornets. He fired his last two rounds, missing with one and taking out another miniature assassin with the last, then he threw the gun as one of the lilliput commandos came diving down at him, firing his laser. He felt the heat as the beam grazed his cheek and then the lilliputian went pinwheeling out of control as the thrown gun struck him a glancing blow. He struck the wall and the tiny floater pak exploded. Forrester dove through the doorway into his private quarters and slammed the door shut, locking it behind him.

Steiger and Delaney were in the lift tube, on their way up, when the alarm klaxon sounded. A second before the tube delivered them to the penthouse floor, the klaxon was silenced. Both men had their guns out. As they came diving out of the lift tube, they heard the unmistakable sound of Forrester touching off one of his antique firearms and it was the sound of the big magnum cutting loose that saved their lives. Stroud involuntarily glanced in the direction of the sound at the moment that the lift tube doors opened and the quick, diving exit of the two temporal agents caught him by surprise. Instinctively, he fired through the open lift tube doors, but Steiger and Delaney weren't there anymore and Stroud screamed as he was engulfed by two plasma bursts.

It took the lilliput commandos scant seconds to blast their way through Forrester's door, but by that time he had already reached his den, where he kept martial mementoes of the past, souvenirs brought back—or rather, brought *ahead*—by the men and women of the First Division. When the lilliputians broke through the door and came flying through into Forrester's private quarters, they found him standing at the entrance to his den, armed with an M-16. As they came flying in and started to fan out, Forrester fired several quick bursts of the .223 high velocity rounds, knocking several tiny invaders out of the air by pure chance, but it was impossible to achieve any kind of accuracy with a fully automatic weapon against such tiny targets moving with such speed.

Steiger and Delaney were racing down the corridor when they heard the M-16 light off. Several quick, sharp bursts were fired, and then the weapon suddenly fell silent. Fearing the worst, they came rushing through the entrance to Forrester's quarters, heedless of their own safety, and Steiger recoiled with a cry of "*Shit!*" as a lilliputian strapped into a tiny floater pak went screaming past him backwards in a line drive, trailing a spray of blood, to strike hard against the wall and explode with a sharp *whuumpf* as his fuel tanks went up.

Forrester stood in the center of the room, holding the M-16 like a baseball bat and swatting at the lilliputians as they buzzed around him like wasps around a nest, the crisscrossing beams of their tiny lasers creating a fine latticework of coherent light around him, making it appear as if he were trapped inside some glowing spider's web.

"*Moses, get down!*" Delaney shouted.

Instantly, Forrester dropped to the floor and Delaney fired his gun. The full-intensity plasma charge streaked across the room, incinerating the lilliputians in its path, slamming into the floor to ceiling window on the far side of the room and melting right through it. Steiger made a running dive and landed right on top of Forrester, covering him with his body, but the remaining lilliputians were in full retreat, swooping out the ruined window with their jets on full power and dispersing in the night like fireflies. Delaney ran over to the gaping hole, but he held his fire. There were people down there and he didn't want to risk hitting any innocent bystanders.

As he turned around, a squad of soldiers came running in, armed with laser rifles and autopulsers, all of which were suddenly pointed in his direction.

"*Freeze!* Drop the gun! Drop it *right now!*"

Delaney rolled his eyes, dropped the pistol and raised his hands over his head. "Don't shoot, I'm one of the good guys," he said.

"On the floor! Flat on the floor *right now!*"

"Well, now that isn't very smart," Delaney said. "I just dropped my gun down there. If I got down beside it, I could pick it up and shoot you, you damn fool."

"I said get down—"

"*Harris, you idiot, put down those guns!*" Steiger shouted, as he got up off Forrester. "It's over!"

"Colonel! I didn't realize—"

"No, of course not!" Steiger said, furiously. "Congratulations, Harris. You've just disarmed and captured Capt. Finn Delaney."

Harris paled. "Capt. Delaney! Sir, I'm sorry, I didn't recognize—"

Forrester groaned and rolled over onto his back.

"Oh, sweet Jesus Christ," said Steiger.

Delaney was at his side in an instant. "Oh, God. Don't move, Moses," Finn said. "Don't just stand there, somebody get a goddamn medic!"

Forrester looked like he'd taken a nap on a barbecue grill. His face and skull were crisscrossed with blackened laser tracks, not bleeding because the heat had cauterized the wounds. There was a hole in his right cheek where a beam had gone in at an angle, exiting through the neck just below his jawbone. Part of an ear had been neatly sliced off. His fatigues looked like they'd been shredded in places and there were numerous pinholes in his shoulders and arms. Miraculously, none of the vital organs appeared to have been hit. He groaned again and tried to sit up.

"Don't move, Moses, help's on the way," said Delaney.

"Screw that," grunted Forrester. "Help me up."

They gently pulled him up to a sitting position on the floor.

"Anyone left alive?" he said.

"I don't know," said Steiger.

"Well, *check*, God damn it!"

"Harris!" Steiger snapped.

"Yes, sir!" Harris rapidly detailed several men. "You, you, and you, come with me, on the double!"

"Somebody give me a cigarette," said Forrester, leaning against Delaney for support.

Steiger got him one and put it between his lips, lighting it for him. Forrester inhaled deeply and then slowly blew the smoke out. The smoke coming out through the hole in his cheek was disconcerting.

Harris came back into the room. His face was ashen. "They're dead, sir."

Forrester looked stricken. "All of them?"

"I'm afraid so, sir."

"Where the hell were *you*?" said Steiger, his voice barely under control.

"Sir, we responded the moment the alarm went off," said Harris, "but there was someone in the tube . . ." He broke off awkwardly when he realized that the someone he was referring to were Steiger and Delaney.

"Yeah, that was us," Delaney said. "Don't blame Harris, Creed. They were incredibly fast. Whoever trained 'em certainly knew what he was doing." He glanced at Forrester. "Next time I warn you about keeping those antiques of yours loaded, do me a favor. Kick me. But why the hell didn't you use a plasma gun?"

Forrester grimaced and pointed at the gaping hole where the floor to ceiling window in the far wall of his penthouse used to be. "That's why," he said, wryly. "I don't see the point in shooting sparrows with a cannon. Besides, bullet holes are a lot easier to fix. Jesus, look at this place!"

The medics arrived and pushed their way through. As they started administering first aid to Forrester, one of them turned to Steiger and said, "We've got to get him to a hospital right now."

"I'm not going anywhere," Forrester began, but Steiger interrupted him.

"The hell you're not," he said. "Doctor, are you willing to certify this man unfit for duty in his present condition?"

"You'd better believe it," said the medic.

"Right," said Steiger. "As of right now, I'm assuming command."

"The hell you are!" thundered Forrester. "You've got a mission—"

"This *is* the mission," Steiger said. "In case it escaped your attention, those commandos who hit you were about six inches tall. And that means the Network is involved in this thing up to their necks. Either that or we're all trapped in a Walt Disney movie. Doctor, get the general to the hospital right away. Harris, take your detail and accompany them. You're not to leave the general's side for so much as a second, got me? If any medical personnel give you any grief about it, refer them to me, but he's not to be alone under *any* circumstances, you got that?"

"Yes, sir!"

"Is there a doctor over there that we can trust?" Steiger asked Delaney.

"Capt. Hazen," said Delaney.

"Yeah, I know her. I'll call her right away and explain the situation. Harris, nobody comes near the general unless Capt. Hazen says its okay. Nobody. That means no nurses administering pills or drip I.V.'s, no cafeteria workers bringing him his breakfast, no orderlies to prep him for an operation, *nobody*. Either Hazen clears it or they don't get near him. Understand? If anything happens to him, it's your ass."

"I understand, sir."

"God damn it, Steiger," Forrester began, but Steiger cut him off again.

"I'm sorry, sir. My first responsibility is seeing to your welfare."

"Forget about my welfare. I'll be fine. You can't leave your team shorthanded!"

"They're not. They've got some very competent help."

7 ————————————————

Hunter thought he might be able to break the wooden chair that he was tied to and work free of his bonds, but unfortunately, there were two problems with that idea. One was that the noise of the chair breaking would be certain to alert Vincent, with his hatchet face and his razor-sharp switchblade. And if Hunter managed to break the chair, it was doubtful that he'd have enough time to slip free of his bonds before Vincent came rushing in. The second problem was that the chair might not break on the first try, and one try was all that he'd have time for. If he tipped himself forward onto his tiptoes and then fell backwards hard, smashing the chair down, it would make a lot of noise even if it didn't break at once and he didn't think that Vincent would give him a second chance.

Hunter wondered what in hell he had gotten himself into. Was Manelli a temporal agent? If so, then why hadn't he simply clocked his captive to the future for interrogation? And what was he doing posing as a 20th century Mafia don? Posing, hell, he was running one of the biggest Family operations on the entire East Coast! It didn't make any sense. The T.I.A. didn't work that way. The only other possible explanation seemed to be that Manelli was in the Underground, but then he had said he wasn't. "No. Not exactly," was what he had said. Now what did *that* mean? Either he was or he wasn't. And why did he seem so interested in Hunter being a deserter, a conclusion he had incorrectly jumped to and one that Hunter had seen no reason to dissuade him from. The idea of Hunter being a deserter from the Temporal Corps had definitely appealed to Manelli. And that would have made sense if Manelli was in the Underground. But then he had said he wasn't. "No. Not exactly." The response was maddening. *Why the qualifier?* It seemed to imply that he was either indirectly associated with the Underground . . . or perhaps with something like it. Only what?

Hunter's mind kept going around in circles and he was getting nowhere. One thing was certain. He'd been careless and now he was in a lot of trouble. If he was going to attempt escape, he'd damn well better get it done soon, before Manelli returned with his silent, deadly looking friend in the violently flamboyant suit. The eyes on that man worried him. They weren't evil eyes, like Vincent's, nor were they expressionless, like the flat-dead stare of a psychotic. They were calm. Confident. Attentive. They were the eyes of a man who did not overreact or panic. The eyes of a pro. A pro with a warp disc. And, once again, that brought Hunter back to the T.I.A. and that made no sense whatsoever. Unless . . .

The door behind him opened.

"Well, well," said a deep, baritone voice. "Capt. Hunter. Imagine meeting you here."

Hunter looked up into the face of Nikolai Drakov and his heart sank. That's it, he thought. I'm dead.

Finn Delaney remained long enough to make sure that Forrester had made it safely to the hospital and that Dr. Hazen was in attendance, with a sizable force of heavily armed I.S.D. men on the premises, then he checked out a floater pak and prepared to clock out to the past, to the coordinates that Gulliver had supplied them with. With Forrester out of commission, Steiger had to remain behind at headquarters and assume command.

"It never should've happened," Steiger had said, after they had viewed the tapes taken from the disabled security system. They saw how the courier, "Stroud," had smuggled the lilliput commandos right up to the penthouse security station in his briefcase and they saw how the attack had commenced, up to the moment that the miniature assassins had knocked out the security system. Steiger was disgusted. "That son of a bitch just walked right in."

"Well, he did have proper credentials," said Delaney. "And no one ever expected him to be carrying an entire commando assault force in that briefcase."

"That's precisely the point," Steiger had said. "We *should've* been expecting it! We'd been warned! Christ, my own brother had been killed by those little bastards and I was *still* asleep at the wheel!"

"You were clocked out on a mission, Creed—"

"It doesn't make any difference, dammit! I should've made sure my people were prepared! I was in command of the I.S.D.; it was *my* responsibility."

"Don't be so hard on yourself, Creed," Delaney said. "What happened to Sandy wasn't your fault. Neither was what happened to the old man. There was no warning with Sandy, no way anybody could have known. And as for the old man, we were expecting the Network to make a try for him, not Nikolai Drakov."

"Yeah, and that's another thing that's got me worried," Steiger said. "You said you actually *saw* Drakov die."

Delaney nodded. "Forrester shot him point blank with a plasma gun."

"So how the hell can he still be alive?"

Delaney shook his head. "Hell, I don't know, Creed. But Andre saw Lucas get killed right before her eyes and he's still alive. I'm not discounting anything. One way or another, I aim to find out the truth."

"Well, while you're at it, keep this in mind," said Steiger. "The Network's got a contract out on Forrester. My brother was killed in what seemed to be a practice exercise for what just went down here. And we still don't know who 'Stroud' was. His credentials were good, which suggests the possibility that he was on the inside. If it turns out that Stroud was an agency mole for the Network, then assuming Drakov is still alive and responsible for this 'lilliput legion,' that means he's working with the Network."

"Jesus," said Delaney, "that didn't even occur to me."

"Maybe you should take somebody back with you," said Steiger.

"There's no point in pulling someone off another team,"

Delaney replied. "We've all got more than enough to worry about. Besides, now that Lucas is back, we're up to full strength again." He paused awkwardly. "Uh, sorry, I didn't mean that quite the way it came out."

"It's all right, I understand," said Steiger. "I just hope you know what you're doing."

"What's that supposed to mean?"

"Just that you and Andre seem pretty convinced that he's really Lucas Priest."

"You're not?"

"Well, I don't know him as well as you two did," said Steiger, "but I'm reserving my judgment until I've had a chance to speak with Dr. Darkness." He sighed. "It's a wild story. I don't know what the hell to believe. Don't get me wrong, it's not that I want to think he's an imposter who's been cleverly coached by someone from the other side, but if it really *is* him, then I'm worried about the consequences of his coming back to life like that."

"Look if I'm out of line, just say so," said Delaney, "but are you sure your concerns don't stem from the fact that Darkness can't do the same thing for your brother?"

"No, I don't think so," Steiger said, after thinking it over for a moment. "I wouldn't have qualified my answer except for the fact that I'm still pretty torn up about Sandy's death. Still, I know the circumstances weren't the same. At least I understand that intellectually. Whether or not I understand it in my gut is something I can't say for sure yet. But either way, it makes no difference. What matters is the truth. Maybe I've been in the agency too long, but I simply can't take anything or any*one* at face value anymore. Be careful, my friend. Watch your step."

"Believe it, Creed, if that *isn't* Lucas, I'll know it. And I'm sure Andre will know it, too."

"Maybe," said Steiger. "On the other hand, maybe she'll subconsciously decide to fool herself. I'm not saying that anything was going on there, it's none of my business, but it didn't take a genius to see that they had some strong feelings for each other. Or at least she did. I'm not sure I'd count too heavily on her judgment right now."

"Point taken," Delaney said. "But even if Andre could be fooled, I don't think I could. Lucas and I go back a long, long time. I know him like I know myself. I know how he reacts, how he thinks. If that isn't Lucas Priest, believe me, he'll wish he *was* dead."

What neither of them had voiced was the unsettling possibility that if Drakov really was alive and creating lilliputians, then he might have created another Lucas Priest, as well. Drakov had studied under the tutelage of a master, the infamous Dr. Moreau, and he had continued where Moreau left off, using his discoveries to genetically engineer such horrifying creatures as harpies, werewolves and vampires. For a man who could acomplish all that, how difficult would it be to create a "fake" Lucas Priest? They had been in his custody before. He could have taken his raw material directly from Lucas himself.

And that could also explain how Drakov had survived. If it was indeed Drakov they were facing. He might have replicated himself. Or perhaps, given the reality bending conditions imposed by time travel, they were encountering Drakov *before* Forrester had killed him. Or what Darkness had done in bringing Lucas back to life had somehow resulted in a temporal disruption that had also cancelled out the death of Nikolai Drakov. Either way, the implications were frightening to consider.

Delaney took one last drag, crushed his cigarette out beneath his boot and programmed the coordinates for "Lilliput Island" into his warp disc. He made a final preflight check of his floater pak. It wouldn't be amusing to have it fail for some reason while he was over the Indian Ocean.

"Right," he said to himself, "let's see if there really is a Lilliput Island."

He clocked out.

He materialized in free fall about a mile above the surface of the Indian Ocean in the year 1702. He immediately fired his jets. Seconds later, he was in controlled flight, soaring above a bank of clouds. He had purposely clocked in at a high altitude, in order to avoid being seen by any passing ships. In some time periods, high altitude transitions could be hazardous due to air traffic, but there was no chance of that here. Still, Delaney knew of one case where a man clocking in at high altitude with a floater pak had rammed a hot air balloon, so it paid to orient yourself at once and pay attention. As he flew past the bank of clouds, he glanced down toward the ocean.

Nothing. Nothing but open sea.

He checked his transition coordinates once more. There was no mistake. So much for Gulliver's insistence, he thought. If Gulliver had been right, there should've been an island down there. Instead, there was only a long, narrow bank of clouds or fog slightly below him and absolutely nothing else in sight for miles, as far as the eye could see. Delaney started to descend a little ways below the cloud bank and fly a quick, wide search pattern, but he didn't think he'd find anything. Gulliver must have been wrong about those coordinates.

And then he saw it, directly below him as he flew down beneath the cloud bank. A small island, approximately the shape of a kidney bean, exactly where Gulliver had said it would be. He blinked. He didn't see how he could possibly have missed it. The cloud bank didn't seem big enough to hide the island from his sight. He looked up. The cloud bank was easily three times as large from below as from above.

Impossible.

He ascended rapidly and went right through the cloud bank once again. And sure enough, from overhead, it was smaller. And even though the wind was blowing briskly in a westerly direction, the cloud bank wasn't moving. Actually, it was moving, but instead of being driven west, it was slowly going around in circles, slowly revolving like a whirlpool.

He had found a confluence.

Directly below him, two timelines intersected. Gulliver's Lilliput Island was in the parallel universe. Somehow, Gulliver's ship must have been blown through the confluence point during a storm. He had been the sole survivor, never realizing that he was in another universe. How could he possibly have suspected such a thing? Or . . . perhaps Gulliver was from the parallel universe to begin with and he had passed through the confluence point when he had escaped from the lilliputians. Either situation was possible. Only how to tell which one had happened? Where did Lemuel Gulliver belong?

Delaney doublechecked the transition coordinates once more. It was now absolutely vital to log the time/space coordinates exactly, or he might never get back home.

"My apologies, Dr. Gulliver," Delaney said to himself. "The island *is* down there. Only 'down there' is a universe away."

He descended through the cloud bank once again and came in at an angle over the island, following the shoreline. It wouldn't take long to do an aerial reconnaissance. The island was fairly small, probably volcanic, though dormant for years. It was heavily forested and Delaney saw nothing that indicated any sort of settlement, no signs that the island was inhabited. He flew lower. And then he spotted it.

Camouflage netting.

From higher up, he never would have seen it. He circled around, powering down his jets and slowing his air speed. There was something down there, hidden beneath a wide expanse of camouflage netting covering an area about the size of half a basketball court. There were numerous gaps in the netting that let the sunlight through, but from higher up, it simply blended in with the rest of the forest. Delaney thought he could see a clearing down there, but he needed to get even lower for a closer look. He flew to the far edge of the netting and slowly started to descend through the trees.

Something stung him.

He slapped his hand to his neck, thinking that it was some insect, but he felt something sticking there, a tiny metal dart, no larger than a splinter. He felt another sharp, stinging sensation in his check and another in his temple, followed by several more in rapid succession. The drug was fast acting and took hold almost immediately. He started to lose control of the floater pak as he circled crazily through the trees, some ten to fifteen feet above the ground, smashing through branches as everything started to blur. Like a pilot with a crippled plane gliding in, out of control, Delaney tried to set down before he lost consciousness. Just before everything went black, he managed to shut the jets off and dropped the remaining few feet into a thicket, his forward momentum carrying him headlong into the bushes.

"They should have been back by now," said Andre, nervously drumming her fingers on the tabletop.

"But they have been gone only a few minutes," Gulliver said.

"They should have been back."

"Perhaps it's taking them longer than they expected."

"You don't understand," said Andre. "We're talking about

time travel, Lem. They said they'd be back in about two minutes. Our time. It could have taken them two *days* to meet with Forrester and pick up the floater paks, and they could still have set their warp discs to clock back in here two minutes after they left." She checked her disc. "And that was fifteen minutes ago."

She smashed her fist down on the table, almost upsetting the wine bottle.

"Damn it! First Lucas disappears, God only knows where to, then Darkness takes off after him and now Finn and Creed are overdue. Something's gone wrong. I just know it."

"What can we do?" said Gulliver.

"For this moment, nothing," Andre said, with a tight grimace. "They're supposed to be coming back here. And Dr. Darkness will be coming back as soon as he finds Lucas. We've simply got to wait, but I hate not knowing what's going on."

"How do you think I feel?" said Gulliver, with a sigh. "At least what you are doing makes sense to you. You understand it, whereas I . . . I can only marvel at these things because I cannot even begin to comprehend them. Time travel; a dead man coming back to life because somehow he didn't die and yet he did; a transparent, ghostlike man who lives upon some other planet, farther away than I can even imagine . . . it all defies belief, and yet I cannot dispute the reality of any of it. I tell you that if this table were to suddenly come alive and start to stroll around the room, I would not be surprised."

"You asked for it," said Andre. "You could have told us what we wanted to know and that would've been the end of it. You can still get out of it, you know."

"Yes, but I would miss the adventure of a lifetime," Gulliver said, with a grin. "Poor Mr. Swift. He so liked my story about the little people. I wonder what he would have made of this!"

"For your own good, you'd damn well better make sure he *never* hears of this," said Andre. "You've told him more than enough already!" She shook her head. "Frankly, I still don't understand why Forrester let you come along on this mission. It's simply too damn dangerous. How did you ever talk him into it?"

"Ah, well, he's a soldier," said Gulliver, picking up a small clay pipe and packing it with some shag tobacco. "And a general, at that. As a ship's surgeon, I have had some experience with serving under military men and I have seen my share of strong-willed commanders. Emotional appeals are wasted on such men. One must appeal to their pragmatism, to their sense of efficiency."

Andre looked at him with interest. "What did you tell him?"

"Simply that removing my memory of what had happened and sending me back home after all that I had seen and experienced would be a waste of a potentially valuable resource," he said, lighting up the pipe and filling the room with the pleasant, rich smell of red Virginia tobacco blended with some Turkish leaf. "Sandy Steiger, may he rest in peace, obviously fulfilled some sort of function here. That it was a military posting was not difficult to surmise from all that I subsequently heard. And after I discussed the matter with General Forrester, I came to a clearer understanding of what it is that soldiers, Temporal Observers such as Sandy Steiger, do. Perhaps I could not fulfill that function myself, but I could certainly provide assistance as a sort of liaison and subordinate. Why waste a man when you can put him to good use?"

"I don't believe it," Andre said. "You volunteered to be a field agent?"

"It seems there is some precedent for this," said Gulliver, with a smile. "Yourself, for instance. The general also explained how certain agents had employed people from the time periods to which they were sent and I submitted that I was eminently qualified. I am better educated than most people in this time and I already have some experience in these matters. I told him that the potential benefits of accepting my services would seem to far outweight the risks and he agreed."

"Lem, you're an amazing man," said Andre, with a smile.

"Indeed, Miss Cross, I quite agree," said a voice from behind them.

As Andre started to turn around, there was the cough of a silenced semi-automatic pistol and the empty wine bottle on the table burst apart into fragments of green glass.

"Please make no sudden moves, either one of you. I don't intend to kill you, but I will if you force my hand."

"Lord, *now* what?" said Gulliver. "And who is *this*?"

Andre stared at the gunman in the custom-tailored, mauve

silk suit and slowly shook her head. "Lem, I haven't the faintest idea."

The first thing Lucas thought was that he had materialized directly in the path of an oncoming train. The ground was shaking and there was a rumbling sound, an incredible din, and a fierce trumpeting . . . and then a Roman legionary knocked into him and sent him sprawling.

"Oh, Jesus . . ." Lucas said, and then there was no time for anything, not even thought, as the elephants came charging.

Another Roman soldier shouldered him aside, not even registering his strange garb in his panic to escape the charging monsters and then Lucas found himself born along by the tide as the Roman phalanx broke and ran before the terrifying onslaught.

He had been here once before. In fact, he was probably here right *now*. It had been one of his first missions and one of his worst ones, as well. He had been clocked out to fight with Scipio's legions against Hannibal of Carthage in one of the bloodiest struggles in history. Chances were that if he looked around, he might even see *himself*, dressed as a Roman legionary, running along with the others. However, there wasn't any time to look. The elephants were upon them and Lucas was plunged right back into one of his worst nightmares. And he knew exactly why.

He had no one to blame but himself. Ever since this awful mission, whenever things had gotten tough, he always referred back to this debacle, the rout of the Roman soldiers before Scipio managed, miraculously, to turn it all around. "You think this is tough?" he used to say at such times. "Try going up against a charging elephant with nothing but a Roman short sword and a spear." Often, he would refer back to his stint with Scipio Africanus whenever he became exasperated. "Christ, it almost makes me wish I was back facing Hannibal and his fucking elephants!"

Well, his telempathic chronocircuitry had granted him his wish. He had become exasperated with Dr. Darkness and the old thought had occurred to him—I really need this, he had thought. Hell, I'd rather be back with Scipio facing Hannibal and his damn—

Elephants!

He leaped to one side and rolled as the massive, trumpeting creature came charging past him, stomping Romans into jelly, and then he rolled again as another elephant missed him by scant inches. And they came on, one after the other, and Lucas found himself scrambling panic-stricken, choking on the dust and leaping around like a grasshopper on speed, trying to avoid the tremendous feet that came down like gigantic grey pistons, threatening to crush him. The dust was so thick that he could barely see. He kept diving to one side, then the other, rolling, jumping, desperately trying to avoid being trampled and then, miraculously, they were past him and he was crouching on the ground, coughing from the dusty fog that enveloped him, his eyes red, his throat raw, every muscle fiber screaming in protest from the strain . . .

. . . and here came the Carthaginian infantry.

A disembodied hand suddenly came out of the dust and grabbed him by the back of his collar, jerking him back hard. The next thing Lucas knew, he was lying on the floor of the apartment on Threadneedle Street, gasping for air and coughing his lungs out.

"That was the silliest display I've ever seen," said Dr. Darkness, standing over him. "Those pachyderms almost pounded you into a pudding. Why the devil didn't you translocate?"

"I . . ." Lucas was seized by another fit of coughing. "I couldn't . . . no time . . ."

"No *time*?" said Darkness, with disbelief. "How much time does it take to think one coherent thought? Well, granted, for you it might take a while, but you could just as easily have thought your way out of that mess instead of wasting all that energy leaping about like a trout thrown up on a riverbank. I've never seen such a ridiculous spectacle."

"I . . . I couldn't think straight," Lucas said, slowly getting his wind back. "It was . . . it all happened so damn fast . . ."

"How the devil did you wind up in the middle of the Punic Wars in the first place? What on earth made you think of that? No, on second thought, don't answer that," Darkness added, hastily. "You're liable to pop back there once again and I have a distinct aversion to large and noisy animals."

"I'm sorry, Doc. Thanks for—"

"Oh, for heaven's sake, don't thank me," Darkness said, with a grimace of distaste. "Now that I've saved your life twice in a row, I feel doubly responsible for it. I never should have taken that survey course in philosophy when I was back in college. It's been getting in my way ever since."

"Just the same, I'm grateful," Lucas said, getting to his feet and brushing off his clothes.

"Don't be grateful, be *careful*," Darkness said. "Be wary of stray thoughts until you learn proper control. You have just had a graphic demonstration of how much trouble they can get you into. I can't be hovering over you all the time like some sort of *deus ex machina*. In order for the field trials to have any validity whatsoever, you must rely on your telempathic chronocircuitry to get you out of trouble, not me."

"I'll try to keep that in mind," said Lucas. He looked around. "Where are the others?"

"How the devil should I know? They were here when I left. At least, Miss Cross and that other fellow were. Everyone seems to be popping off somewhere."

"Andre? Gulliver?" said Lucas. He looked in the other rooms, but the apartment was empty. "Andre wouldn't simply leave like that. And Steiger and Delaney were due back. Now there's no one here but us. That isn't like them. Something's happened."

Then he noticed the remains of the shattered wine bottle. He glanced at Dr. Darkness with alarm.

"How much time has elapsed here since you left?"

"Ten, fifteen, twenty minutes perhaps?" said Darkness. "I'm really not quite sure."

"What do you mean, you're not quite sure?"

"I can't be bothered with trifles, Priest," said Darkness, irritably. "When one routinely deals in light years, one doesn't sweat the occasional ten minutes."

"Well, something happened here in those ten minutes," Lucas said, tensely, "That bottle didn't break, it burst apart, as if . . . ." his voice trailed off as he started looking around the apartment, trying to estimate trajectories, and finally, he found it—a bullethole in the wall next to the armoire.

"Look at this!" he said. "Doc, they're in trouble! You've got to help me!"

"Look, Priest, I thought I already explained that—"

"Dammit, Doc, I haven't got time for this! I don't care about the validity of your field tests; I've got to find out what happened here. I can't fade out the way you can. If I went back to see what happened, I'd be visible and there's no telling what I might be clocking into; but you could find out what happened without anybody seeing you."

"Yes, well, I suppose I could do that," grumbled Darkness. He grunted. "Perhaps you're right. Under the circumstances, I can't expect you to cope with all of this yourself. Do you want me to find out what became of Steiger and Delaney, as well?"

"It could be important, Doc. Please."

Darkness sighed. "Very well." He grimaced wryly. "Do you think I could depend on you to remain in one place long enough for me to do that?"

"I'll try to think good thoughts," said Lucas, sarcastically.

"Yes, do," said Darkness. "I'll be right back."

He disappeared and almost immediately reappeared, standing directly behind Lucas.

"I'm back."

Lucas jumped, startled. "God, don't *do* that!" He took a deep breath. "You certainly cut it close. You only left about a second ago!"

"So?"

"So what if you'd arrived a second earlier and seen yourself leave?"

"So what? As long as I didn't tell myself what I'd found out in order to save myself a trip so that I couldn't have found out what I told myself I'd found out in the first place, it wouldn't have caused any problems whatsoever."

"Huh? You want to run that past me again?"

"Never mind. The important thing is that you were correct in what you had surmised. Something *did* happen here. Miss Cross and Gulliver were abducted at gunpoint by some character right out of a Frank Sinatra movie."

"Frank who?"

"Never mind. He looked like a 20th century gangster dressed by a Hollywood designer. His .45 automatic was what made the bullethole you found. He shot at the bottle, apparently to impress them with the fact that he wouldn't hesitate to shoot if they resisted. They seemed sufficiently impressed. He made them surrender their warp discs, then he replaced them with some he had brought with him. Evidently, they were preprogrammed with the desired transition coordinates."

"What the *hell* is going on?" said Lucas. "Where did they go?"

"I haven't the faintest idea," Darkness said.

"Great," said Lucas, with resignation. "Just great."

"That isn't all," said Darkness. "I tached to the 27th century, as well, to check with your headquarters. I spoke briefly with Steiger. There's been an attempt on Forrester's life. He's critically wounded. Steiger's had to remain at headquarter's and assume command."

"Good God," said Lucas. "What happened?"

"Steiger said a renegade T.I.A. agent smuggled in a commando assault force in a briefcase and . . ." Darkness stopped and frowned. "*In a briefcase*? No, wait, that can't possibly be right. . . ."

"Lilliputians!" Lucas said.

"I beg your pardon?"

"Lilliput commandos!" Lucas said. "They murdered Steiger's brother, right here in this very room. They were after Gulliver. They must have—"

"Wait a moment!" Darkness interrupted. "Lilliputians? Gulliver? I knew I'd heard that name somewhere before. You're talking about a novel by Jonathan Swift, for God's sake!"

"I can explain," said Lucas. "You see, Gulliver encountered Swift after he escaped from Lilliput Island and—"

"Never mind," Darkness said, holding up his hand to stop him. "This plot is becoming positively Byzantine. I'll simply try to follow along as best I can."

"Fine. What about Delaney?"

"He should be here."

"Well, he's not."

"Obviously."

"So where is he?"

"How the devil should I know?"

"Didn't you *ask*?"

"Steiger simply said that Delaney had to go on without him."

"Did you tell him what happened to Andre and Gulliver?"

"No, I thought I'd keep that information to myself," Darkness said, sarcastically. "Of course, I told him. He was understandably distressed, but he said there was nothing he could do."

"No, of course not," Lucas said. "He's second in command. He can't leave HQ with Forrester out of commission. Finn must have gone on ahead, assuming we'd be here when he returned from scouting Gulliver's coordinates for Lilliput Island. Only he hasn't returned and Andre and Gulliver have been captured. The question is by whom?"

"The obvious answer would be the S.O.G.," said Darkness.

"Yeah," Lucas nodded, "the Special Operations Group might have located another confluence and crossed over undetected, but there's another possibility, as well. It could be the Network."

"The Network?" Darkness frowned. "What the devil is the Network?"

"Something I've only learned about since my return," said Lucas, grimly. "Andre was telling me about it. You know about the Underground? Well, the Network is like an Underground on the inside of the T.I.A., a secret agency within a secret agency. They're like moles within Temporal Intelligence, only instead of working for some foreign power, they've struck out on their own and set up a sort of black market, transtemporal corporation."

"Enterprising of them," Darkness said. "And entirely predictable. It was only a matter of time before something like this happened."

"If you're finished with the puns, we've got to figure out what the hell to do about it," Lucas said.

"You have any suggestions?" Darkness said.

"Yeah, but it's going to be risky."

"You're talking to a man who's liable to discorporate at any moment," Darkness said, wryly. "Don't tell me about risk. What's on your mind?"

"I want you to go back to the time Andre and Gulliver got snatched again," said Lucas. "You've got to try and read those warp discs Andre and Gulliver were given, find out where they went. But you've got to make sure nobody notices. We mustn't do anything that could disrupt the scenario. Otherwise there's no telling where they might wind up. Meanwhile, I'm going to check out those coordinates that Gulliver gave Finn."

"You think that's wise?" said Darkness. "You still haven't fully adapted to your telempathic chronocircuitry. You've been very fortunate so far. You took a hell of a chance translocating all the way back to Earth by yourself. Suppose something had gone wrong? You might have materialized in space and died in seconds."

"What do you want me to do, Doc? You went and turned me into a human time machine without even bothering to tell me about it. Now you want me to say 'mother, may I?' every time I draw a breath just because you're worried about your precious prototype? Well, screw that. I died back in 1897 with a .50 caliber ball through my chest, remember? The way I see it, Doc, this isn't life, it's only special effects. We'll rendezvous back here exactly five minutes from now. And if I'm not back by then, you're on your own."

8 _____

Finn groaned and opened his eyes. Shafts of painfully bright sunlight streamed down on him through a canopy of tree branches. He squinted against the glare and tried to turn his head. It felt as if someone had given his hair a sharp yank. He tried to raise his head and found he couldn't do that, either. In fact, he couldn't move at all. He had been tied down, immobilized by a large number of thin, crudely braided ropes that were firmly staked to the ground. He could have broken any one of them with ease, but there were far too many of them. His floater pak had been removed and he had been dragged out of the thicket and turned over on his back, then spread-eagled on the ground in the middle of a small clearing, like a butterfly pinned to a board. He felt something moving across his chest.

Footsteps.

A tiny figure moved across his chest and stood silhouetted against the sunlight, looking down at him. Then two more little figures came up to stand beside the first one. He could not make out their features. All he could see were three shadowy figures, no more than six inches tall, standing on his chest. Two of them were aiming miniature laser rifles at him.

"Who are you?" one of them said, raising his small voice so that Finn could hear him clearly.

"Who the hell are *you*?" countered Finn.

The tiny man crouched down on Finn's chest and a second later, Finn yelped with pain. The lilliputian had taken a fistful of his chest hair and yanked it out.

"You little son of a—"

One of the other lilliputians whacked him in the chin with the butt of his tiny rifle, then brought it up to his shoulder and aimed right between Finn's eyes.

"Now you just lie very, very still, answer my questions and speak softly," said the first lilliputian, crouching on one knee on Finn's chest, "or my men will start shaving off pieces of your anatomy with their lasers. You understand?"

Finn grunted.

"I'll take that as a yes," the lilliputian said.

Finn strained to raise his head a little against the restraining ropes, so that he could see his tiny interrogators better. The little man doing all the talking had long, black, wavy hair that fell down to his shoulders like a lion's mane and was held in place by a cloth headband. He was bearded and shirtless, wearing a black shoulder harness resembling crossed bandoliers. It held a miniature laser pistol on one side and several power magazines in loops on the other. He was dressed in loose camouflage trousers bloused over tiny jungle boots. His small physique was lean and heavily muscled, ripped to the bone. His two companions looked about the same, like jungle commandos who had been out in the bush too long.

"One more time," the lilliputian said, "who are you?"

"Capt. Finn Delaney, Temporal Intelligence. You want my serial number, too?"

"That won't be necessary," said the lilliputian, with a smile. "I believe you. However, if I stop believing you, my men will start causing you considerable pain. Now then, Captain Delaney, what are you doing here?"

"I came looking for you, you little pipsqueak—Aahhh!"

One of the other lilliputians had fired his laser, barely grazing Finn's left ear. Finn strained hard against the ropes and the little commandos on his chest danced a jig to keep their balance. Almost immediately, Finn heard a multitude of rapid little tapping sounds on either side of him. With his peripheral vision, he could see other lilliputians on the ground, using tiny sledge hammers to pound in the stakes he had loosened with his movements. The one who seemed to be the leader let go of Finn's chest hair, which he had seized with both hands to keep his balance when Finn had started to strain against the ropes.

"Please don't do that again, Captain," the lilliputian said. "I don't really want to kill you, but I will if you leave me no choice."

Delaney couldn't believe it. He was being threatened by a man who was smaller than his shoe size.

"How did you find us?" the lilliputian said. "How did you locate the confluence?"

"Gulliver gave me the position of the island," Finn said.

"Gulliver? Impossible. He didn't know anything about the confluence."

"Of course, he had no way of knowing about the confluence," said Finn. "He must have simply sailed right through it without realizing he was crossing over from one universe into another. He took a sextant reading when he escaped from here. He must have done it the moment he came through the confluence. The thing I can't figure out is which timeline he came from in the first place. I don't suppose you'd happen to know?"

"No, Captain, I wouldn't. And at the moment, I don't really care. My main concern right now is deciding what to do with you. What, precisely, were your orders?"

"What orders?"

"Come on, don't play stupid. You're an advance scout for an invasion force. How many others were sent out with you? How long before you're overdue?"

"I came here alone."

"You expect me to believe that?"

"I don't really give a damn what you believe," Delaney said. "If the Temporal Army was going to invade this island, they'd have been on you like a fox on a duck by now. And if you really believed there was going to be an invasion, you wouldn't still be here. You'd have killed me and gotten the hell out."

"You're probably right, Captain," said the lilliput lieutenant. "Getting off this island would have been smartest thing for us to do. Unfortunately, my men and I had no means of getting off this island, so if an invasion force is coming in hard on your heels, we're simply going to have to fight. Unless, of course, your people are planning to wipe out this entire island with a warp grenade, in which case I guess we're shit out of luck. And so are you."

"Wait a minute," Finn said. "If you have no way of getting off this island, then how the hell did you get to the 27th century to make that assault on HQ?" Delaney said.

"That wasn't us," the lilliput lieutenant said.

"Oh, yeah, I guess it was some other bunch of lilliputians," Finn said, sarcastically.

One of the other lilliputians quickly raised his rifle and aimed at Finn's other ear, but the lieutenant raised his hand, holding him off. "That wasn't us," he repeated. "We're stuck here. Or at least we were til you showed up with your floater pak and warp disc."

"No offense, but I don't think they'd fit you."

"No, but they fit you and we could easily fit inside your clothing. All we have to do is kill you, program your disc, get inside your pockets and your shirt, down inside your sleeves and trouser legs, hit the button and we're out of here."

Delaney licked his lips nervously. "Yeah, I guess that ought to work. So what's stopping you?"

"Unfortunately, none of us knows how to program a warp disc," said the lilliputian.

"I see," Delaney said. "So that's why I'm still alive."

"As one soldier to another, Captain, I'm sure you can appreciate that my first responsibility is the safety of my men," the tiny commando said. "If killing you would ensure their welfare, I wouldn't hesitate to do it. However, I hope that won't be necessary."

"Yeah, I hope so, too," said Finn.

"Then perhaps we can reach an understanding," the lilliputian said. "If you transport us off this island, somewhere safe, we'll let you go and you'll never see or hear from us again. Otherwise, we'll have no choice but to kill you and use your body to transport us, taking a chance on trying to program your warp disc without really knowing what we're doing."

"That could land you in one hell of a lot of trouble," Finn said.

"We're already in a hell of a lot of trouble," the lieutenant said. "We've been abandoned here. We're too small to build and sail a seaworthy boat or even a raft. Stuck here on this island, we're sitting ducks. There's no place we can run. We'll just have to take our chances."

"If I agreed to help you, how do you know I wouldn't turn on you the moment you set me free?" said Finn.

"Before we cut your ropes, most of us would get inside your clothing, along with our weapons, of course. That would make things very uncomfortable for you if you tried to cross us."

"Yes, I'm sure it would," said Finn, visualizing dozens of tiny lasers going off inside his clothes. He shuddered and the lilliputians swayed to keep their balance on his chest.

"I see I've made my point," the lieutenant said.

"Yes, indeed you have," said Finn. "But what guarantee do you have that I wouldn't come after you with reinforcements? After all, if I transported you somewhere, then I'd know where you were, wouldn't I?"

"True, but that wouldn't help you find us. On a deserted island like this, we're vulnerable. But in a crowded city, with lots of nooks and crannies for us to hide in, you could search for years and never find us."

"Makes sense," Delaney said. "Only what guarantee do *I* have that you'll let me live once I've taken you wherever you want to go?"

"None," said the lilliputian. "You've only got two options. Refuse to help us and we'll kill you, take our chances trying to work your disc ourselves and use your body as an escape vehicle. Or cooperate and we might let you go. It's up to you."

"That doesn't leave me much choice, does it?" said Delaney.

"We weren't given much choice ourselves," said the lilliputian.

"All right, you win," Delaney said, stalling for time. "Cut me loose."

"Not just yet," the lilliputian said. He raised two fingers to his mouth and gave two sharp, piercingly high-pitched whistles.

There was a bustle of activity on either side of Finn and the next thing he knew, little wooden rung ladders crudely lashed together from twigs were put up against his sides and a score of grubby little miniature jungle commandos with tiny rifles slung across their shoulders started to climb the ladders up to his chest. They swarmed across him and crawled into his trouser pockets and down inside his shirt. They fastened ropes to his belt and lowered themselves down inside his trouser legs. Finn struggled hard to suppress his instinct to shudder. It felt like rats going down his clothes.

"All right," said the little lieutenant after his men had "boarded" Finn. "We're going to cut you loose now. But I'm warning you . . . don't make any sudden movements. In fact, don't move at all unless I tell you, otherwise my men will open fire."

Finn felt as if his skin were crawling. He suppressed another shudder, swallowed hard and nodded. "Right, you got it."

The lilliputian nodded to the two men who stood on either side of him on Finn's chest and they brought up their rifles and fired, using the beams to slice the little ropes holding Finn down. Delaney could see that the laser rifles they were using were, in fact highly modified surgical scalpels. He didn't even want to think about what they could do if the lilliputians down inside his clothes cut loose.

After a few moments, they were done and Finn lay motionless as they climbed into his breast pockets. Then their leader moved up across his neck and climbed down inside his collar, at the shoulder. He unholstered his pistol and held it up against Finn's ear.

"All right, very slowly now . . . sit up."

Finn did as he was told.

The lilliputian commander straddled his shoulder with his legs down inside his shirt, hanging onto his collar with one hand and holding the pistol ready with the other.

"Okay, so far so good. Now very slowly, stand up."

Finn stood awkwardly.

"Tell those little bastards to stop squirming around," he said.

"They'll stop. They're just as nervous as you are, believe me. Remember, you don't want to make them too nervous, right?"

"Right," said Finn, gulping as he felt a tiny gun barrel poke his groin. "Okay, you're calling the shots. Where do you want to go?"

"Program your disc for New York City, the month of September, 19—"

"Finn!"

"Lucas!"

Lucas Priest had suddenly appeared standing across the clearing from him.

"*Who the hell is that?*" the lilliputian leader said in Delaney's ear.

"Friend of mine," Delaney said, under his breath.

"*Tell him to stay where he is!*"

"Finn, for God's sake, where the hell have you—"

"Stay where you are!" Delaney shouted as Lucas started to come toward him.

"What . . ." Lucas stopped where he was. "Finn, what is it?"

"Just don't move!"

Lucas frowned. "All right, I won't move." He shut his eyes and fought back a wave of vertigo. "Finn, what's the matter?"

"I've got lilliputians down my pants."

"You've got *what*?"

"Lilliputians," said Delaney. "They're all over me. In my pockets. Inside my clothes. And they've got lasers."

Lucas looked closer and saw that Delaney's clothes did, indeed, look a little lumpy. And some of the lumps seemed to be moving. He couldn't help himself. He started chuckling.

"What the hell's so goddamned funny?" said Delaney.

Lucas burst out laughing.

"Stop that!" shouted Delaney.

"*Don't shout*!" said the lilliputian. "You want to burst my eardrums?"

Lucas found it impossible to keep a straight face.

"Clock out, damn you!" shouted the lilliputian.

"I don't think so," Finn said.

"You don't think what?" said Lucas.

"I wasn't talking to you. I was talking to the little pipsqueak sitting on my shoulder—*Ow!*"

The lilliputian had slugged him in the ear with his tiny pistol. "Now!" he said. "Clock out now or you're dead!"

"You kill me now and none of you will ever make it out of this clearing," said Delaney. "The situation's changed, my little friend. Right now, I'm the only thing keeping you and your men alive. Kill me and you've all had it. My buddy there will burn you the minute my body hits the ground. You'd better give it up."

"Surrender?" said the lilliputian commander. "And wind up

being dissected in one of your research labs? Not on your life. So long as we've got you, your friend won't dare to make a move."

"Looks like it's a standoff then," Finn said.

"I don't think so," said the lilliputian. He stuck two fingers in his mouth and gave a long, piercing, high-pitched whistle.

Finn felt movement inside his trouser legs. Several of the lilliputians hiding there had let go of the ropes and dropped down onto his boots. Lucas stared wide eyed as several lilliputians came bounding out from the bottoms of Finn's trousers, tiny laser rifles aimed straight at him.

"That was not a good move," said Finn.

Lucas disappeared.

The lilliput commandos on the ground glanced around, confused, then suddenly, one by one, they were snatched up into the air, crying out briefly before they vanished from sight, their tiny rifles falling to the ground.

"What the—where did they go?" their commander said. "What—*ahhh*!"

Lucas suddenly materialized at Finn's side, and with a deft motion, he plucked the lilliputian leader out from under Finn's shirt collar. His other arm was held tightly across his body, holding squirming lilliputians trapped between his forearm and his chest.

"Now then," said Lucas, holding the struggling lilliputian leader up between his thumb and forefinger, "I suggest you drop your weapon and order the rest of your people to evacuate Captain Delaney's clothes and fall in right down there, or I'll drop these men to the ground and stomp on them. And that goes for you, too."

"Never mind us!" shouted the commander to his other men. "We've had it! Shoot! Shoot! Save yourselves!"

Finn had a bad moment, but the scorching fire never came. Instead, the men inside his breast pockets threw out some rope and rappelled down the length of his body to the ground. The others came out of his trouser pockets and the inside of his shirt, sliding down tiny ropes to the ground as Finn stood there, feeling like the north face of the Eiger.

"Nobody's ever going to believe this," he said, shaking his head as the lilliputians dropped their weapons in a pile and fell into platoon formation at his feet.

"What I can't figure out is how the hell they got into your clothes in the first place," Lucas said, gazing down with wonder at the three ranks of lilliputians down below him, standing in formation with their hands clasped atop their heads.

Delaney sighed and grimaced ruefully. "Don't ask, okay?"

"Dear Lord, *now* where are we?" Gulliver asked, with exasperation.

"I don't know, Lem," said Andre, turning around slowly and examining their surroundings.

Both of them were handcuffed. The man in the tailored mauve suit had made Gulliver cuff Andre's hands behind her back, then he'd cuffed Gulliver himself and fastened his own warp discs around their wrists, slightly above the steel bracelets. Then he clocked them through one at a time to . . . where?

They had materialized in the center of a large room, beneath a skylight. They seemed to be standing in some sort of empty warehouse or abandoned loft. Above them, the hangarlike ceiling was a crisscrossing webwork of supporting girders and steel beams on which small kleig lights were mounted. Andre turned and saw a row of large rectangular casement windows in the wall behind her at about eye level. They were the kind that opened outwards from the bottom. A warm, humid breeze wafting in carried the sounds of traffic and the stifling smell of air pollution. Through the windows, she could see the West Side Highway and the Hudson River, with New Jersey on the other side. It was starting to get dark.

"We're in New York City," she said. "The 20th century, I think, but I'm not sure about the exact time—"

"Never mind the time," said a voice from behind them. "Get back away from the windows."

The man in the mauve suit had materialized behind them and as they turned around, he beckoned them away from the windows with his gun. It was a big, black semiautomatic pistol, Andre noticed, and it was cocked. It was a 10-mm Springfield. That, along with the style of the man's suit and her brief glimpse of the city outside, confirmed her guess about the time period. Late 20th century, early to mid 90's. The dark-haired man watched them from behind tinted, aviator-style glasses. His manner was calm, self-assured, and thoroughly professional.

"You're with the Network, aren't you?" Andre said.

"That's right," the man said.

"Who are you? Are you with the agency or did they bring you in from the outside?"

"What's the difference?" he said, flatly.

"One of degree, I suppose," said Andre. "One merely makes you a criminal. The other makes you an agent who's gone bad. In my book, that's about ten times worse."

"Really?" he said, still in that same flat, world-weary voice. "And how long have you been with the agency?"

"A couple of years," she said.

"A couple of years," he said, amused. "A whole couple, huh?"

"Before that I served with the First Division."

"Ah. One of Moses Forrester's legendary Time Commandos, eh? Saved the world a few times, did you?"

"I did my part."

"How commendable. Excuse me if I don't share your zealous sense of duty. You see, unlike you privileged elite, I was never sent out on glamorous short-term missions to return to luxurious quarters at Pendleton Base, where I could live in a style normally reserved for command staff officers. See, we 'spooks' spend years on the minus side, living in primitive squalor, gathering the intelligence that enables you glory hounds to function and only getting brought in from the cold when our chemically increased lifespans threaten to become an inconvenience. And then we're only brought back long enough to be briefed for a new assignment in the field. More years on the minus side that inexorably grind on into decades. And always there's the struggle for funding to maintain field operations—"

"Oh, bull," said Andre. "The T.I.A. has the largest budget of any government agency—service branches included!"

"We do a bigger job than any government agency, service branches included," the Network man said. "You have any idea what it takes to maintain a field office? No, of course not. What the hell do you care? They expect a section head to set up a field office and maintain it with just a small staff of agents, as if all we had to do was read newspapers and monitor the electronic media, never mind that many of the places we're sent to haven't even heard of electricity, much less mass media. We're expected to feed intelligence to the Observers, investigate and report all anomalies to Temporal Army Command, monitor all activity within a temporal zone that a regiment couldn't adequately cover. And with the parallel universe involved now, we're supposed to handle all those added complications, as well."

He snorted derisively. "You tell me," he continued. "how are we supposed to do that without recruiting additional personnel from the temporal zones we're assigned to? And those people have to be paid somehow out of a budget that doesn't allow for them. Elaborate, costly procedures must be followed to keep them from suspecting what we're really doing. Special, painstaking precautions, also very costly, must be taken to avoid causing any temporal disruptions of our own, because supposedly that's what we're here to prevent. And somehow we're supposed to keep our sanity while trying to do a job that simply can't be done."

"It sounds to me as if you're trying very hard to justify yourself," said Andre. "It also sounds like you should have been relieved a long time ago. You should've been brought in. You need rest and you need help. You're a burnout case."

"Yeah? Well, maybe I am. Maybe there was a time when doing my duty was as important to me as it is to you. But as you've surmised, I've been at it for a long, long time now. And let me tell you, it's like pissing in the wind."

He leaned back in the chair, took a deep drag off his cigarette and exhaled the smoke in a sigh.

"You see, it's kinda hard to convince the folks back home that what goes down in some temporal backwater makes any difference to them. I mean, why should they care about a field office in 11th century Jerusalem? Why should they give a damn about some war in 19th century Africa or political instability in 20th century Latin America? That was all ancient history, right? Now the rising interest rates, the falling value of the dollar, the collapse of the service economy, bank failures, those things make a difference to them. They're relevent, you see. Why should they pay taxes to support operations hundreds or thousands of years removed from their own reality? All they can see is their own world winding down. They simply can't see that it's all connected. They're fools. They're like a bunch of mindless lemmings, running full tilt toward the edge of a cliff. So if they don't give a damn, why the hell should we?"

He backed away from them, keeping them covered with his gun, until he came up against a wooden table and some chairs. He pulled a chair out, sat down and casually crossed his legs, never once taking his eyes off them. He took out a pack of English cigarettes, shook one out and lit it with a lighter held in his free hand. He offered the pack to Andre, but she shook her head. He shrugged and put it away.

"It's all falling apart, you know. I figure it probably started coming to pieces back around Julius Caesar's time and it's been growing progressively worse ever since. The miracle is that it's all stayed together this long. Somewhere back in Roman times, some idiot decided that man's role on this earth was to conquer nature instead of being a part of it, so we've been bludgeoning nature to death ever since. And several thousand years later, we've just about finished the job."

"Time travel was the final straw," he continued, in his sleepy sounding voice. "The Greeks used to say, 'Those whom the gods would destroy, they first make mad.' Well, we've become the gods and we've driven nature mad. It's fragmenting into split personalities. Parallel timelines. And now that it's started, there's just no way to stop it. It's going to be like a chain reaction, building and building and building. No stopping it. No stopping it at all."

"What in heaven's name is he talking about?" Gulliver said, under his breath. "Do you understand any of this?"

Andre nodded. "I'm afraid I do," she said. "And I'm afraid he has a point, too, despite his twisted logic."

"Twisted logic?" the Network man said.

"I'd call it twisted," said Andre. "Things may be falling apart, but that's no reason to stop trying to do anything about it. You talk as if there's some kind of virtue in not caring, in simply giving up. Nothing can be done, so why bother? Live for today, forget about tomorrow, right?"

"That's only human nature," he said, with a shrug. "When the bombs were falling on London during World War II, people made love in the bomb shelters. Knowing that death could come at any second, they tried to wring as much out of the passion of the moment as they could."

"That wasn't why," said Andre, shaking her head. "That's what I mean about your twisted logic. They did it because the procreative urge is often activated during times of great stress and extreme danger. Because their innermost instincts, knowing, as you said, that death could come at any moment, were driven to reaffirm life. Faced with imminent extinction, the human animal fights to procreate, to create new life to carry on the struggle. That's why things have stayed together this long. Not because it was some sort of miracle or blind luck or entropy or whatever the hell you want to call it, but because we're a race of fighters and dreamers. We know things aren't going well, but we have a dream that they'll get better and we fight to make that dream come true. Because when you get right down to it, that's all there is. If you stop fighting for your dream, then it really is all over. If you give up your dreams, you die."

The sound of slow hand clapping echoed through the loft. "Bravo, Miss Cross! Spoken like a true dreamer! Bravo, indeed!"

Andre spun around toward the door at the far end of the loft. The freight elevator doors stood open and Nikolai Drakov had stepped out, dressed in an elegant, dark, wool, velour topcoat and a conservative worsted suit with a very fine pinstripe. His tie was impeccably knotted, his shirt was raw white silk and he wore a dark blue scarf draped around his neck. He looked more like a corporate attorney than the last surviving member of the terrorist Timekeepers, former leader of the notorious Time Pirates and master of the monstrous hominoids. Andre stared at him with disbelief.

"Yes, Miss Cross, I really *am* alive, as you can see," he said, with an amused smile, giving her a slight bow from the waist. "Only the good die young, as they say."

He turned around and motioned to someone behind him in the elevator. Two men came forward, supporting a third between them, a man with his hands and arms firmly tied behind his back. They dragged him out and shoved him forward, so that he fell sprawling full-length on the floor. He moaned and raised his battered face to look at Andre.

"My God," she whispered. "Hunter!"

9

They had brought their twenty-six tiny prisoners back to the apartment on Threadneedle Street, all bound with their own little ropes and carefully wrapped up in a section of the camouflage netting that had concealed their camp. Finn slowly unrolled the netting, taking care not to damage any of their little prisoners; then he gently laid them all out one by one on the table top, as if they were wounded combatants in a field hospital. They all suffered this treatment stoically, saying nothing, apparently resigned to whatever fate awaited them.

"Maybe we can find some sort of a valise or something to transport them," Lucas said. "Something soft. We can line it with some cloth or toweling, make sure they don't get tossed around too much."

Delaney took out another parcel in which he had wrapped up the weapons they'd been carrying along with their floater paks and some of the supplies they'd found at their base camp.

"Check the closets," he said. "Maybe there's some bags in there. I just want to get the prisoners off our hands as soon as possible. I'm worried about Andre and Gulliver."

"I'm worried about them, too, Finn," said Lucas, "but we've got to wait for Darkness. He's the only one who'd know where they were taken."

"That's quite an interesting collection you've got there,"

said Darkness, suddenly materializing behind them. He projected himself forward through space/time in a rapid series of translocations, leaving behind a trail of ghostly afterimages. He stood over the table and gazed down at the tiny prisoners. "If you're anxious to be rid of them, I'll take them off your hands."

"You?" said Lucas. He narrowed his eyes suspiciously. "Why? What would you do with them?"

"Oh, I was thinking I could dress them up in little suits of black or white and use them to play chess," said Darkness, with a perfectly straight face.

"Oh, for cryin' out loud!" said Delaney. "We haven't got time for jokes!"

"Who's joking? They'd make a dandy chess set. Only I'd need thirty-two and you've got only twenty-six. Think you could manage to rustle up another half a dozen?"

"Forget about it," said Delaney. "What's happened to Andre and Gulliver?"

"They were abducted."

Delaney rolled his eyes. "Yeah, right. We already *know* that. Where were they *taken*?"

"New York City," Darkness said. "The 20th century. September 13, 1992, to be exact."

"Are you sure?"

"I am always sure, Delaney," Darkness said, wryly. "I do not make idle pronouncements. I observed the settings on their warp discs, and to be doubly sure, I followed them. They were clocked to an old warehouse building on Washington Street. They're in a loft, on the top floor. The man who took them prisoner is some sort of renegade T.I.A. agent, a member of the Network. I didn't hear him say his name, but he's a tall, slim, dark-haired, rather bored-looking individual dressed like a giant boysenberry. He was holding them there alone, apparently waiting for someone."

"He was waiting for General Drakov," a small voice said from behind them.

They turned to face the table where the lilliputian prisoners were all laid out.

"What did you say?" Delaney said.

The lilliputian commander struggled to sit up. "I said, he was waiting for General Drakov. That warehouse on Washington Street was one of our base camps. And the man your friend described sounds like Victor Savino. I've met him. He controls a criminal organization known as the Family through a man named Domenico Manelli."

"Savino?" said Delaney. "Vic Savino? Tied up with the 20th century Mafia?" He glanced at Lucas with astonishment. "Savino's the T.I.A. section chief in that temporal zone. Steiger's mentioned him dozens of times. They started out together. The man is something of a legend in the agency."

"And he's with the Network," Lucas said. "That means Drakov is not only still alive, but he's hooked up with the Network somehow. The most dangerous enemy we've ever faced, and our own people are involved with him. Christ, I don't believe it!"

"It doesn't make sense," Delaney said, shaking his head. "Why would the Network be involved with Drakov?"

"Because he has something they want," the lilliputian commander said. "Us. Hominoids, tailor made to your specifications. All it took was just one demonstration and they let Drakov name his price."

"Why are you telling us all this?" Delaney said.

"Because I'd like to see the bastard burn," the lilliputian said, to a chorus of grumbling assent from his men.

"Why?" Delaney said. "And why should we believe you?"

"The son of a bitch marooned us on that island," the lilliputian leader said, bitterly. "I've seen him squash men underfoot as 'an object lesson in discipline.' We were never people to him. We were cannon fodder. A toy mercenary force that used live ammo. It was kill or be killed. When the hit on Gulliver went bad and he escaped, Drakov decided to evacuate the island. We're all that's left of the original regiment, the 'first generation,' as he called us. And he hung us out to dry. The second generation helped him do it. They just left us there for you to find."

"You mean he knew we were coming?" said Delaney.

"He said it was only a matter of time," the lilliputian leader said. He grimaced. "No pun intended. When he found out Gulliver had escaped with the help of an Observer, he realized that Gulliver would be interrogated and you'd eventually find the confluence and discover the islands. He said that it would be a pity if there was nothing left for you to find."

"So he left you there," Lucas said, "to kill us when we arrived."

The lilliputian nodded. "He said that our only chance to stay alive would be kill you. We'd have all died anyway. Our commanding officer was killed. A snake got him. I was the exec." He snorted. "Some great commandos we turned out to be. There were five hundred of us in the first generation. We're all that's left."

"Well, Lieutenant, regardless of whatever Drakov told you, you're not going to be killed," said Lucas. "We're going to clock you to our headquarters in the 27th century. And you're going to be treated humanely, like prisoners of war. Special arrangements will obviously have to be made for your detention, but nobody's going to kill you. I guarantee it."

"Wait, Lucas," said Delaney, "let's think about this for a minute."

Lucas frowned. "What do you mean? What's there to think about? We have to deliver the prisoners. Surely, you're not suggesting that we—"

"No, no, of course not," said Delaney. "You know me better than that. I was merely thinking that we might be overlooking an opportunity here." He glanced at the lilliputian leader. "Lieutenant, how'd you like a crack at your old friend, Drakov?"

"Finn, no!" said Lucas. "Absolutely not! I know what you're thinking and you can just forget about it!"

"Why?"

"*Why*? Are you serious? We can't simply clock to the 20th century with a suitcase full of lilliputians! It's too risky! How do we know we can trust them?"

"When you get right down to it, we don't," said Finn. "But I believe him. Everything he's told us fits with what we already know about Drakov. And if the Network is involved, we're going to need help. We can't ask headquarters for backup because we don't know who we can trust back there."

"Maybe not in the T.I.A., but we can trust our own people, the First Division," Lucas said.

Delaney shook his head. "They wouldn't have anyone to spare. You don't know what it's been like, Lucas. Ever since Forrester uncovered the Network and set out to break it, it's been all-out war. The only people he can trust in the entire agency are our old First Division people and there simply aren't enough of them to go around. Most of them are on adjustment duty, just like we are, and most of the rest are engaged in ongoing undercover work, trying to help expose new Network cells and break them up. We're not only trying to preserve the continuity of the timeline, we're faced with hostilities from the parallel universe and from within the T.I.A., as well. And with the old man in the hospital, Steiger's going to have his hands full. We can't ask him to spare us any reinforcements, Lucas. And even if we could, there'd be no way to be sure that word of their clocking out to help us wouldn't leak out and someone would clock back ahead of them and warn Savino."

Lucas nodded. "Yeah, you're right. I guess it's going to have to be just you and me, like in the old days. Only this time, we've got the Doc along to help us."

"Just one moment," Darkness said. "When did *I* become a temporal agent? Somehow, I don't recall enlisting."

"Don't hand me that, Doc," Lucas said. "I don't recall asking to be brought back from the dead and made into an experimental human time machine, either! Now if you want to see how your prototype functions in the field, then I suggest you come along and help, otherwise I'll just go and do it myself!"

He disappeared.

"Lucas! What the . . . where did he go?" Delaney said.

"Oh, hell," said Darkness. "I'm afraid he translocated to the 20th century."

"You mean—"

"Yes, I'm afraid so," Darkness said, with a sigh. "He was thinking about going and doing it himself and that's precisely what he did. I fear I didn't quite get all the bugs out of system. It does tend to interpret one's thoughts rather literally."

"Well, don't just sit there, for God's sake! Go and help him! He could be in trouble!"

"Not if he keeps his wits about him," Darkness said. He grunted. "That'll be the day. I'd better go and help him."

He vanished.

Delaney quickly programmed new transition coordinates into his warp disc. He glanced down at the lilliputians.

"If the offer's still open," said the lieutenant, "we accept."

Delaney threw open a closet door and took out a brown

leather valise. He grabbed several shirts out of the closet and stuffed them down into the bottom. "All right," he said, setting the valise on the table and carefully cutting the lilliputians' bonds. "Get inside. But if you try anything, so help me, I'll do the Mexican hat dance on this bag. Let's go."

For a moment, Andre was too stunned to move. First Lucas had miraculously come back from the dead, and now Reese Hunter. But then she realized that this man couldn't possibly be the Reese Hunter she had known, the one who had been brutally murdered by the Timekeepers in 17th century France. This could only be his twin from the parallel universe, an officer in the Counter Insurgency Section—their counterpart to the Temporal Intelligence Agency.

They had met when Forrester had sent them on a mission through a confluence, into the parallel universe, where Nikolai Drakov had pretended to defect only so that he could hijack the S.O.G.'s Project Infiltrator along with its brilliant director, Dr. Moreau. It was from Moreau that Drakov had learned how to create his deadly hominoids. Capt. Reese Hunter had been sent out to stop him and he had met the Time Commandos when they were all taken prisoner by Drakov and his homicidal henchman, Santos Benedetto.

They didn't really know each other, and yet, in another sense, they did. This Reese Hunter was not the same man who had helped Andre to avenge her brother's death, but he was identical to that Reese Hunter in almost all respects, as if they had been cut from the same mold. He, in turn, had also known an Andre, although the Andre he had known in his own universe had been killed while on a mission, just as the Lucas Priest and the Finn Delaney he had known had died. During the time they they had shared the same prison cell at Drakov's headquarters on the island of Rhodes, they had discovered that they "knew" each other well through having known their counterparts. It was an eerie sort of intimacy.

When they had escaped, they had taken Hunter prisoner. There had been no choice, of course. He was the enemy. But once they had crossed over back into their own timeline, Hunter had escaped with a stolen warp disc and they hadn't seen him since. Now there he was, lying on the floor at Andre's feet, badly bruised and battered. He was from the other side, but at the same time, he was indistinguishable from the man who had helped her and changed her entire life. They were the same, right down to their DNA. As he raised his face to look at her, Andre could not suppress a gasp. And then, involuntarily, she moaned softly.

"Oh, Reese! What have they done to you?"

He squinted up at her through swollen eyelids. "*Andre*? Is that really you?"

Drakov chuckled. "It's rather like old home week, isn't it?" he said. "It really is amazing how fate keeps throwing all of us together. The late Professor Mensinger doubtless had an equation of some sort to account for how the Fate Factor keeps selecting us out of random temporal zones and maneuvering us together to resolve our mutually disruptive influence. Well, perhaps this time we can settle things, once and for all."

Andre looked up at him from where she knelt on the floor, beside Hunter. "Drakov, how can you possibly be alive? I *saw* Forrester kill you!"

"Did you, indeed?" he replied, in an amused tone. "Somehow I've always thought that it would happen the other way around. I trust I died well?"

For a moment, she wondered if Drakov had somehow cheated death like Lucas had. With Nikolai Drakov, it seemed that almost anything was possible. His birth had been a temporal anomaly. He had been conceived when a very young Moses Forrester, fresh out of boot camp and on his first assignment in minus time, had been seriously injured and separated from his unit. He had been nursed back to health by a beautiful young Russian gypsy girl named Vanna Drakova. Stranded, crippled and with a damaged implant, young Forrester had thought that he was trapped forever in the past. By the time an S & R team finally found him, Vanna was pregnant with his child. Forrester, afraid that Vanna's child would be aborted, never mentioned it and the Search and Retrieve team took him away into the future, never to see the girl he loved again.

Nikolai was born in the middle of a brutal Russian winter storm while Moscow burned during Napoleon's retreat. He had survived when most other infants would have died in such severe conditions. His seemingly miraculous survival and his unusual health were due to the antiagathic drugs that were still active in his father's system, Forrester having received the anti-aging and immunizing treatments shortly following his induction into the Temporal Corps. From what little the uneducated gypsy girl could tell him about his father, Nikolai had formed a picture of some supernatural, demon lover who had abandoned both of them.

For years, he felt that he was cursed, a demon issue, and when his mother was murdered by a knife-wielding rapist who had given Nikolai the scar upon the left side of his face, the bitter resentment and the fear had turned to savage hatred. Years later, when he had found out the truth about his father from a woman known as Falcon, the infamous leader of the Timekeepers, Drakov had vowed that he would never rest until Moses Forrester was dead and the timestream was irreparably split. He was, of course, insane. And he was also dead. Andre had seen him incinerated by a plasma blast. So how could he possibly still be alive? And then the only possible explanation struck her.

"My God, you've done it to yourself," she said. "You've created a hominoid from your own genetic template!"

"Very good, Miss Cross," said Drakov, with an appreciative nod. "Very good, indeed. Only that should be hominoids, plural, not singular."

She paled. "How many?"

He smiled. "Ah, now that would be telling, wouldn't it? And what's life without a little mystery?"

She stared at him, astounded. "Does . . . does that mean that you . . . that you're . . ."

"That I'm what?" said Drakov, smiling. "The original Nikolai Drakov or a hominoid? Interesting question. You see, under normal circumstances, a clone would essentially be a sort of carbon copy, yet not necessarily the same as the original. Such things as culture, environment, experience and so forth play an important part in the formation of a personality. It's not merely a matter of genetics. However, a hominoid is considerably more than just a clone. There is genetic manipulation and cybernetic surgery, among other esoteric procedures. And when you add time travel child rearing into the equation, what I call 'time lapse maturation,' carefully supervising the development through the years and using implant education to program specific memory engrams, why, then what you might very well wind up with would be a clone who has the same experiences, the same memories, and the same exact personality, carefully cultivated from identical genetic stock. And in such a case, how could you tell the difference? If I were the original Nikolai Drakov, I would naturally know that I was the original. Yet on the other hand, if I were *not* the original Nikolai Drakov, but I had been given the same memories and personality, how would I ever know?"

"So what are you saying?" said Andre. "That what Forrester killed was a hominoid?"

"Perhaps," said Drakov, smiling slightly, enjoying her confusion. "And perhaps not. Suffice it to say that he killed *a* Nikolai Drakov. But, as you can see, there are more where that one came from."

"Dear Lord, I understand absolutely none of this," said Gulliver, miserably. "It seems that I have come full circle somehow. Will this madness *never* cease?"

"Never fear, Mr. Gulliver," said Drakov. "For you, it will cease all too soon. You've really become quite an inconvenience. You seem to live a charmed life. I've never met a man who was more inept, yet so difficult to kill. It defies all explanation."

"Leave him alone, Drakov," Andre said. "He has nothing to do with this."

"My dear Miss Cross, he has *everything* to do with this," said Drakov. "If not for him, you would never have stumbled upon this little venture of mine until it was far too late for you to do anything about it. As it is, I was forced to move ahead of schedule and alter my plans somewhat. Altogether, you've been very irritating."

"I think you'll find us a lot more irritating before it's all over, Nikolai," Andre said.

"Really? Oh, I see. You're no doubt anticipating rescue by your two gallant young comrades, Steiger and Delaney. Well, you may have quite a wait. Knowing those two as I do, I imagine the first thing they did upon questioning young Mr. Gulliver was to go looking for my island base. If they've been unfortunate enough to find it, they will have also found the reception committee that I left behind for them. Somehow, I doubt you will be seeing them again. In any case, for you, Miss Cross, it *is* all over. Savino, bring her."

Savino came up behind her and grabbed her by the arm, lifting her up and shoving her away from Hunter.

"Savino?" she said, staring at him. "Vic Savino?"

"That's me," he said. "Get moving."

"Traitor." She spat in his face.

He punched her in the jaw and knocked her to the ground.

"Coward!" shouted Gulliver. "You craven coward, hitting a woman!"

Despite his hands being cuffed behind his back, Gulliver rushed Savino, but Savino merely stepped aside and tripped him, sending him sprawling.

"Enough of this nonsense," Drakov said, irritably. "Bring her, I said!"

Savino grabbed Andre and manhandled her into the elevator. As he got in after them, Drakov beckoned to the two men he had brought with him. He indicated Gulliver and Hunter.

"Kill them and dispose of the bodies in the river," he said.

"No! Wait!" shouted Gulliver.

The elevator doors closed.

The two men came forward, reaching inside their custom-tailored jackets.

Dr. George Ericson, the chief hospital administrator, was not pleased with Lt. Harris and he let him know it in no uncertain terms.

"Now look here, Sergeant—" he began.

"Lieutenant," Harris corrected him, testily. It was not an auspicious beginning.

"Lieutenant," the administrator said, his tone clearly indicating that whether it was sergeant or lieutenant made not the slightest bit of difference to him. "This has to stop immediately. I can't have you turning this hospital into an armed camp."

"This hospital is on a military base, sir," said Harris, wryly. "It's right in the middle of an 'armed camp,' as you put it."

"I fail to see what that has to do with anything," Ericson said, impatiently. "You have literally invaded this hospital with your armed guards. It's disturbing the patients and the staff feel practically beseiged. We simply cannot have this. I cannot allow you and your men to go on harrassing the patients and the staff, making everyone coming in and out submit to being searched, checking identification, really, it's quite intolerable. By what authority do you—"

"By the authority of the acting base commander, Col. Steiger, sir," said Harris, interrupting him. "That gives me all the authority I need. As to invading this hospital, sir, that's precisely what we're here to prevent."

"You're disturbing the patients—"

"I don't really think that we're disturbing any of the patients, sir. Most of them are military personnel in the first place and would certainly understand the need for security under the circumstances. The only patients who can even see any evidence of additional security on the premises are those who were up on General Forrester's floor and they've all been moved. Our people up there are doing all they can to make their presence as inconspicious as possible."

"Nevertheless," Ericson persisted, "this entire so-called security operation of yours is an unwarranted intrusion and it's interfering with the function of this hospital. It simply won't do. I cannot allow it to continue."

"I think what's happening, sir," Harris said, evenly, "is that your doctors are complaining about being searched everytime they come into the hospital or pass one of the interior checkpoints we've established. And frankly, sir, that's tough. You might remind them that one member of the hospital staff has already been murdered by an infiltrator. We're here to see that it doesn't happen again."

"Well, I take the strongest possible exception to this," the chief administrator protested.

"I'll make a note of it, sir," said Harris.

"Don't you condescend to me, Sergeant—"

"That's Lieutenant," Harris said.

"Whatever. I demand to speak to your superior officer at once!"

"That would be Col. Steiger, sir," said Harris.

"Fine, I'll speak to him."

"As you wish, sir."

"Well?" said Ericson.

Harris sighed wearily. "Well, *what*? Sir."

"I'm waiting."

"For what?"

"For you to go and get Col. Steiger, of course!" the chief administrator said, as if Harris were a total idiot.

Harris lost his patience. "What the hell do I look like to you, an errand boy? You think the acting base commander's going to come running just because you snapped your fingers? In case it's escaped your attention, Dr. Ericson, the base is on full alert and the reason General Forrester is in this hospital is because there have already been several attempts on his life and the last one damn near succeeded! Now I'm here to do a job and I don't intend to leave my post simply because some prima donna doctors have been inconvenienced. Now if you want to speak to the acting base commander, I suggest you go through the proper channels and request an appointment. If Col. Steiger thinks that your request warrants sufficient priority, he'll see you, but frankly, I wouldn't hold my breath. Now get the hell out of my face. I've got work to do."

The chief administrator looked as if he were about to have apoplexy. "How *dare* you speak to me like that? Who do you think you are? I'll have your stripes for this!"

"I haven't *got* any goddamn stripes," said Harris, rolling his eyes. "I'm a commissioned officer. Now I'm really trying not to lose my temper, but—"

"You are the most arrogant, insolent, and uncooperative young man I've ever met!" Ericson said, puffing himself up like a blowfish. "Now I *demand* to see Col. Steiger this very instant, do you hear me? This very instant!"

"That's it," Harris said, "I've had it. If you're not out of here in three seconds, I'm placing you under arrest. One . . ."

"*Arrest*?" The adminstrator's face turned purple and his eyes bulged. "*On what charge*?"

"Two . . ."

"You must be out of your mind! You wouldn't dare—"

"Three, Donnelly, Kruger, place this man under arrest."

As the two men moved in to take the astonished hospital administrator into custody, a well-dressed man hurried past the checkpoint, carrying a briefcase.

"Wait a minute!" Harris called after him.

"Can't stop now!" the man called back over his shoulder as he hurried on. "I'm Dr. Blake, I'm due in surgery! It's an emergency!"

"Stop!" shouted Harris.

The man ignored him.

"Stop that man! Right now!"

Donnelly and Kruger forgot about the hospital administrator and rushed after Dr. Blake, drawing their weapons as they ran.

"Now see here!" the chief administrator shouted as he hurried after them. "You men! Stop! You can't do that! That man's on his way to an emergency surgery! You can't—"

"Ericson!" Harris shouted. "Get back here!"

Dr. Blake suddenly dropped his briefcase on the floor, sliding it towards the lift tubes. Then he pivoted around sharply, drawing a plasma pistol from a shoulder holster.

"Look out!" yelled Kruger.

Donnelly dived to the right while Kruger leaped to the left as "Blake" fired. The plasma charge took Dr. Ericson full in the chest as he came running up behind them. He screamed as the searing heat enveloped him and then an instant later, his charred remains fell to the floor. As the briefcase stopped sliding, there was a faint, explosive pop and the lid flew open. A bright, incandescent glow came from within the briefcase.

Harris fired his weapon and dropped "Blake" in his tracks, but even as he did so, a swarm of lilliputians equipped with floater paks came rising up out of the briefcase.

"Jesus Christ," Harris said, grabbing for his communicator. "He's got a chronoplate in there! Donnelly, Kruger! *Fire! Fire!*"

As the two men laid down a crossfire in the hospital corridor, Harris shouted into the communicator.

"Mayday! Mayday! Assault in progress at Post 1!"

The lift tube doors revolved around and a group of hospital staff members stepped out right into the line of fire. Three of them were killed instantly, the rest dispersed, screaming and beating at their flaming clothing or clutching at themselves where a dozen miniature lasers had sliced through bone and sinew as easily as if it were warm butter.

The lilliputians swarmed into the lift tube and more kept on coming from the briefcase. Four security men came running down the hall and two of them went down at once. Donnelly, trying to get around the screaming wounded, caught several laser beams in his head and upper torso. He fell to the floor without a sound.

"Harris, this is Steiger. What's going on down there?"

"It's a goddamn invasion!" Harris shouted into the communicator as reinforcements from the other hospital entrances started to arrive upon the scene. "We're got casualties down here! I've got several men down! They're coming through a temporal transit field, lilliputians, hundreds of them! I can't get to it! They've gotten to a lift tube and they're headed up your way!"

"Damn it!" Steiger swore. "How the hell did they get through? Destroy that field, Harris! Cut 'em off, right now, no matter what it takes!"

"Right," said Harris, gritting his teeth. He dropped the communicator and took out his plasma sidearm. "My goddamn fault. My own, stupid, goddamn fault . . ."

He held his plasma pistol out before him, took a deep breath and starting running down the hall, right into the line of fire. He screamed, "Get down! Get down!" and fired as he ran, his pistol cycling rapidly. The lilliputians returned his fire, but he kept on coming, right into the deadly web of laser beams, aiming at the briefcase that a small band of lilliputians was frantically trying to shove into an open lift tube. Harris kept on coming, screaming as he charged them, firing into their midst, incinerating them as they swarmed up out of the temporal transit field and destroying the skirmish line they'd quickly set up in the lobby, pinning his men down. He was within fifteen feet of the lift tubes when his plasma pistol cycled through, the charge pak exhausted.

With a roar of rage, he flung it at them and made a flying dive over their heads, crushing a half a dozen of them beneath him as he fell. Smashing at the lilliputians with his fists and sweeping them out of the way, he scrambled for the briefcase, reaching inside and with his last breath, fumbling for the controls. He didn't make it. He died before he could shut down the field.

Steiger was running flat out down the hall, shouting instructions as he went.

"They're on their way up! Cover the stairs and fire exits! Cordon off the area around all access points to this corridor! Nobody gets through! Heads up, people! Here they come!"

The first tube came up and the chime rang softly as the door revolved. Steiger's men fired as it slid open. The interior of the lift tube was slagged with plasma, but not before some of the lilliputians managed to get out, some coming out low, on foot, firing as they ran, while others came out high, swarming out in their floater paks and rapidly dispersing, firing down at the men in the corridor below them.

At the same time, a cry went up from down the hall. A squad of airborne lilliputians was coming up the fire stairs. The men covering the stairs immediately opened fire as Steiger ran from one point of conflict to the other. A filament-thin laser beam lanced past his left temple, missing his head by a quarter of an inch. He threw himself to one side, struck the corridor wall, and spun around. A lilliputian in a floater pak came down at him from just below the ceiling, like a fighter on a strafing run, his tiny autopulser cycling rapidly. Steiger fired and the lilliputian burst into flame, then exploded as the tanks on his tiny floater pak went up. Steiger shielded his face as little bits of burning shrapnel rained down on him.

Behind him, down the hall, the corridor was in flames. The lilliputians were outgunned, but the same plasma weapons that enabled Steiger's men to shoot down such small and rapidly moving targets were also setting the hospital on fire. The spinklers had gone off, but they were not sufficient to the task and Steiger couldn't risk sending in the fire brigade until the battle was all over. It wasn't simply a question of defeating the tiny invaders; they had to do it within the next few minutes or else the fire would endanger the patients on the lower floors.

He rushed to the stairwell. Several of his men were dead, some killed by the tiny commandos, but at least two were killed by fire from their own men, trying to shoot down airborne lilliputians who were darting among them like angry wasps. The walls and stairs were blackened and burning as Steiger came through the door, but none of the lilliputians had gotten past his men. There was a pitched battle in the stairwell as the tiny invaders were being driven back.

And then another cry went up. They were coming out of a second lift tube. Steiger and his men ran out into the hall. Perhaps two dozen lilliputians were in full flight, hurtling towards them down the corridor. Steiger's men and the lilliputians opened fire simultaneously. The man on Steiger's right screamed briefly as a laser burned through his brain and he fell dead on the floor. Half a dozen lilliputians went up in a blast of plasma, several of them spinning end over end, in flames and out of control, exploding as they hit the corridor walls and their propellant tanks went up.

A few of them got past Steiger and he winced with pain as a laser burned his shoulder, then he was turning and sprinting after them. They were headed down the corridor, straight for Forrester's room. Several of them hovered around the door lock, providing covering fire while two of them aimed their lasers at the lockwork. They burned through the door in a matter of seconds. Steiger and his men ran directly into the deadly laser fire, firing into the beams with their plasma weapons to break up their collimation.

Steiger couldn't believe it. The lilliputians seemed to have no regard whatsoever for their own survival. Like miniature kamikazes, they flew right at him and his men, corkscrewing in erratic loop-de-loops with their jets on full power. It was like trying to shoot down a flight of crazed hummingbirds. The man on Steiger's left fell. Steiger bent down and wrenched the plasma rifle out of the dead man's grasp, but there wasn't even enough time to slap a fresh charge pak into it. He brought up the rifle stock sharply, smacking a lilliputian in full flight. The lilliputian caromed off the rifle stock like a baseball and tumbled end over end, his jets damaged and out of control. He slammed into another tiny commando and they exploded in mid air, the shrapnel from the floater paks lacerating Steiger's face. He didn't even feel it. He bolted straight for Forrester's room, but the lilliputians had already flown inside. They swooped down over the bed, their lasers playing over the shape beneath the covers. As Steiger burst into the room, he heard someone yell, "GET BACK!" and he recoiled as the blue mist of Cherenkov radiation flooded the room.

The awesome weapon's transponder tapped directly into the energy field of a neutron star by means of an internal chronocircuitry link with an Einstein-Rosen Generator in outer space. The result was a limitless supply of "ammunition" in the form of energy leeched through a time warp from a star. The magnetic field generated around the muzzle formed an invisible forcing cone that allowed selective fire—a stream of neutrons fired on either a tight beam or a wide dispersal "spray." The entire room glowed blue for an instant and the

attacking lilliputians disappeared, their atoms disrupted by the
neutron stream.

The bed also disappeared, as well as the night table, the drip
I.V. stand, the lamp and the entire wall. A cold night wind
blew in through the gaping hole where the wall had been. The
edges of the hole were as smooth as melted glass. Forrester
stood in the corner of the room, with his back against the wall.
He lowered the strange looking weapon. It resembled a small
flamethrower, with a knurled pistol grip and an unusually
shaped muzzle, only without the attached hose and tanks.

Steiger walked over to the hole in the wall. It was about
twelve feet across and eight feet high. Steiger stepped up to the
edge and looked down 110 stories. The wind plucked at his
hair and clothes, its coolness soothing to the wounds on his
face.

"Jesus Christ," he said, softly.

Forrester came up to stand beside him, holding the disruptor
in his right hand. It was difficult to believe that something the
size of a sawed-off shotgun could have done such damage.

"I think we've got a slight problem here with over penetration," Forrester said, wryly. "Darkness always did overdo
things. Sure works, though. If he ever gets all the bugs out, I
might actually consider making these standard issue."

Steiger simply stared at him.

"You look terrible," said Forrester.

"Yeah," said Steiger. He took a deep breath and let it out
slowly, then snapped on his communicator. "This is Steiger.
All posts, report."

"Post 1, sir. Lafferty here. All secure down here."

"Casualties?"

Four dead, two wounded, sir. Should I send in the fire
brigade, sir? We've got alarms going off all over the place."

"Yeah, send 'em in. Make sure we get all the wounded out
and stand by to evacuate patients. Get additional personnel in
if you have to. Steiger out."

"Post 2, sir. Cpl. Steinberg reporting. Everybody's dead.
I'm the only one left. But we're secure, sir. That is, I'm secure.
I guess. I mean . . . hell, I don't know, I—"

"Pull yourself together, Steinberg. You all right?"

"I've been hit, sir, but it's not serious, I don't think. I mean,
I'll manage."

"Good man. Hang in there, we'll get someone to you as soon as we can. Stand by."

And on it went. Every single post, men dead, men wounded, but the attack had been repulsed. Fortunately, none of the hospital patients had been hurt. The lilliputians had known exactly where to go and they had struck directly at the top floor. Now they were all dead. They had given no quarter and asked none. Steiger and Forrester went out into the corridor, filled with smoke and flames, steaming from the sprinklers interacting with the heat, blackened from the plasma blasts, scarred by laser fire, littered with bodies.

"Oh, God damn it to hell," said Forrester, his voice breaking slightly. "All this just because of me."

"Don't do that to yourself, Moses," Steiger said. "This is a war. And the Network has a lot to answer for."

"And they're going to answer for it, believe me," Forrester said grimly. "We were lucky this time, but the entire top part of this building will have to be evacuated. Christ, how many of them were there?"

"I don't know," said Steiger. "It seemed like hundreds. But we stopped 'em. We stopped 'em cold."

"Yes, for now," Forrester said. "But I can't risk another attack like that. I can't stay here. It's too dangerous to the other patients and the hospital personnel."

"But you haven't been released for duty—"

"After this, I don't think you'll get any arguments from Dr. Hazen or any of the staff," said Forrester. "Get me out of here, Creed. I'm going back to headquarters. We've got a lot of work to do."

10 _____

Lucas materialized in the middle of Washington Street. For a moment, he did not know where he was; then a blast from a diesel truck's air horn caused him to leap to one side, narrowly avoiding being run down.

"Get outta the road, asshole!" the trucker yelled out the open window as he rumbled by.

Lucas looked around. The area he stood in resembled a war zone. The street was pockmarked with pot holes. The sidewalks were cracked and buckling. The warehouses all around him were shuttered and boarded up and covered with graffiti. An abandoned car was rusting on its wheel hubs, the wheels long since stolen. The rest of the car had been stripped, the windows shattered and an uprooted traffic sign had been hurled through the windshield, like a harpoon transfixing a whale—an eloquent commentary on the mindless fury and frustration of the scuttlefish who crawled these streets at night.

And it was getting dark.

"New York City," Lucas said, realizing where he was. "Damn. I've done it again."

He groaned and brought his hands up to his head, pressing them flat against his temples. His head felt as if it were about to burst. The pain rivaled the worst hangover he'd ever had. It kept fading in and out, as if someone were flickering a switch on and off.

He cursed Darkness and his damned telempathic chrono-circuitry—although without his interference, Lucas knew he wouldn't even be alive. Still, it was a mixed blessing. Each time he thought he had a handle on it, he'd somehow lose control and flip through time and space like some sort of leaf blown on a temporal wind. And the more often he did it, the greater the strain seemed to be. Obviously, he required a period of recuperation after each translocation. Darkness had warned him about that.

Curiously, the amount of time and space he covered during each translocation seemed to make no difference. Whether he translocated from one side of a room to another or from Darkness's secret laboratory headquarters all the way to Earth, it seemed to feel the same. The sensation upon arrival was not altogether unlike what most people felt upon making transition via the old chronoplates or the warp discs that superseded them, although the vertiginous feeling was minimized somewhat with the warp discs. The initial translocation—the departure—took place so fast that it was impossible to notice it happening. It occurred literally with the speed of thought. But immediately upon arrival, there was the unpleasant sensation of vertigo and a curious coldness, as if a chill mountain breeze were blowing through his body, whistling in between the bones and organs, making every single nerve fiber shiver. And he had noticed that the effects seemed to be increasing every time.

He often wondered if Darkness even had a clue to what he was doing. That the man was a genius on a level beyond anything that anyone had ever known was indisputable, but at the same time, and perhaps because of that, he was also utterly incomprehensible. He often agonized over the ethical implications of his work, yet the rights of individuals meant nothing to him. This was not the time to be concerned about such things, Lucas realized. He was in a dangerous neighborhood and it was getting dark. Somewhere nearby, Andre and Gulliver were being held prisoner by the Network. And Lucas had no weapons.

Where the hell was Darkness?

The shadows lengthened as night fell on the city. This wasn't the kind of darkness that I had in mind, thought Lucas. Why hadn't Darkness followed him? He looked up and down the street. He had absolutely no idea where Andre and Gulliver were being held. There were warehouses and old factory buildings along both sides of the street. They could be in any one of them.

Then he saw a sleek black Cadillac, a stretch limousine, turning slowly into the street. It was definitely not the sort of vehicle one expected to encounter in this area of town. He quickly translocated behind the abandoned car. The limo pulled up in front of an old brick warehouse building with graffiti all over the doors and two men got out, dragging a third between them. The front door on the other side of the car opened and another man got out. Even at that distance, Lucas recognized the massive figure of Nikolai Drakov.

He watched Drakov and the others go into the building. The limousine waited at the curb, its motor running. Lucas gasped, slumping down behind the wrecked car as the pain washed over him again, coming and going, coming and going, like waves crashing on a shore. Everything started to spin around. He sagged against the car and slip down to the street.

"Hey, mah man . . ."

"He's wasted."

"Yo, got any money, my man?"

He felt hands on him, turning him around, patting down his pockets.

"Yo, man, check out the boss threads, man! I gotta get me them threads!"

"Fuck the threads, where the hell's the *money*? Hey, dude, where the hell's the money, dude?"

"Get away . . ." Lucas said, clumsily pushing at them, desperately trying to focus and ignore the pain.

Something went *snik* and he felt the sharp point of a switchblade pressed up beneath his chin.

"Awright, muthafucker, where's the bread? I *cut* you, man. C'mon, where you got it stashed?"

"Maybe in his boots."

"Check his belt."

He felt their hands fumbling at his clothes and he tried to resist, but the knife blade pressed up against the underside of his chin again. He struggled against the pain and dizziness, trying to focus in on his attackers. They were little more than just a blur, but he could tell that there were three of them. Slowly, they resolved into distinct figures. One was white, two were black, dressed in tatterdemalion, street-punk style—studded and fringed leather, motorcycle jackets with chain trim, patched jeans, engineer boots or brightly colored, hightop sneakers and T-shirts or bright tank tops with printed designs. They had pierced ears, spiked bracelets, chains, studded choker collars. One wore his hair in a short Mohawk, another had a crew cut and the third had shaved his head completely. Lucas felt his boots being pulled off, then his trousers. One of them started opening his shirt.

Sheeit, man, he ain't *got* no money!"

"Ain't got no damn watch, no rings, *nuthin,* man! Someone musta already rolled 'im!"

"I'm gonna do him," said the one with the knife.

"Shoot, forget it, man. C'mon, least we got the clothes."

"I wanna cut him."

Lucas felt hot, stinking breath on his face.

"So cut him and c'mon, man, I ain't got no time for this shit!"

The one with the knife knelt over him, his eyes glittering wildly.

Lucas suddenly reached out and his fingers closed tightly around the hand holding the knife. He struck out hard with his other hand and smashed the punk's windpipe. The punk's eyes went wide with pain and sudden terror as he made gagging, choking noises and sagged down to the sidewalk, gargling on his own blood.

"Hey, what the— "

Lucas came up with the punk's knife in his hand.

"Son of a bitch!"

The punk with the shaved head reached up and unsnapped the leather epaulet on his motorcycle jacket, pulling down the steel chain he wore around his shoulder. The other one dropped the clothes they took off Lucas and reached into his back pocket. He pulled out a butterfly knife and opened it with a quick flick of the wrist.

They moved apart and came at him from two sides. Lucas hefted the switchblade, found its balance point, shifted his grip and flung it with a quick, underhanded motion. It struck the punk with the butterfly knife, sinking into his torso, right under the rib cage. He grunted with surprise, clutched his chest and collapsed onto the street. The remaining punk snarled and brought the chain down hard. Lucas took the blow on his upraised forearm, wincing as the shock traveled up his arm. He twisted his wrist, grabbed the chain, yanked sharply and smashed the punk in the face before he could regain his balance. The punk lost his grip on the chain and staggered backwards, bleeding from his broken nose. He gave Lucas a terrified look as he scrambled back, then stooped, snatched up the black fatigues and took off down the street at a dead run.

"You bastard! My clothes!" shouted Lucas, throwing the chain after him furiously. Only his boots remained lying on the street. "Great! Just fucking great!"

There he was, alone in one of the worst areas of 20th century New York. Andre and Gulliver were being held prisoner by Nikolai Drakov, and he was standing in the middle of Washingon Street in his underwear with two dead bodies at his feet. All he needed now was for a police car to come by. Although that wasn't very likely. The police knew better than to cruise a neighborhood like this.

Lucas glanced down at the two dead punks. They looked none to clean, but the one with the Mohawk was just about his size. With a grimace of distaste, Lucas stripped off the punk's clothes. He slipped on the tight-fitting black jeans and the motorcycle jacket, after wiping some of the blood off. He hoped he wouldn't get lice, but if he did, it wouldn't be the first time. He walked over to the other corpse, pulled the switchblade free and picked up the butterfly knife the punk had dropped. As serious weapons, they left a lot to be desired, but they were better than nothing.

He glanced back toward the building Drakov had gone into just in time to see him coming out again. The man with him had to be the Network man Darkness had described. He was pushing Andre ahead of him into the limousine. There was no sign of Gulliver.

"Darkness, damn it, where the hell are you?" Lucas said, watching as they got into the car. "Delaney . . ."

But there was no sign of them. He had to do something. The limo was pulling away from the curb and making a U-turn in the middle of street. His gaze fell on the trunk.

All right, he thought, here goes nothing. Desperately hoping that his telempathic chronocircuitry could compute the time-space coordinates and the trajectory from the input of his senses, Lucas stared hard at the trunk of the departing limousine, *willing* himself into it.

He tached.

Gulliver shook his head, backing away as the two gunmen came toward him. "No, please," he said. "Don't . . ."

The men grinned, aiming their guns. Suddenly, both guns flew out of their hands and disappeared.

The gunmen stared, dumbfounded, and then a voice spoke from behind them.

"Are you gentlemen looking for these?"

Dr. Darkness stood behind them, flickering like a strobo-scopic ghost. He held out his hands. A gun rested in each palm.

"Hey!" said Finn Delaney.

Both gunmen spun around to see Delaney, who had materi-alized within a foot of them. He reached out quickly and slammed their heads together. They both collapsed to the floor.

"That was a little tight there, Doctor," said Delaney. "Another foot closer and it would've gotten messy."

Darkness shrugged. "How was I to know that they'd be standing there?"

Gulliver shut his eyes and almost sobbed with relief.

"Delaney!"

Finn glanced down at the figure sprawled out on the floor. "Well, well," he said. "Look what we've got here. I believe we've recaptured an escaped prisoner."

"Damn you, Delaney, get me loose," said Hunter.

"You know this man, Delaney?" Darkness said.

"I knew his twin," Delaney said. "Dr. Darkness, meet Capt. Reese Hunter, of the Counter Insurgency Section of the Special Operations Group." He bent down over Hunter and cut his bonds with his commando knife. "You look like hell," he said.

"I feel like hell," said Hunter. He got up to his feet and winced.

"Where's Andre?" said Delaney, using his laser to burn through Gulliver's cuffs.

"Drakov took her," Gulliver said.

"Yeah, you just missed 'em," Hunter said.

"Damn! What about Lucas?"

"Lucas?" Hunter said, rubbing his sore wrists. "*Lucas Priest*? I thought he was dead."

"It's a long story," said Delaney. "I don't suppose you have any idea where he took her?"

Hunter shook his head. His gaze fell on Darkness and he stared. "Say, pilgrim, am I still punchy or am I actually seeing *through* that guy?"

"Yeah, well, that's a long story, too," Delaney said, taking the two guns from Dr. Darkness. One was a Browning Hi-Power, the other was a Czech CZ-75. "Premium hardware for this time period," said Delaney, examining the pistols. He glanced at Hunter. "You know how to use these?"

"9-mm semiautos?" Hunter said. "Yeah, I can manage. Why, don't tell me you're actually going to arm an escaped prisoner?"

"I'm going to take a chance," Delaney said, handing him the Hi-Power. "Now you can shoot me in the back with that thing or you can help. It's up to you. Drakov isn't just our enemy, he's yours as well. I figure any business we've got between us can wait til this is finished. What do you say?"

"All right. I'm in. I've got a score to settle with that man."

"Truce?" Delaney said, offering his hand.

"Truce," said Hunter. They shook.

Hunter hefted the Hi-Power in his hand. He jacked out the magazine and checked to see that it was full, then slapped it back in. He tucked the gun into his waistband in the small of his back.

Delaney beckoned to Gulliver. "Lem, come over here. Take this one," he said, handing him the black CZ.

"I have never seen such a gun," said Gulliver, dubiously.

"This one's a lot easier to shoot then anything you might have seen," Delaney reassured him. "It has two different carry modes, double action or cocked and locked. You're only going to worry about one, the double action. If you want to shoot, all you do is point the gun and squeeze the trigger, simple as that. You can fire fifteen shots without reloading."

"*Fifteen*? Without reloading?"

"As fast as you can pull the trigger," said Delaney. "But don't fire all fifteen. It's better to shoot in groups of three. Now the trigger pull on the first shot is going to be a little stiffer than on the succeeding ones, so be prepared for that. And use two hands, like this."

Delaney demonstrated a proper combat stance and showed him how to sight.

Gulliver gingerly took the pistol and followed his example.

"Good. It will kick a bit, but don't let that throw you."

Hunter watched the brief instruction session with curiosity. "Are you sure he knows what he's doing? Just what time period is he from, anyway?"

"Well, that's—"

"Yeah, I know. A long story. Never mind. Forget I asked."

"Sorry, Hunter, but you're on a need-to-know basis. You *are* from the other side, after all."

"Yeah, sure. It's just that I'd feel better about this if we had a little more help."

"We do," said Delaney. He picked up a leather valise that was sitting on the floor on the spot where he'd clocked in.

"What's that?" Hunter said.

"A little more help," Delaney said. "Very little."

The limousine turned left on the Avenue of the Americas, known to native New Yorkers simply as Sixth Avenue, then headed north towards the fashionable neighborhood of Soho, short for "South of Houston."

"Where are you taking me?" said Andre.

"Patience, Miss Cross," said Drakov. "All will become self-evident before too long."

"Why, Drakov?" she asked. "Why work for the Network? What are you after?"

"I should think that would be obvious, Miss Cross," said Drakov. "The Network pays me very well and I find their logistics support extremely helpful. They are very well orga- nized, you know. Quite impressive. Not even the Timekeepers operated on such a scale. There is, in addition, a certain delightful irony to being subsidized by what is essentially a branch of my father's own organization. And in that, regard, we have certain mutual goals in mind, don't we, Mr. Savino?"

She glanced at Savino with contempt. "Steiger said you were a section chief in the 20th Century, but I never made the connection. From the way he talked about you, I never would have believed you were a traitor."

"A traitor?" said Savino, in that same, curiously unemo- tional tone. "That's interesting. To what or to whom am I a traitor? To the country? How? I haven't sold the country out. To the agency?" He shook his head. "I haven't sold the agency out, either. In fact, I've been instrumental in bringing a considerable amount of revenue into the agency. True, I'm not exactly playing by the rules, but the idea of a clandestine intelligence organization playing by any set of rules is patently absurd."

"Oh, I see," said Andre. "I guess I just didn't understand. And taking part in a plot to assassinate the director of the T.I.A., that's nothing more than interdepartmental politics, right?"

"Forrester brought it on himself," Savino said. "I'm sure he never paused to consider the complexities that gave rise to an entity such as the Network or the conditions that make its existence necessary. I doubt he ever gave any thought to the consequences involved in dismantling the Network."

Andre snorted derisively. "Are you seriously trying to tell me that the Network is a *necessary* organization?"

"Absolutely," said Savino. "That's something your friend and mine, Creed Steiger, will probably never understand. You probably can't understand it, either. You both seem to share the same delusion. You believe in absolutes. You think there's such a thing as right and wrong."

"How foolish of us," Andre said, sarcastically.

Savino shook his head with resignation. "You people in the First Division always had it easy compared to what we had to do. By the time you got involved, your objectives were clearly delineated. You weren't sent in unless there was a specific situation to be dealt with and you always knew what the parameters of your missions were, thanks to us and the Observers. We did the scut work. We pinpointed the temporal anomalies. We gathered the intelligence that made it possible for you to do your job."

"And you feel you didn't get enough credit or compensation, is that it?" Andre said.

Savino shook his head. "No, not me. Maybe some people in the Network feel that way, I can't speak for everybody, but I've never felt like that. In the old days, when Steiger and I were starting out as field agents, we weren't after glory or compensation. Doing our duty was enough. Besides, we were young. We got off on the adventure. But as time went on, the thrill wore off. And I began to realize something. That what we were doing was like trying to stop a horde of locusts with a fly swatter.

"It was impossible to do the job that we were being asked to do and still play by the rules," Savino continued. "The thing was, nobody really cared when it came right down to it. The legislators gave a lot of lip service to 'working for the cause of peace' and 'bringing the Time Wars to a halt,' but when it came time for appropriations for funding temporal defense plants in their districts, guess which way they voted? When it came time to make spending cuts so they could say they were trying to balance out the budget, did they cut appropriations that funded jobs in their own districts? Did they maybe refuse to vote themselves their annual salary increase? No, they cut services everywhere they could, instead. And they kept chipping away at our budget every year. But they still wanted us to keep doing the same job, a job that kept on getting more and more impossible to do. And they wanted us to do it by the book. Even that was so much lip service. Most of them didn't care one way or another, so long as the job got done and nobody got caught."

"Steiger cares," she said.

"Yeah, well, he would," Savino said. "He wound up working with a man named Carnehan after a few years. Name mean anything to you?"

"Col. Jack Carnehan," she said. "*Codename:* agent Mongoose."

Savino nodded. "Yeah. He was the best. A goddamned legend. But crazy. A real danger junkie. And there was one other thing that made him different. He really believed that the good guys always win."

Savino's lips twisted into a wry, sad little half smile.

"It was amazing, really. In some ways, Carnehan was like a kid who never grew up. He kept on playing the same games, only at some point, the games started to be played for keeps and he just never noticed. Steiger bought into the whole trip all the way. I suppose I can even understand it. Old Jack had a lot of style. Charisma with a capital C. And Creed was young. He fell under the man's spell."

Savino was staring straight ahead, his eyes slightly unfocused, as he recalled the past. His face and voice were touched with melancholy. It was the first real emotion Andre had seen in him.

"The thing was," Savino went on, "Carnehan didn't really play by the rules, either. He didn't exactly break them, but he sure bent a lot of them all to hell. The same as you commandos do. You call it 'throwing away the book.' Improvising in the field. Well, hell, that's all we ever did. We threw away the book and improvised."

"You did a lot more than that," said Andre. "You crossed over the line." She glanced at Drakov and saw him listening with an amused expression on his face.

"Crossed over the line," Savino repeated, mockingly. "Where *is* the line? And who decides where it should be drawn? You? Me? Forrester? Some legislator who's never been on the minus side and hasn't got the faintest idea of what we're up against? Don't you understand? It's all arbitrary."

"Well, if you believe that, then I guess anything you do becomes justifiable," said Andre. "And obviously, you've worked very hard at believing it. You really sold yourself a bill of goods, Savino. I just hope it didn't cost you too much."

They made a right on West Eleventh Street and pulled up in front of the black double doors of Il Paradiso. Savino draped his jacket over Andre's shoulders, covering the handcuffs, then helped her out of the car. As he took her arm and drew her close, she felt the sharp point of a stiletto digging into her side.

"A nightclub?" said Andre. "What's this, another Network front?"

"No, actually, this club is operated by the Mafia," Drakov said.

"The Mafia?" Andre said, with disbelief.

"Sort of a sideline for the local capo," Drakov explained. "It allows him to rub elbows with the artsy set and feel sophisticated." He held the door for them. "Oh, by the way, most of the employees of this establishment are perfectly ordinary citizens with little or no knowledge of the proprietor's criminal activities. Attempting to give alarm or otherwise involve any of them would only endanger them needlessly. And you wouldn't want to do that, would you, Miss Cross?"

Savino pricked her slightly with the knife and she winced. "All right, you've made your point."

They went inside.

The club wasn't open yet, but the young employees were all bustling about, getting everything ready. There were several bartenders behind the garish, guitar-shaped bar, peeling lemons, slicing limes, setting bottles into the wells and turning on their beer taps. Waitresses were setting up tables and a crew of roadies were up on the elevated stage, stacking amplifiers, assembling a giant drum kit and making sound checks with the mikes. A gorgeous young woman in a black lycra skirt, high heels, a T-shirt with the club's name and logo on it, and moussed and silver-streaked blond hair approached them.

"Excuse me, sir, we won't be open for another . . . oh, it's you Mr. Savino."

"Is the boss in?" Savino said.

"Yes, sir, Mr. Manelli's upstairs."

They went up a carpeted flight of steps, past a massive bouncer whose biceps strained the seams of his pink silk tiger print shirt. The bouncer greeted Savino politely, calling him sir. It was clear that while Drakov wasn't known here, Savino was definitely part of the heirarchy.

Upstairs at Il Paradiso was where the "in group" congregated. A second bar catered to the celebrities and the beautiful people, who descended to the dance floor now and then to give a thrill to the rabble down below. The private upstairs lounge extended over the tables down below, ending in a railed balcony that overlooked the dance floor and provided an unrestricted view of the stage. Manelli was seated at a table in the corner, surrounded by his entourage, heatedly discussing something with two men sitting across from him. He looked up as they approached and excused himself, striding quickly across the room to meet them.

"What the hell is going on, Savino?" he said. "I had a meeting and I couldn't even get into my own office, for Christ's sake! There's some kinda weird lock on the door—"

"I told you we'd be using the office for a few days," Savino said, calmly.

"You didn't tell me you were going to change the lock! Hell, you changed the whole goddamn door! I try to take a meeting in my own damn office and I can't even get the door open! It made me look like a goddamn idiot."

"I told you we were going to use your office until further notice," said Savino.

"Yeah, but you weren't here and what am I supposed to say

to people when I can't conduct business in my own damn office? How do you think that makes me look?"

"I don't give a damn how it makes you look," Savino said. "You tell them the office is being repainted or something. I don't care what the hell you tell them, Domenic, but I don't want to hear you questioning my instructions again, is that understood?"

They spoke in low voices and to anyone watching them, it would have appeared as if Savino were a subordinate being dressed down by Manelli, instead of the other way around.

"You're pushing me, Savino," said Manelli, tensely. "You're pushing me real hard. I don't like being pushed. And I don't like not knowing what my club is being used for." He gave Drakov a long, appraising look. "I go to great pains to keep my other business separate from the club, Drakov. There's a reason for that. I like to keep a low profile and we're very visible here. Now my people tell me you've had several sealed crates delivered to my office and stored there. I want to know what's in them."

"Lilliputians," Drakov said.

"What?"

"Lilliputians. They're miniature people, about six inches tall. I'm using the crates as troop transports."

Manelli stared at him long and hard, the muscles in his jaw twitching. "All right, if that's the way you want to play it, have it your way."

He glanced from Savino to Drakov and pointed his index finger at them. "The club's about to open and I don't want any difficulties tonight, but I want you and whatever's in those crates out of here first thing in the morning, you understand? And I want that cockamamie hi-tech lock off my goddamn door. You got til noon. And that's more slack than you deserve. At one second after twelve, I'm going to have my boys bust down that door and crack open those crates. And if what's in there is what I think is in there, the Network's going to find out that the cost of doing business just went up. *Way* up. Kapish?"

He turned and went back to his table without waiting for a reply. Savino took a deep breath.

"He thinks we're dealing arms," he said. "Manelli always

was a pain in the ass to keep under control. He's going to be trouble. And trouble is something I don't need right now."

"Relax," said Drakov, walking up to Manelli's office door and pressing his palm against the flat metal plate. The lock clicked open. "After tonight, it will be finished. And what you do about Manelli will be entirely up to you."

He entered the office and Savino shoved Andre in after him. The two large wooden crates stood open on the floor. They were empty. Manelli's desk and chairs had been moved back against the wall and in the center of the floor, glowing faintly, was an activated chronoplate.

11 ———————————

Lucas huddled in the trunk of the Cadillac limo, feeling nauseous and trying to ignore the pounding pain in his temples. The trunk was roomy, so he wasn't painfully cramped, but the motion of the car over the potholed streets didn't do much for his disposition. Several times, the car stopped for traffic lights, but this last time, he felt the car pull over to the curb and after a moment heard the doors slam. He hesitated, and then he felt the engine start up once again and the car started to pull away. He tached.

Someone leaned on a car horn and Lucas quickly rolled underneath a parked truck as the yellow cab sped by, missing him by inches. Fighting the dizziness and the painful pressure in his temples and chest, he quickly scanned the sidewalks from his shelter beneath the van and spotted Drakov and Savino shepherding Andre into the nightclub. His head was throbbing and he felt as if he were going to throw up. It was worse than the worst hangover he'd ever experienced, much worse. All he wanted to do was simply lie there on the filthy street and wait for it to go away.

His worst fear was that what had happened to Darkness would somehow happen to him. Although the process that each of them had undergone was different, the principles were essentially the same. Darkness had, inadvertently, permanently tachyonized himself with the result that his atomic structure was unstable. The particle-level telempathic chronocircuitry that had become a part of Lucas was designed to prevent tachyon translation from upsetting his atomic stability, at least that was what Darkness claimed, but there was no denying the side effects he was experiencing. And they seemed to be getting worse. What would he do if he eventually became permanently tachyonized, like Darkness? Would he be able to retain his sanity, knowing that he could discorporate at any moment? What the hell, thought Lucas, by rights I should have died back in the 19th Century. Any way you look at it, I'm on borrowed time.

He heard heavy footsteps above him in the truck, then the sound of something heavy being moved across the truckbed. Ignoring the stabbing pain in his head, he tried to focus on the booted feet that stepped down to the street from the rear of the truck.

"Easy . . . easy . . . okay, that's got it. Go ahead, jump down, I'll hold it."

A moment later, another pair of feet, shod in running shoes, jumped down from the truck bed and Lucas watched as two leather-jacketed roadies manhandled a PA column speaker into the club. He listened for a moment, heard nothing more above him, then slid out from beneath the truck. He looked into the back and saw that the truck was just about completely unloaded. Nothing remained except some tool boxes, several coils of cable hung up on the walls, and some spare mike stands. Lucas jumped up into the truck and grabbed several coils of insulated cable.

"*Hey*! What the hell are you doin' in there?"

A spikey-haired young man in a red leather jacket and black jeans stood at the back of the truck, a cigarette drooping from the corner of his mouth.

"Get the fuck out there!"

"Hey, back off!" said Lucas, angrily. "I'm the club electrician, awright? There's a problem with the fuckin' wiring and they sent me out to get some more cable. Is this garbage the best you guys got?"

"What's wrong with it?" the roadie said, defensively.

"What's wrong with it?" Lucas echoed him, sarcastically. "It's the wrong gauge, the damn insulation's frayed, no wonder we're shorting out in there. Ah, to hell with it, I'll patch something up." He jumped down from the truck. "You guys oughta be more careful about this stuff. Someone could get a nasty shock. It ain't even code. Got a spare smoke?"

The roadie reached into the pocket of his jacket and took out a pack of Marlboros. He shook one out and offered. Lucas took it and the roadie lit it for him with a cheap, disposable lighter.

"Well, is it gonna be all right?" the roadie said.

"Yeah, if I get to it sometime tonight," said Lucas. "Thanks for the smoke."

He went into the club, carrying the coils of cable.

"You sure you know where you're going?" Hunter asked Delaney.

"If Darkness says Andre was taken to a place called Il Paradiso on West 11th Street, then that's where she is," Delaney said.

"Right, I understand that," Hunter said. "What I don't understand is *how* he knew that."

"Well, it's a long—"

"Don't say it." Hunter shook his head with exasperation. "Hell, forget I even asked. I'm just along for the ride, right?" He took the Browning Hi-Power out of his waistband and racked the slide, chambering a round. "Wish I had something with a bit more firepower, though. Don't suppose you'd have a spare laser or an autopulser in that bag of yours?"

The cabbie glanced nervously up at the rearview mirror. Why? Why did these things have to happen to him? There he was, sitting at a light and minding his own business, anxious to get the cab back to the garage and go home for the night, have a few beers and go to bed, when this big red-haired guy walks right up to the cab and sticks some kind of weird looking cannon right through the driver's window. The cabbie glanced up into the rearview mirror when he heard the sound of the slide being racked. He saw the gun and the taxi swerved, almost hitting a bus.

"Never mind what's in my bag," Delaney said. "And you . . ." he glanced at the name on the hack license, ". . . Emilio, just keep your eyes on the road and everything will work out fine. Got it?"

"S-sure thing, mister! Anything you say!"

"Shut up and drive."

"Y-yes, sir!"

For this I left Miami, the cabbie thought. Drunks throwing up in the back seat, muggings, punks spraying graffiti on the inside of the cab, irate truckers smashing his windshield with tire irons because they thought he cut them off, and now gunmen hijacking him to the West Village. To hell with it, he thought, this was the last straw. If he managed to live through this night, he was quitting and going back to bussing dishes in Florida. New York was crazy!

Steiger stood in the hospital corridor with Forrester, surveying the damage. It was extensive. The walls were pinholed by laser fire and scorched by plasma. The ceiling was coming down in places, there were gaping holes in the floor and the hospital personnel were still removing bodies. But that wasn't what concerned them most. A cordon of armed men stood around an open briefcase lying on the floor, by the lift tubes. Inside it, assembled and glowing faintly, was an activated chronoplate.

"Did any of them get back through?" said Steiger.

"Yes, sir," said the corporal in charge of the men standing guard around the plate. "A bunch of them that got caught in a crossfire down here broke through and escaped through the field. I thought it best to secure the chronoplate and not disturb it, sir."

"Well done, Corporal," Steiger said. He crouched down over the plate. "The screen's been damaged," he told Forrester. "On purpose, it looks like. Whoever assembled this was pretty clever. They rigged it so you couldn't read the transition coordinates off the screen and they modified the border circuits so the plate could be assembled inside the case, instead of taking it out like you're supposed to. Cute. That means there's no way we can find out where they came from. And it also means the temporal field has to be smaller than normal. But the question is, how much smaller?"

Forrester gave Steiger a sharp look. "If you're thinking of going through there, Creed, you can forget about it," he said. "It's much too dangerous. It could be a trap. Besides, as you just pointed out, we don't even know if the altered field will be large enough to transport a full-grown man."

"Yeah, you're probably right," said Steiger. "It would be much too risky."

He straightened up, turned, then quickly snatched the corporal's autopulser rifle and, holding it close against his body, hopped into the open case.

"*Steiger!*" Forrester shouted, but it was too late. The border circuits of the chronoplate flashed and Steiger was briefly bathed in the eerie, bright green glow before he disappeared from sight.

"A chronoplate?" said Andre, glancing down at the softly glowing border circuits assembled on the floor. She looked up at Drakov. "Don't tell me the Network couldn't spare you any warp discs, Nicky. I thought you were on such good terms with them."

Drakov gave her an acid look. "I detest that name," he said. "And if you are seeking to provoke me, Miss Cross, it won't work, no matter how irritating you become."

He jerked his head toward the desk and chairs on the far side of the room. Savino pushed her over to one of the chairs and roughly shoved her down into it.

Drakov pulled back his sleeve and glanced at the warp disc on his wrist. In relatively modern industrial time periods, it was simplest to disguise a warp disc as a pocket watch or a multifunction wrist chronograph, which it most resembled. More primitive time zones demanded that a warp disc be disguised as some piece of ornamental jewelry, such as a pendant or a bracelet, with its face and control studs concealed.

"It's almost time," said Drakov.

"We going somewhere?" Andre said.

"Eventually, Miss Cross, eventually. And for your information, you may be interested to know that I still have a plentiful supply of warp discs of various size classifications left over from that shipment I hijacked from Amalgamated Techtronics." He smiled at the expression on her face. "You thought you recovered most of them, didn't you? Shall we bet that according to the invoices you were given by the factory, most of the missing warp discs were accounted for?"

"How could you know that?"

"You would be surprised, Miss Cross, at how often there are so-called 'accidental overruns' on Temporal Army contracts.

Very inconvenient for the management. It upsets the accountants no end and creates a problem of cost efficiency, especially since the Army will only pay for what it ordered and no more. Fortunately, there are 'independent contractors' who are quite willing to assist in liquidating accidental overruns."

Andre stared at him with astonishment. "Are you telling me they sell restricted ordnance under the table, on the black market?"

"Yes, rather amusing, isn't it? I discovered that quite by accident. Imagine, I went to all the trouble and risk of hijacking warp discs when all I had to do was buy them direct from the manufacturer." He chuckled and consulted his disc once again. "In any case, a chronoplate was precisely what I needed in this particular instance. I required a temporal transit field linked through two terminals, each of which would be destroyed as it fulfilled its function. And that sequence is due to be initiated any moment now . . ."

The border circuits of the chronoplate began to flicker brightly, then they flashed with an emerald glow and tiny soldiers wearing miniature floater paks started to materialize just above the border circuits. They rose up into the air, still within the transit field, and as more flying lilliputians appeared below them, the ones rising up toward the ceiling peeled off and flew in a counterclockwise circle around the room. Drakov watched them, smiling to himself, then his smile abruptly faded as the last lilliputian peeled off from the formation.

"What is it?" said Savino, seeing the expression on his face.

"Where are the rest of them?" said Drakov. "That's only a fraction of the number I sent through."

They waited, but no more lilliputians came through. The ones already in the room continued to circle just beneath the ceiling, like bees buzzing around a hive.

"Maybe they didn't make it," said Savino. "We figured there'd be losses, didn't we?"

Drakov shook his head, frowning. "Yes, but not so many." He licked his lips nervously and checked the time again.

"Come on, come on, where *is* it? That damn plate should have blown by now!"

He was watching the glowing border circuits, waiting for the glow to disappear, which would mean that the link on the other end had been broken by the chronoplate being destroyed.

Andre couldn't take her eyes off the circling lilliputians, flying round and round just beneath the ceiling like miniature airplanes in a holding pattern. Circling around the chronoplate, almost as if they were waiting for something.

"*Damn* those little bastards!" Drakov shouted. He looked up at them with fury. "You were in full retreat! And you forgot to blow the terminal, you miserable, little . . ."

He reached into his jacket and pulled out a plasma pistol. He raised it, aiming at the chronoplate, and at the same instant, the border circuits flashed once more and Steiger came tumbling through, onto the floor.

"*Creed! Look out!*" Andre shouted. She came out of the chair and launched herself at Drakov in a running dive.

Drakov fired.

The band had set up on the stage and the musicians were running through a final sound check with all the instruments and mikes. There was a massive wall of amplifiers stacked behind the band and everything was turned up full. There was a bank of synthesizers, two electric guitars, an electric bass, a gargantuan clear plastic drum kit with two huge basses, rows of accoustic and electric tom-toms, cymbals and an array of gongs and bells, and the ensemble was rounded out by the lead singer, an androgynous young man with snow white hair down to his shoulders and a strut a 7th Avenue hooker would have envied.

He paraded back and forth across the small stage, prowling like a panther in a cage, shrieking into the mike with such abandon and such force that Lucas winced, wondering how he could possibly sing like that and not scream himself hoarse. The sheer volume of the band was deafening. With his roadielike appearance, no one bothered to approach him. And with the volume of the music, conversation would have been impossible.

This was where it started, he thought in passing as he quickly scanned the club. The heavy metal sound, which over the years became the dominant form of music, absorbing both the fringe and mainstream styles, always on the cutting edge of technology until it eventually metamorphosed into cyberpunk, the ultimate union of the musician and his instrument, where the synclaviers and percussion circuit boards were actually hardwired into the musicians' bodies.

The band stopped playing for a moment to make some minor adjustments, and the silence after such an auditory barrage was almost a shock. Lucas took advantage of it to approach one of the club's employees, a beautiful young woman in a black lycra miniskirt and a T-shirt emblazoned with the club's logo.

"Excuse me," he said, and the aftereffects of the band made him speak much louder than he needed to, but she seemed used to it. "I'm looking for those people who just came in here, two guys and a girl—"

"You with the band?" She gave him a cursory glance and went back to applying black fingernail polish to her nails.

"Yeah, and so's the girl. I'm supposed to get—"

"Upstairs."

"What?"

"Upstairs, they went upstairs."

"Oh. Thanks."

He headed for the staircase, but as he got there, the big bouncer stood in front of him with his beefy arms folded across his chest.

"Where do you think you're goin'?"

"Upstairs," said Lucas.

"Oh, yeah?"

"Yeah."

The bouncer shook his head and rolled his shoulders back, flexing his lats and chest muscles. "I don't think so."

Lucas tried to go around him, but the bouncer stepped in front of him, putting his hand up against his chest and shoving him back. At that moment, the band started up again. Lucas didn't waste time trying to argue. The music was too loud, in any case. He simply kicked the bouncer in the groin with all his might and then swung the rolls of cable hard across his face as he doubled over with pain. Then he ran up the stairs two at time, taking advantage of the noise. He reached into the pocket of the leather jacket, took out the switchblade and flicked it open.

He reached the top of the stairs and looked around quickly. There was no sign of Andre or Drakov or the other man. But Manelli, sitting at his table in the corner, looked up and saw him, spotted the switchblade in his hand, quickly tapped

Vincent on the shoulder and pointed at Lucas. Vincent and the other man quickly got up and started coming toward Lucas, reaching inside their coats. Lucas didn't think that they were reaching for cigars. He took the rolled cables and slung them hard at the man furthest away from him. Instinctively, the man threw his hands up to protect his face. The cables struck him and he staggered back against the balcony railing, lost his balance, and the wailing of the electric guitars drowned out his scream as he went over.

Lucas didn't stop. He continued moving forward fast after he threw the cables and just as Vincent cleared leather with his big, black Beretta, Lucas was on him, grabbing his gun hand with his left hand and with his right hand, driving the knife deep into his solar plexus and up underneath his ribs.

Vincent's breath hissed out of him and his eyes opened wide in shock, as if he was unable to believe that someone with a knife had actually kept coming when he had a gun. Then he was collapsing to the floor and Lucas had the gun. Manelli was coming up out of his chair, the girl beside him was screaming, the sound drowned out by the band, and then her scream suddenly became sharply audible as the band stopped, having seen the first gunman fall from the balcony. There were more screams coming from downstairs now and Manelli was reaching inside his coat. Lucas raised the Beretta and shot him in the chest.

And then all hell broke loose.

The yellow cab pulled up in front of the entrance to Il Paradiso, and the moment they stepped out, the terrified driver mashed the pedal to the floor and peeled out into traffic, fishtailing and nearly causing a collision between two other cars, whose drivers blew their horns in loud, prolonged blasts of protest.

"Nervous fella," said Hunter. "He didn't even wait to collect his fare."

People were starting to cue up outside the club, waiting for the doors to open. Their costumes ranged from the casual to the outrageous. Spikey hair in shades of blue and purple, studded and fringed leather, cheeks dusted with glitter, young men wearing eyeshadow and black lipstick, girls with their heads shaved bald. A sign advertised that a band named Flesh was playing there that night.

Hunter glanced at the kids on line, then at Gulliver's green transit fatigues, the black base fatigues that Delaney was wearing, the holstered laser on Delaney's belt and the plasma pistol strapped to his upper thigh.

"Think we're too noticeable?" he said.

Darkness suddenly appeared beside them.

"Unless you expect me to take care of everything for you, you'd better get in there right now," he said.

"*Wow!*" shouted a longhaired young man in a headband, faded jeans and a camo fatigue jacket festooned with military pins and insignia. He pointed at Darkness, standing there and flickering like a ghost on a television screen. "Check *him* out!"

A gum-popping black girl in spike heeled boots and Danskins nudged Delaney with her hip. "Yo, Rambo," she said, touching her tongue to her upper lip, "can I play with your big gun?"

"Come on," Delaney said, grabbing the bewildered Gulliver's arm and pulling him along toward the entrance to the club.

"We'll take a raincheck, honey," Hunter said to the black girl, then hurried after Delaney.

Darkness had disappeared again and the bewildered young longhair in the camo jacket kept pointing at the spot where he had stood and insisting to his friends on line, "He was right *there*, man! Seriously. Then he beamed out, just like on Star Trek!"

Two large club employees who looked like bikers stood at the door. They saw Delaney and Gulliver coming, looked at each other and shook their heads.

"Christ, look at this," one of them said. "It's Chuck Norris and Buckaroo Banzai."

"Awright, hold it right there!" the other one said, pointing at them. "Look, you can't bring those sci-fi toys in here, Mac, somebody might think that it's a real—"

Delaney unholstered his laser and shot a beam straight at the sidewalk between the biker's legs.

"*Ho-ly Shit!*"

The biker leaped backwards and as Delaney continued resolutely toward the door, the other one swallowed hard and hastily opened it for him. The sound of the band making its final sound check came through and the kids on line shouted gleefully and started to push through after them. As Delaney,

Gulliver and Hunter pushed past a startled cashier, a body fell from the balcony and landed on the dance floor. The band fumbled to a stop and somebody screamed.

Above them, on the balcony floor, someone fired a shot. And almost simultaneously, there was the unmistakeable *whump* of a plasma blast. Holding his laser pistol in one hand and the leather satchel in the other, Delaney ran for the stairs.

"Hold it!" gasped the white-faced bouncer, hunched over and clutching his groin.

Delaney slammed into him with his shoulder and sent him crashing to the floor, not even slowing down as he ran up the stairs.

"Unnnh!" groaned the bouncer, huddling on the floor. "That's it. I quit!"

Steiger hit the floor and rolled just as Andre struck Drakov. Drakov's shot slammed into the chronoplate, destroying it. He kicked Andre away savagely and raised his pistol once again.

Steiger fired.

Drakov threw himself to one side as the plasma blast struck the door and burned right through it, but before Steiger could fire again from his position on the floor, filament-thin laser beams came lancing down at him, striking him in the shoulder, grazing his left ear, hitting his legs and narrowly missing his groin. He cried out with pain and looked up, seeing the flock of lilliputians circling above him like tiny vultures.

"Jesus!"

He quickly rolled across the floor as a webwork of fine beams came stabbing down at him. Andre was trying to crawl out through the burning doorframe. People outside were screaming. Steiger kept rolling, following Andre out the door as the lilliputians came swooping down after him.

Delaney reached the top of the stairs just as Steiger came rolling through the burning doorway with lilliputians swarming after him. Delaney opened the leather sachel.

"Go! Go! Go!" he shouted.

The ragtag lilliputians came rising up out the bag like fighters off a carrier deck, darting up at the lilliputians swooping down on Steiger. Drakov came through the burning doorway and Delaney fired at him with his laser. The beam struck Drakov's shoulder. He cried out and returned the fire.

Delaney leaped to one side, hit the floor and rolled. Lilliputians were swooping through the air like miniature airplanes dog-fighting. Some of the lilliputians who had been marooned back on the island spotted Drakov and swarmed after him. Drakov sprinted for the balcony. As Delaney aimed, Drakov dove over the railing headfirst, activating his warp disc. As the astonished band members watched, a dozen laser beams pierced him as he fell, and then he suddenly vanished in midair.

Lucas dragged Andre underneath a table, pressed the barrel of the Beretta up against the chain linking her handcuffs and shot it off. Steiger stopped rolling and got to his knees in time to see a figure standing in the burning doorway of Manetti's office, leveling a gun at him. In an instant of shocked recognition, he hesitated, his eyes wide with disbelief.

"*Savino!*" he said.

Three shots cracked out, one after the other, and Savino jerked, then toppled backward into Manelli's burning office. Gulliver stood at the head of the stairs, his semiautomatic gripped tightly before him in both hands.

"Nice shootin', pilgrim," Hunter said, clapping him on the shoulder, "but I'd keep my head down if I were you."

Pandemonium reigned inside the club. Fine beams of deadly coherent light crisscrossed in midair, creating a lethal lattice-work of laser fire that filled the balcony floor and lanced down at the stage below. The musicians fled the stage as their amps were struck by laser beams and starting arcing, sparks shooting out from them. Smoke filled the club and the fire alarm went off. The young people who had pushed into the club were milling about below in panic, trying to fight their way back to the door while those behind them continued trying to push their way in until shouts of "Fire! Fire!" turned them around as well and sent them streaming back out into the street.

Lucas crawled over to where Manelli fell, took his gun and handed it Andre.

"Where's Drakov?" he shouted.

"I don't know! He must've clocked out!"

"*Damn* it!"

"Gulliver!" shouted Andre, pointing to where he was huddling underneath a table, clutching his gun and looking up uncertainly, not knowing who to shoot at as the lilliputians fought and died above him. "We've got to get him out of here!"

"Him?" said Lucas. "Hell, *we've* got to get out of here!"

As they scrambled over to where Gulliver was taking shelter, Hunter crouched down over Savino's body amidst the flames in Manelli's office.

"All right, you son of a bitch, where *is* it?" he said through gritted teeth as he pulled back Savino's right sleeve. Was he left handed?

He pulled the warp disc off Savino's left wrist. Now all he had to do was figure out if it was failsafed. The flames were getting very close. He could feel his hair crackling.

"*Hunter!*" shouted Delaney, from the doorway. He squinted from the smoke. The office was a conflagration. He could not get through the door. Flames licked at Hunter's clothes. "*Hunter, are you crazy? Get the hell out of there!*"

"I'm workin' on it, pilgrim." He defeated the failsafe function and quickly punched out a transition code and activated the warp disc.

"*Hunter!*"

The ceiling fell in.

Hunter materialized in the middle of the living room floor of his elegant Upper West Side townhouse. He immediately started rolling around to put out his flaming clothes. Gasping, he tore off his jacket and then rushed, still smouldering, into the bathroom. He turned on the shower and jumped in. His clothes hissed and steamed as the cold water soaked them down. He stayed there for a long time, breathing heavily as the cold water beat down on him, then he stepped, dripping, out of the shower and stripped off his soaked and ruined clothes.

He'd just barely made it. He expelled his breath and inhaled deeply, trying to calm down. That had been close. As close as he'd ever come. He'd have to move now. He could no longer remain in this time period. Even if the Time Commandos didn't find him once again, there were still people in Manelli's organization he'd have to be on the lookout for. He'd made too many contacts. Too many enemies. He had been in a rush to establish himself and had become too visible. That was a mistake he would not repeat again.

As he changed into a fresh suit of clothes, he quickly ran

over in his mind what his next few steps would have to be. How many of his assets could he liquidate quickly? If he converted some of his wealth into precious stones, he could take them back into the past with him, but if he was able to make a few astute investments, they could mature while he clocked ahead into the future and pretended to be his own descendent. No, he thought, far too complicated and too risky and not enough time to set it up, in any case. That was another mistake. He'd not prepared an escape plan in advance. Foolish, very foolish. He'd become overconfident and it had almost gotten him killed.

The hell with it, he thought. Be smart. Take what you can get your hands on now, cut your losses and get out while you still can. But first, there was one last thing he had to do.

He knotted his silk necktie and slipped into a brand new jacket. He quickly opened his safe and took out his important papers, domestic and Swiss accounts, stock portfolios, emergency cash, standby forged documents and several different passports. Then he picked up the Browning Hi-Power he had dropped on the carpet when he'd clocked in from the club. He jacked out the magazine and checked it, then he slapped it back in and racked the slide.

Krista was surprised to see him when she opened her door. "You! But I thought . . . How did you get up here?"

"I slipped the security man downstairs a hundred bucks to let me up," said Hunter, smiling. "Told him I had a special gift for you, a surprise for your birthday."

She glanced at him, uncertainly. "But . . . I . . . I don't understand. It's not my birthday."

"Well, I brought you something anyway," said Hunter. He took out the Browning and shot her right between the eyes.

The street was slicked down from the fire hoses blasting water at the club. Finn Delaney, Creed Steiger, Andre Cross, Lemuel Gulliver and Lucas Priest stood among the crowd being kept back behind the barricades as the firemen gathered up their equipment and the police officers took statements. With the weapons hidden underneath the coats they'd stolen from the cloakroom, they were careful to stay back out of the way. Reporters from the print and electronic media were milling about. There was some kind of story here, but no one quite knew what to make of it. There was a good deal of confusion. The police detectives were not surprised to hear that there had been some sort of shootout inside the club before the fire broke out. They knew about Manelli and his Family business. What they were having a hard time reconciling were the statements of some of the eyewitnesses.

"I'm tellin' you, Lieutenant—"

"Sergeant. Sergeant Lubinski."

"Whatever. Look, I'm tellin' you, man, I know it sounds crazy, but there were these little people . . . tiny little people—"

"You mean like dwarves?" said the detective, frowning. "Midgets?"

"No, man, no, smaller, about like this . . ." The white-haired lead singer of Flesh held his hands about six inches apart, one over the other.

"Like what?" said Lubinski.

"Yeah, like this, man, they were about six inches tall, and they were flyin' around in these tiny, little rocket belts and shootin' lasers, it was fuckin' incredible—"

"*Lasers?*" said Sgt. Lubinski. "*Tiny, little rocket belts?*"

"Yeah, it was outrageous, man, there were, like, dozens of 'em, no, more, and they were, like, having a war in there, like dogfights, you know? Swoopin' around and blasting away at each other and—"

"Now wait a minute . . ."

"Look, I know it sounds crazy, but—"

"Just hold on a second," said Lubinski. "You're with that group, Flesh, huh? Aren't you guys the ones who went ape and burned down that club in Jersey a few months ago?"

"Hey, look, that wasn't our fault, man!"

"Yeah, right. And what did you take before?"

"What did I take?"

"Yeah, what are you on?" Lubinski said. "Dust? PCP?"

"Oh, man! Come on, don't give me this! Look, I'm straight, so help me, I swear to God! Look, ask anybody, there were these little people—"

"Seems like you guys in the band were the only ones who saw any little people, chum," Lubinski said, wryly. "Everybody else saw some kinda laser light show that went out of control, and one of your own roadies told us that the club electrician said your wiring wasn't up to code."

"Look, you gotta believe me, man, it wasn't us, I swear! I'm tellin' you, there were these little people flyin' around—"

"I know, I know, with rocket belts and lasers," said Lubinski, rolling his eyes. "I think you'd better come along with me, ace. You got the right to remain silent . . ."

Delaney glanced at Lucas and smiled. "Somehow I don't think they're going to believe that fella, do you?"

Lucas shook his head. "No. Too bad. They were a good band, too. Sure brought down the house."

EPILOGUE ═══════════════

"I simply can't get over it," said Forrester, staring at Lucas Priest and slowly shaking his head. "I just can't believe you're alive."

"How do you think I feel, sitting here with people who saw me die and helped to bury me?" said Lucas.

They were gathered in Forrester's newly refurbished quarters, sitting in the living room for an informal, postmission debriefing over drinks and coffee. There was still some construction going on outside as workmen repaired the damage from the lilliput assault and installed new, state-of-the-art security systems, the necessity of which Forrester had finally reluctantly admitted. In the morning, Forrester was due to go in for surgery to repair the damage done to his face and kneecap. The other wounds, fortunately, had not been very serious, but the hospital was less than enthusiastic about having him back as a patient.

"It seems crazy," Lucas said. "I've been going over it and over it and I still haven't been able to accept it, somehow. I know that Andre saw that jezail bullet make hash out of my chest, and I know that Finn helped bury me, but I didn't die! That was never part of my experience. It was part of theirs. So what does that mean? Does it mean that *another* Lucas Priest died in my place? Some . . . some alternate version of

myself that was only a potential future for me relative to where
I was before Darkness snatched me, a potential future which
was realized for everybody here but me, because I was
sidetracked? I can't figure out what happened. Did I sidestep
my own fate and get away with it somehow? Or am I the
temporal anomaly here? Is my existence the metaphysical
result of some sort of compensation by the Fate Factor? Am I
some kind of parallel Lucas Priest who came into existence the
moment my 'original self' died? Just thinking about it gives me
the shakes."

"There's still another possibility, you know," Delaney said.
"One that suggests the laws of temporal relativity are a lot
more flexible than we might think."

"What do you mean?" said Andre.

"In effect," Delaney said, "what Dr. Darkness did was
essentially the same thing that we've been doing all along. He
effected a temporal adjustment."

"No, wait, that can't be right," said Lucas, "because there
was never a temporal disruption in the first place."

"How do we *know*?" Delaney said.

"What do you mean, how do we know?" said Lucas. "It's
obvious, isn't it? Our presence there in 19th century Afganistan
was never part of the original temporal scenario. We went back
there to effect a temporal adjustment, so anything that happened to us couldn't possibly have been disruptive because we
were never part of the original scenario to begin with."

"How do you know?" Delaney said. "How do you know
that by going back into the past, we didn't become part of the
original scenario?"

He paused, trying to formulate the concept.

"The fact that we're capable of going back in time and
becoming involved in so-called 'past' events would seem to
indicate that, in a sense, it's all happening now, only that 'now'
is not an absolute, concrete concept. It's completely relative,
depending on where you are and what you're doing. I mean,
how do you define 'now?' How do you capture it? Even as you
perceive that something is happening now, it's already happened, hasn't it? Something has to *be* in order for you to
perceive it, but once you've perceived it, it is no longer
something that is in a state of *being* it's something that has

been. The act of your perceiving it has, in a sense, relegated it to the past."

"Come on, Finn, that's just semantics," Steiger said.

"Is it?" said Delaney. "Look, one thing I learned in R.C.S. when we got into advanced zen physics is that all perception of time is, in a sense, nothing but semantics. I know that's a complicated concept, but bear with me. Mensinger compared the timestream to a river. And no matter where you are in relation to that river, it's in the act of flowing. Mensinger also made the analogy that a temporal disruption is like something that acts against the current and the result of such a disruption depends on its degree.

"We've always assumed that presence in the past by people from the future was relatively safe, so long as it remained nondisruptive," he continued. "That fits in with what Mensinger believed and it's what allows us to effect temporal adjustments. But we've also always worked from the assumption that our presence in the past had a negligible effect, or essentially no effect at all, so long as it remained nondisruptive. That we were somehow separate from the original scenario, like someone standing on the outside and looking in. But what if that was wrong? What if the mere fact of our presence in the past made us a part of the original scenario, whether we did anything disruptive or not?"

"I'm not sure I understand," said Andre. "How does that change anything?"

"In some ways, it doesn't," said Delaney. "It still allows us to effect temporal adjustments, and in fact, it supports our ability to go back into the past without disrupting it significantly, by lessening the temporal impact of our presence. It might account for the continued resiliency of the timestream considering the growing influence of the Time Wars over the years and the potentially disruptive presence of such things as the Network and the Underground, not to mention the confluence effect."

"But how does that relate to me?" said Lucas.

"I was getting to that," said Finn. "If, by going back into the past, you become part of the past, not just a potentially external influence, but an internal one as well, then anything that happens to you could be potentially disruptive to the scenario, not necessarily from our standpoint, but from the standpoint of the future. Because what we're concerned with is what happened to you in the period between your so-called death in 1897 and right now. But people a hundred years from now would be concerned with what happened in 19th Century Afghanistan and its effect on the timestream all the way down the line to where they are, or will be, and that includes not only anything we do right now, but anything we might do, or be meant to do, for the remainder of our lives, because that will be part of their past."

"I see," said Forrester. "So what you're saying is that Priest's death might have been the temporal disruption, not his survival?"

"It's possible," Delaney said. "And the more I think about it, the more sense it seems to make. He's survived and there hasn't been a timestream split as a result of that, so far as we can tell. Now maybe that's because he wasn't historically significant enough for his survival to have caused a serious temporal disruption. But on the other hand, maybe his death would have resulted in a temporal disruption further up the timeline, as a result of something he wouldn't have been able to do if he hadn't lived, something he hasn't done yet. In that case, what Darkness did in saving him would be a temporal adjustment to restore the continuity of the timeline."

"Wait a minute," Lucas said. "If that's the case, then that would mean that Darkness knew my death would cause a temporal disruption."

Delaney nodded. "Think about it," he said. "Consider everything that he's accomplished, Lucas. Consider what he's done to you. Consider that our most brilliant scientists can't even begin to understand the principles behind some of his discoveries. Hasn't it occurred to you that Dr. Darkness could be from the future?"

"Wow," said Andre.

"I never even thought of that," said Steiger. "But you could be right. Assume that, and everything else falls right into place. All the things he knows, everything he's done, all the questions about him that we've never had any answers for . . ."

"Yes, and speaking of answers," Forrester said, "Darkness has a lot to answer for."

"You might as well forget it," Steiger said. "Knowing him,

he probably wouldn't tell you anything, especially if what Finn just said is true."

"Where is he, Lucas?" Andre said. "I never saw him again after what happened at the club."

Lucas shook his head. "I don't know where he is. Back at his secret headquarters out beyond the galaxy. Maybe he's discorporated, which would mean he's everywhere. Or maybe he's standing right here beside us, vibrating faster than light and laughing up his sleeve. Who knows?"

"Well, whatever the truth may be," said Steiger, "I'm glad to have you back, Lucas. And you can have your old job as exec back anytime."

"I'll be the one who decides that," Forrester said. "And I don't think I want to change things. Right now, nobody outside this room knows that Lucas is alive and I'd like to keep it that way for now. It might give us an edge." He glanced at Lucas. "Besides, I don't think you'd care much to have every scientist on this planet wanting to examine you."

"No, I think I'll pass on that," said Lucas. "But what about Gulliver?"

Forrester picked up his communicator and spoke into it. "Is he here yet?"

"He's been waiting for the past ten minutes, sir," came the reply.

"Send him in."

A moment later, Dr. Lemuel Gulliver, dressed in smartly creased, black base fatigues and wearing the single chevron of a Pfc., came into the room, snapped to attention and saluted.

Forrester returned his salute and said, "At ease, Private." He glanced at the surprised expressions on the faces of the others and smiled. "I'd like you all to meet the newest member of the Temporal Observer Corps. He'll be clocking back home soon to assume his new post. Sit down, Gulliver, and have a drink."

Forrester waited until the greetings and congratulations had stopped, then he continued with the debriefing.

"That still leaves us with some very disturbing loose ends," he said, and they all fell silent.

"First and foremost, there's Drakov." Forrester never referred to him as his son anymore. "You can imagine how I felt when I learned that he was still alive. I thought that was all finished, but now apparently he's replicated himself and the threat's been multiplied. I've issued orders to all Observer outposts and every team in the field to keep a lookout for him or any of his hominoid selves, with orders to shoot to kill on sight. I fear we haven't heard the last of him. Or the Network. But at least we've driven them out of the agency. All loyal personnel are volunteering to be scanned and the rest of them are going underground. Still, they're not finished with us, and in many ways our job is bigger now than it ever was before. But I'm resolved to see it through."

They all nodded in silent agreement.

"Last, but not least, there's the question of the lilliputians," Forrester said. "Your report says that they're unaccounted for. What the devil do you mean, they're unaccounted for?"

"Well, after the battle in the club, we never saw any of them again," Delaney said. "The two groups of lilliputians went at each other pretty hard. I'd guess that most of them were killed and the survivors perished in the fire."

"You'd *guess*?"

"A guess is the best that any of us can do, sir," Andre said. "That's why, officially, the report reads that any possible survivors were unaccounted for."

Forrester sighed and shook his head. "I'll have to assign extra Observers to that time zone and have them keep an eye out. Although how they'll ever find any lilliputians in a warren like New York City is beyond me. Still, it'll have to be attempted. If any of them survived, and if they should start to reproduce . . ."

"I'm not sure that we have anything to worry about there, sir," Lucas said. "All the lilliputians we saw were male. That doesn't mean there aren't any female lilliputians hidden away somewhere, but it would stand to reason that Drakov would want to control their population and not encumber himself with lilliputian offspring. Besides, all the hominoids we've ever encountered have been mules, incapable of reproduction."

"And if any of them did live through the fire," Delaney said, "I feel sorry for the little bastards. 20th Century New York is a hard city to survive in if you're normal sized. They'll have to keep out of sight and struggle for survival, with not only humans to be wary of, but stray cats and dogs, and the city's teeming rat population . . ." He shook his head. "I wouldn't give you much for their chances of survival."

• • •

"Tyler! Seth! What was all that noise?"

"Nothing, Mom!"

She opened up the door to the boys' bedroom and saw them sitting on the floor, surrounded by all their G.I. Joe and Rambo action figures and all the military paraphernalia that went along with them.

"What was that crash I heard?" she said.

"Oh, nothing, Mom," said Tyler. "We were just playing."

She gave a quick glance around the room to see if anything was broken.

"Well, try to play quietly, okay?" she said. "We've got company, remember?"

"Sure, Mom. We're sorry. We'll try to be quiet."

"Good. See that you do."

She closed the door.

The two boys exchanged glances, then Tyler got up and went over to the door, opened it a crack and peered out.

"It's okay," he said. "The coast is clear."

His brother reached underneath the bed and pulled out the food they'd swiped from the kitchen of the co-op apartment. Several of the "action figures" suddenly came to life and started to attack the food.

"Boy!" said Seth, grinning ear to ear. "This sure beats having hamsters!"